Vision of Love

A Center Stage Love Story

Act Two

by

Kathryn R. Biel

VISION OF LOVE

Paperback ISBN-13: 978-1-949424-21-8

This book is a work of fiction. Names, characters, places, and incidents are either products of the author's imagination or are used fictitiously and any resemblance to actual persons, living or dead, business establishments, events or locales is purely coincidental.

Cover design by Sue Traynor

Dedication

To the cast, crew, and staff of the Mac-Hadyn
Theatre
The show must go on.

Chapter 1: Tabitha

I'm ten seconds in, and this is the weirdest first date ever.

I'm not even supposed to be on a date. I'm supposed to be having a girls' night in with my former bandmate. But Angie and her partner, Sergei, are delayed in their return to New York City, and Angie had made other plans for us tonight anyways. Apparently, this was supposed to be a double date with them and Sergei's friend. Instead, it's just the two of us.

God, he's grumpy.

He literally "humphed" at me when I introduced myself, barking out his own name. Henderson Quade. Maybe I shouldn't have made that comment about his accent, but Angie did tell me I'd love it. Of course, I'd been expecting Russian, or at least Eastern European, like Sergei's. I was not expecting Australian, which, let's face it, has a Chris Hemsworth vibe.

It's, like, auto-sexy.

And he is cute, though if he doesn't do something about his attitude, it won't get him far. Especially not tonight. I don't even want to be here. I'm jet-lagged and missing my daughter, and then there was that incident with the goat in the Central Park petting zoo ...

It hasn't been the best of days.

Two people recognized me today, and I don't know how to feel about it. I'm trying to fly under the radar here so no one knows I'm in New York right now. On the other hand, am I now so irrelevant that I can fly all the way from LAX to LaGuardia, traipse all around Manhattan, and only *two* people recognize me?

What a day.

I really don't need *another* bad date story to be the cherry on top. Hell, my last bad date ended up with me being lied to in the back of a limo and subsequently pregnant.

Okay, this date will *not* be like that one. I swear. Let's take another look and see if there's anything here to be salvaged.

Auburn hair. Probably about 5'11", which is a little short for my liking, but not terrible. A light beard. Blue eyes. If I had to guess, I'd say he was in his thirties. I bet he smells rugged and spicy.

He narrows his eyes slightly at me. Okay, it's a little early in the evening to try to lean in and smell him. I sit back and see his gaze drop down and return quickly. If I'm not mistaken, there was a bit of an eye roll in there. It can't be what I'm wearing, can it?

I look down at my form-fitting dress and strappy heels. You can take the girl out of LA, but you can't take the LA out of the girl. Even if you do dye her golden locks a medium brown so she can walk down the streets unrecognized by the paparazzi who used to follow her every move.

Of course, when you take the girl out of LA in the middle of February and plop her down in Manhattan, the odds are very good that she will not have appropriate clothing for the weather.

Thank God Angie left a coat behind that's warmer than anything I own. It still looks lightweight compared to his peacoat. He's wearing jeans and a turtleneck sweater. Not exactly dressed to impress, though. I'm definitely used to men who are better groomed. Maybe it's an East Coast thing?

He takes a deep breath in. "So, tell me a little about yourself."

He sounds like he's starting a job interview. What's next? Where do I see myself in five years? Okay. It's not like I'm really looking for anything. Hell, I live in California. Even if he were the love of my life, it's not like there would be any way for this to work out.

Not that I do love or long term anyway.

And seriously, what am I supposed to tell him? Do I lead with the fact that I'm in New York for three weeks while my daughter bonds with her baby daddy, who is a megastar, and that no one can know he fathered a child out of wedlock? Father, my ass.

Lying sperm donor is more like it.

Perhaps I tell him that despite my darkened tresses, it is I, Tabitha Stetson, aka Tabby Cat from the superstar group, the Sassy Cats. Does he know that already because of Angie? Usually when people know that, they lead with it.

Somehow, I doubt either one will turn this date around. I decide to go with a tamer version of choice A.

"Relax, buddy. This isn't an interview. It doesn't have to be anything. I'm looking for something to take my mind off the fact that my daughter is with her father for three weeks and I don't know what to do without her."

I see his shoulders drop a little. Is that relief? Or is it revulsion that I have a kid?

"Oh, how old's the ankle biter?"

"Ankle biter?"

"Child. Kid. Tyke. Little one."

I laugh nervously, trying to cover the fact that I feel like an idiot. I mean, he's speaking English too. Maybe it's because that was not how I expected him to reply. "Um, she's three. She'll be four next month. I love her to pieces, and this is the first time she's been away from me for this long. But her father is ... working ... here in New York, so I brought her out to spend some time with him."

"I take it you're not together?"

I cock my eyebrow. Like I'd be on a date if we were? What a weirdo. "We were barely together long enough to fertilize the egg."

"Right. Okay. Well, is there anything else inappropriate I can ask? I'd like to get that out of the way now." He flashes a quick grin, and it changes his whole face.

I'd been beginning to think all he could do was scowl.

I smile. "No, it's fine. I made my bed."

"Literally," he says dryly. Another grin flashes, lightening his words and making my stomach do a little twist. "Maybe we should get a drink." Henderson nods to the waitress who is hovering patiently.

"Or multiple?" I glance at the menu. "Oooh, the cantaloupe mimosa looks delish." Wait—can I even order that? It's nighttime. Do I look stupid? Is he going to tell people that Tabitha Stetson is so uncouth that she ordered a breakfast drink at dinner?

But it's what I want. Couth be damned.

Henderson orders a beer. He looks like a beer guy. Maybe couth would be lost on him anyway. He's definitely rougher around the edges than the guys out in California. I bet he's never had a manicure. I look down at his shoes. They're worn, brown lace-up boots.

"Are your shoes warm? Mine aren't. I had booties that I bought for the trip, but I stepped in a puddle today, and they're soaked. My feet practically turned into popsicles."

Henderson looks down at my feet. "I don't think those are helping the situation. It's the middle of winter, you know."

This time, the eye roll is obvious.

"I know," I laugh nervously. "I didn't bring the right clothes for the weather. Or a date. I borrowed Angie's coat, but her feet are about two sizes smaller than mine. Believe me, I did try to squash my feet in those boots because they looked so warm. So this was all I had that was appropriate for going out." I'm prattling on. Henderson looks so ... disinterested. I'm not used to having to work this much to get attention.

Either he really doesn't know who I am, or he's playing super hard to get. Unless he's a professional actor, it's got to be the first thing.

"Right, well, the summer in Upstate New York is perfect. Hot during the day, a little cooler at night," Henderson supplies. "But beautiful in general."

Huh? What the hell is he talking about? The comment is so out of left field; it has nothing to do with anything. "Okay." I don't know what else to say.

And the date just went back to being weird.

His scowl is back.

I don't like his scowl. I'd much prefer to see that smile of his.

I could do without the eye roll too.

Luckily, the waitress comes to the table with our drinks. I glance quickly at the menu. "Vegetable curry, please."

He orders the peri-peri chicken, whatever that is. "I had you pegged for the avo sandwich."

It takes me a beat to realize he's talking about the avocado sandwich. "No bread. At least I'm trying to get back to that. Paisley loves toast, so I've fallen off the wagon for the past two years. I've probably eaten more bread since she was born than I have in my whole life combined." I shrug. "The price of being—" I cut myself short before I can finish with "in showbiz." It sounds so pretentious. "You know, health conscious."

Ugh. When did I become so lame?

Maybe I was always this lame, but because I was famous, no one cared.

Henderson does not seem at all impressed or awestruck. He's not looking at me with that *look*. In fact, he's barely looking at me at all. Is it the kid talk? Maybe I shouldn't talk about my daughter. Or maybe it's because I mentioned carbs.

Guys in California are aware of their carbs. Maybe New York guys don't care about what they eat. Whatever it is, I don't seem to be making any headway with him.

I'm tempted to drain this drink and several others, just so I can make this night go away. While that's not the most stellar of plans, I need a little something to make me less awkward. I take a gulp of my mimosa.

Henderson clears his throat. "I'm sorry. I'm a bit grumpy. I'm usually not this uptight. I mean, don't get me wrong, I'm always uptight. Just not this much."

"So it's not just me?" I look at him intently. I don't think I've ever been so out of sync with someone. And that says a lot considering the amount of men who have attempted to make "music" with me over the years. "Why are you extra uptight tonight?" I lean forward, resting my chin on my fist. I want him to look me right in the eye when he admits he's nervous about being on a date with me.

He shakes his head slowly. There's another eye roll. I should take a drink every time he does that. Of course, I'd probably have alcohol poisoning before dessert.

"A pipe burst in the apartment above mine this afternoon, causing a deluge, and I'm not sure about the condition of my things. I don't have a lot, but I'd prefer what I have to be dry." He casually shrugs one shoulder. "I'm not holding my breath for my landlord to fix it anytime soon, either."

I relax back into my chair. It's not me. It has nothing to do with me. Maybe I haven't lost my touch. "Oh, my God, that's the worst. I remember when I was a kid, my mom got the bright idea that we were going to move to Minnesota. It was like the reverse *90210*. Of course, it was because she was following a guy there. He flew out to Cali, and we all drove back to his house together. It took *days* to get to St. Paul, and when we arrived, we discovered the pipes had burst in his house. It was like stupid cold, like negative one-hundred, and all the radiators blew up because Mr. Wonderful turned his heat off to save money. Everything was covered in icicles. Mom took one look and dragged me out to the car, and that was the last we ever saw of St. Paul."

"What about the bloke?"

I shrug. "What about him? I couldn't believe that she even committed to that much. I'm sure there was someone else the following week."

"Oh," he says softly. His eyes drop to his beer. "Yeah, my mum's a bit of a mess herself. Never was able to pull herself together."

So, he knows what it's like. He should understand where I'm coming from then. "Yeah, so I don't want to do that to Paisley. I haven't really dated since she was born. I've been trying to lie low. Stay out of the spotlight, you know. It never used to bother me—in fact, I loved being seen. But now that I have Paisley, I don't want her life negatively affected by decisions I make. I'm not going to go parading a new guy every week. I know what that's like."

He looks up and his gaze locks on mine for a brief second. "Me too. It's how I ended up here. My dad met my mum during a study abroad year in Australia. She thought he was there to stay. He was not. And then he took me on a trip to America, and we never went back. It was ugly and messy and unfortunate."

Wow. This is the most depressing first date I've ever been on.

"Things are getting real deep real quick. Let's talk about something lighter. I don't want to talk about serious adulty things."

"Fine, but one more serious thing—Paisley?"

Yes, I named my daughter Paisley Elvis Clementine Stetson. I realize it's a mouthful, but not without reason.

"For Paisley Park. You know, Prince's company."

We sang with Prince one time. It was one of the highlights of my life. Yes, the Sassy Cats were big enough to sing with Prince. We weren't actually allowed to make eye contact with him, except for during the performance, but at least we were up on stage with him.

And now I'm being set up on a blind date, hoping he doesn't get up and leave because he's so bored with me.

Oh, how the mighty have fallen.

"Right. Okay. Makes more sense. Prince was a real genius. So you don't leave your tot often?"

I want to tell him that I do have a nanny—Maria—who is a tremendous help, but that doesn't sound like something you say on a first date. You also don't share that the nanny used to work for your baby daddy and his wife, raising their son. You especially don't share that the baby daddy is none other than Jonathan Spencer Maxwell.

God, even thinking his name makes me want to roll my eyes. I take a sip of my mimosa instead. What a pretentious prick. But when you're a mega movie star with boyish good looks and the ability to charm the pants off of anyone—myself included—you can make everyone call you by three stupid names.

"I mean, I have help, but this is the first time she's gone with him for this long. Three weeks. It's just me, all by myself, for three weeks."

"Do you want to spend it alone? I'm not saying you should, but I hear some mums just want peace and quiet." He gives me an apologetic smile, as if he's sorry he dragged me out when I could be staying in.

I mean, he sort of did.

Despite his grumpy exterior, I can see some kindness. A genuine feeling. Someone who's not looking for something from me. He's really just here for me. And even though he's just met me, he seems real in his concern. I barely know what to do with that.

I smile back at him. "I like having adult time. I don't actually like being alone that much. I just want to be able to go the whole night without asking if you have to go pee pee in the potty."

That finally cracks his grumpy exterior once and for all, and his grin spreads from ear to ear. "I promise, you won't have to mention going pee pee in the potty." The words are slow and measured coming out of his mouth. I'm guessing that's not a phrase he uses often—or ever. It's comical from him.

"Is it a problem that I have a kid?" I don't know how to date as a mother. Let's face it, most of what I did before I got pregnant with Paisley wasn't really dating. It was more like hooking up. While in my head I've turned over a new leaf and am looking for more, in reality, I probably don't have more to give than the occasional hookup.

Especially not with someone who lives on the other side of the country.

Still, now that Henderson is starting to relax a bit, I should give him a chance. The night is way too young, and he is way too cute to rule anything out.

Chapter 2: Henderson

I was nervous there for a bit. She's not at all what I expected.

When my best mate Grayson Keene first called, asking me to come to this dinner, I wanted nothing to do with it. He's the face of The Edison. I'm only the managing director. He's the one with the charm and charisma and the schmoozing capability.

I'm the practical one.

When he said I had to come to dinner to try to secretly convince a has-been pop star to commit to starring in one of the shows this summer at The Edison Theater, it was a hard pass. So not my thing.

But he'd begged.

Carson Reuben from *Backstage Magazine* had gone out on a limb to make this introduction. And now Grayson was stuck two hours north in my other hometown of Hicklam, taking his mother to the doctor. The dinner in the West Village at Jack's Wife Freda fell squarely in my lap. It's a solid restaurant, which may be the only high point to the evening.

Still, my initial instincts to run far and fast were confirmed the moment I asked the hostess for my table and from behind me, I heard the shrill squeal, "Oh my God, Angie was right. I do love your accent. I'm your date for the night."

I'm sure I rolled my eyes. It was only a matter of time before she asked me to say "shrimp on the barbie."

I don't know how she knew it was me, other than the accent, but I was on the lookout for a thirty-something brunette. Grayson hadn't been able to remember her name, other than it started with a T and "she was in one of those girl groups, like Fate's Daughter, or something like that." He's not always the best with details. That's more my end.

Now, maybe it's because I'm on my third coldie, or maybe because she's grown on me, I'm not as irritated.

Not in the least.

As she's explained away the impractical shoes and the desire for privacy, as well as the bit with her mum, I'm seeing a vulnerable side that most performers don't let the world see. Her blue eyes sparkle as she talks about her daughter, as well as her desire to have adult time. She's well-groomed and coiffed, yet somehow looks natural at the same time.

Then it hits me. She's not performing. This is Tabitha, pure and unadulterated. She's not on stage. She's not thinking about her group. And she absolutely has no idea that this is any sort of audition. I bet if she did, the walls and the façade would go up in an instant.

Which also means that there's probably no way in hell she's interested in giving up her domestic life for a stint at The Edison this summer.

I feel as if I'm standing at the base of Mount Everest with nowhere to go but up. Remind me to throttle Grayson when I see him again.

Yet, I know The Edison needs this. Her. Last season was a nail-biter if ever there was one. Grayson's mum got in way over her head financially with those renovations, and it's a wonder they—we—didn't lose the theatre lock, stock, and barrel. We actually finished in the black by a larger margin than we ever could've dreamt. We'd be idiots not to harness that momentum by landing a big name for this summer.

Specifically, *I'd* be the idiot. I take a beat while the waitress delivers our food. In a former life, I'd been in front of the curtain rather than behind it. Time to dust off those skills and channel my inner Grayson.

"Where are you located normally? Somewhere warm, I take it?" I smile a little, willing my face muscles to relax. Tabitha is striking to look at. I'm surprised, despite her incognito sunglasses, no one recognized her when we came in.

"Southern California."

"Oh, is this your first time in New York?" I know it's not, not with her history, but since she hasn't brought it up, I'm going to play dumb for a bit. Put her at ease.

"Not at all, but I haven't been here in about five years. Not since before Paisley was born."

I tilt my head. What's the deal with the dad? Is the kid going to be an issue this summer? Does the dad live here? "Did you say she's with her dad for three weeks? What'll you get up to in the meantime?"

She shrugs and looks down. "I guess some relaxing, visiting friends. Maybe a spa day or two. Shopping. Definitely shopping. I'm buying boots and warm socks." She nods, as if these things are truly fulfilling. "Anything I can do to keep me from missing Paisley."

"Museums? Broadway shows? Do you like the theatre?"

"Oh, yes. I always flew out to see Angie in her shows. That was before she did *Hollywood Dance Off!* of course."

This is not the first time she's mentioned this Angie person. "Angie?"

"Yeah, Angie. Angie Aliberti? She's one of my best friends, even if I don't get to see her as often as I'd like. I saw her out here in *A Chorus Line* and in *West Side Story*. She was so perfect as Anita. I think that's what helped her win *Hollywood Dance Off!*, all that Broadway training."

Angie Aliberti is her friend.

Duh. Of course she is. I'm sure all the Backstreet Boys know N'Sync. Obviously the group Angie was in, the Sassy Cats, would know the members of Fate's Daughter. While I've only vaguely heard of Fate's Daughter, I do know of the Sassy Cats. Mostly because of Angie Aliberti. My stomach flips. Angie Aliberti is big time.

Now if I could land *her*, that would be a beauty. Absolutely great. Also totally out of my league. Way more than The Edison could handle.

But I'm not here to sweet talk Angie Aliberti. "Yes, I've heard of her, natch. I catch a lot of theatre here. It's sort of my thing."

"Natch?"

"Naturally. Obviously." I try not to roll my eyes.

"Right, naturally. So ..."

I can't tell if she wants to be recognized or not. I've got to play this right. Time to double down.

"I saw her on Broadway first, and then know she went on to television. I don't really follow her career or anything. I don't watch much telly." It's the truth. "I spend half my year here in the city and the other half upstate. I work for a seasonal family business up there, and it doesn't leave much time for recreation."

"So are you in the off-season now?"

"It's ending. We're starting to head into the season. We're discussing casting, and auditions will start next week. There's always something to do on the business end down here in the city."

Immediately, she perks up. I see the veneer go down. "Auditions? Auditions for what?"

Time to cast the reel.

"I'm the managing director of a small, award-winning theatre. It's about ninety miles north of here, in a little town called Hicklam."

"Ninety miles? That's so far."

I'm surprised that's what grabs her focus. Even though she's warming up, and I have to admit I'm starting to enjoy myself, I'm really no further along on my mission.

"Only if you're walking it. It's about two hours on the train or by car. Not too bad at all. The worst part is getting in and out of the city. Once you hit Westchester County, you're in the clear."

"Man, in LA it can take you two hours to go five miles."

"That sounds terrible. Why would you want to live there?"

"Because the weather is beautiful every single day." She laughs. "I never have to worry about getting hypothermia from stepping in a puddle."

"This is true. But the fires and mudslides can prolly be a bit problematic, no?"

"That and the earthquakes, and when Trader Joe's is out of my favorite organic popcorn."

The waitress deposits another round at our table. I lift my coldie in salute, chuckling. "Here's to first world problems."

Tabitha tilts her champagne flute back at me. "To first world problems. May your feet be dry and warm, and your traffic be light."

"And may your popcorn be in stock."

And with that, this is no longer a chore.

Not in the least.

All too soon, we're done with dinner and our third round of drinks. I still haven't laid the pitch for The Edison. I need to stall and buy more time.

Plus, I want to get her to open up about her career so I can get her to sing for me. We've been duped by the whole "of course she can sing" line before.

I don't care if she was in a marginally popular group that had a hit record once. It was probably auto-tuned within an inch of its life. Until I hear her pipes, I will proceed with extreme caution.

Grayson will thank me later.

A large crowd at the table next to us lets out a rowdy cheer of "Opa!" It's then that the brilliant idea crashes on me like a tidal wave. "You up for something fun? One of the true gems of New York City?"

I stand up and offer her my hand. She looks from my hand to me and then back again. "I guess?" She takes my hand gingerly, as if she's afraid.

"I've got a fun place for us to go to. It's only about five blocks away. Can you manage it in those shoes?" I really don't want to pay for a cab. It's not like The Edison has the cash flow for unnecessary expenses.

In a related story, I don't have the cash flow for unnecessary expenses.

"Sure. I may whine and complain the whole way, but I can manage. Worst case, you can carry me."

She's kidding. At least I hope she's kidding.

Chapter 3: Tabitha

*O*w. *Ow. Ow.*

These shoes are definitely not made for walking. That's not even considering the cold and slush on the sidewalks. Gross. A small whimper escapes my lips.

"Did you actually just whine?"

"No, aaaah." Each step is like a thousand knives in the ball of my foot. How did I ever spend hours dancing in heels like this? Perhaps my laid-back Cali-style is getting its revenge. I think I'm developing a bunion. Definitely a blister. "I'm okay." I'm not okay.

"We are literally a block and a half away. Can you make it or not?" There's a terrified edge to his voice that betrays his fear that he is *actually* going to have to carry me.

I'm a diva, but I'm not that much of a diva. Though if he offered ...

"I'll be fine. I will, however, be accepting all offers of a foot rub this evening." As I say this, a homeless man sitting on the sidewalk looks up.

"I'll take that job, honey."

I stop in front of him. I hadn't even seen him there, a pile of rags in a doorway. Oh, that poor man. Quickly I open my purse and pull out … well, I guess he's going to be a hundred dollars richer tonight.

"No, thank you, but please take this. See if you can find yourself someplace warm to stay tonight. It's too cold out here."

"Lady, there ain't even a Code Blue." He narrows his eyes. "Don't I know you from somewhere?"

I can say with absolute certainty that I have never seen this man before in my life. It's highly unlikely that he recognizes me. I glance back at Henderson, who shrugs.

"I don't think so," I say measuredly.

"Are you sure? You look like a cat on a hot tin roof. Meow." He swipes imaginary claws at me.

The pain in my feet suddenly does not matter; all that matters is that I get away from this man. Of all the times to be made. And by this guy! I don't want Henderson to see this side of me. Not yet. I'm liking that he's just here for me and not my fame.

I glance back at the man sitting on the ground. How did he recognize me? But he did. There's no doubt about it. "Cat on a Hot Tin Roof" was one of our biggest hits. Second only to "Here Kitty Kitty."

God, those song titles were the stupidest things ever.

"Huh. That was weird. I can't believe he meowed at me." I *can* believe he meowed at me. People do it all the time when they recognize me. They throw the cat paw hand gesture in too. "Poor man. I hope he can get some help."

"That was very generous of you. Did you really give him a Benjamin?"

Heat rushes my face. Not many people have that kind of money to throw around. I shouldn't be showing off in front of him.

"I meant to pull out a twenty." I laugh nervously. "It's fine. I'm sure he needs it more than I do. Plus I'm a little tipsy. I tend to get very generous when I drink."

It's true. I once gave a total stranger my Prada bag. It was so last season and I was over it, but it was still a nice thing to do for a woman who admires your purse in a bar.

"Remind me to get you loaded and then talk to you about some investment opportunities in my business."

I lace my arm through his, partially because I'm unsteady on my feet, which have remembered to hurt, but also because I'm cold. And seeking shelter from anyone else on the street who might recognize me.

And because I'm tipsy, and he's cute.

All in all, it seems like a smart thing to do.

Henderson's body is warm and firm. He's strong under that casual exterior. What's best about Henderson is he doesn't know who I am. He's not with me for the star power. He's not after me for something. Hell, he even paid for dinner like a true gentleman.

I think, if he likes me at all, it's for me, and not because I am famous.

Or used to be famous.

All these things make Henderson quite attractive in my book. I hope wherever we're going has some intimate, dark corners.

"Here we are."

I look up to see clean glass doors with the word "Oppa" above the opening in neon pink. It's a bustling pub.

"This place can be a lot of fun. It's pretty quintessential New York. Eclectic and funky and traditional all at the same time."

It's definitely not LA.

It's also not Gymboree or Mommy and Me Yoga.

The main room is surprisingly full for a Thursday night. Henderson steps in front of me to navigate the crowd, taking my hand in the process. It feels so warm compared to the popsicle at the end of my arm. "Let's try downstairs."

I nod, not attempting to yell over the noise. It's been a while since I was anywhere this crowded. Clad in Angie's coat, I don't feel as confident as I normally would if I were in my own clothes. How was I to guess that Angie would be setting me up on a blind date? I'm kicking myself again for not packing appropriately.

I'm also regretting my hair color. No one even recognizes me, except for a bum on the street.

Though, I guess that's the point, right?

But still, I don't feel like myself right now.

Not that I know who that even is anymore. Am I still a pop star? Am I a pre-K mom? I don't have a career right now, but I feel like I should. On the other hand, I'm not qualified to do anything other than be a performer. I barely got through high school. My skill set is definitely ... lacking.

"Hey—you okay over there? You look stressed. Is it this place?" Henderson squeezes my hand gently as he leads me to a small square table on the far side of the basement bar. "Let me go get a drink. What do you want?"

I probably should stick to something light. "Maybe wine?" I crane my neck to try to see what they have on display. "How about a ..."

Henderson's already making his way up to the bar.

Okay then. I glance around. This place is actually pretty cool. The walls are black with white doodles and sketches all over them. There's a drawing of a picture frame around the quote, "Trust me, you can dance. - Vodka."

It makes me smile because dancing has never been my forte until I've had a few shots. That was sort of problematic with the Sassy Cats because our concerts required *tons* of dancing. Eventually I got it, but I hated every minute of it. Mostly because, like school and stable relationships, it doesn't come easily.

I look around some more. This is a karaoke bar. I haven't been to one of these since we were in Tokyo.

Man, that was a crazy night.

This will be totally different, being here with a complete stranger. I probably won't even get up to sing.

"One cab sav. Hope it's all right." Henderson places the glass in front of me as he sits down. He's got another beer.

"This is a karaoke bar."

"Yeah. It's usually a bloody good time here. Amazing energy from the crowd."

"Do you sing?" Maybe he's a performer. He's involved in a theater, right?

He shrugs. "I'm fair. My mate is a performer, so he really kills it. I don't sing if he's gone up first. I'm used to being on the other side of the stage. Why? You sing?"

He really doesn't have a clue who I am. Yet, he's here, buying me dinner and drinks. Are we here because he actually wants to get to know me for me?

Nah, he probably just wants to hook up.

Too bad for him my days of doing that are over. I mean, last time I did that, I ended up with a surprise gift nine months later.

I may not have done well in school, but that's a lesson even *I* can learn.

"A little. I'm out of practice, unless you consider the *Paw Patrol* theme song."

"I don't even know what that is, but c'mon. It'll be fun."

I shrug. "Maybe. We'll see."

But as soon as the music starts, I know I'll be getting up there. I have to. I can feel the energy coursing through my veins, just like it did every time I was about to get up on stage with the Sassy Cats.

I don't even know that I loved performing that much. I loved the energy and the adoration from the crowd. That was where I got my high.

A high I no longer feel.

As much as I love Paisley, life with her is different.

When I'm on stage and people are yelling and screaming for me, it fills me up. It makes me feel whole.

It's the only time I feel that way.

Even in my most perfect moments with my daughter, I'm not full.

And I've been running on an empty tank for so long, trying to do what's best for my daughter.

It's time for mama to put some gas in her tank.

Chapter 4: Henderson

This is the pits, lying to Tabitha.

If I believed in dating and love and all that crap, she'd be the exact type of person I'd want to spend time with. She doesn't take herself so seriously. Not like the actresses I'm used to dealing with.

I still can't believe she gave that man a hundred dollars. Without even blinking.

Either she has no concept of money, which is a strong possibility, or she's a genuine, generous person.

Little details can tell a lot.

On the other hand, she's hiding a lot from me. If she thinks this is a potential date, wouldn't she be a bit more forthcoming about her past? She sings *a little*. Granted, I wasn't a big Fate's Daughter fan. Okay, I wasn't a fan at all, but if they had a hit song, she had to have done a fair amount of singing.

I'll be interested to see what song she picks. I wonder if it will be her song? If it is, I'm so out of here.

No way I'll get up there myself.

Many moons ago, I thought I had a decent voice. It wasn't a skill I cultivated, though, because I was determined to be a "serious actor." In my head, "serious actors" did not dare sing and dance and do musical theatre. Although I did have a role or two where I had to sing a few bars and always held my own.

Grayson even told me that if I took some vocal lessons and worked at it, I'd be in contention for decent parts. I wasn't going to lower myself like that.

It turned out to be a colossal mistake. It's how I ended up being the managing director at my mate's theatre rather than being on stage myself.

So yes, singing is a sore spot for me.

As are actresses in general.

If I didn't love the thrill of a production—and if I were qualified to do anything else—I'd find another job. But there's something in seeing your vision go from pages on a script to being a living, breathing, kinetic thing that moves people to tears.

I'm addicted to that feeling.

"Wanna do a duet?" Tabitha asks hopefully. That's not a good sign. If she doesn't think she can sing on her own in a setting like this, then carrying a stage performance is doubtful.

"Why don't you go first while I apply some liquid courage?" I lift my beer and take a sip.

Okay, a large gulp.

The first singer of the night gets up there, singing a rousing and off-key version of "September" by Earth, Wind, and Fire. Tabitha's got to be stronger than that.

I hope.

If not, Grayson's a dead man.

"Whatcha gonna sing?" I ask when Tabitha makes her way back to the table after signing up.

"Can't tell you. It's a surprise." She winks at me and finishes her wine.

"Another cab sav?"

Tabitha nods. "Please. I need some help before I bust out my inner Mariah."

I choke a little on my beer. Please no. Very few people have the skills to sing like that, and if she did, she wouldn't be a has-been pop star—she'd still be a star.

She puts her hand on my arm. "Just kidding. I'm not that drunk, and I don't know that there's enough liquor in here to get me that drunk. I know my limits and 'Vision of Love' is way beyond it."

I sag back in my chair for a beat, placing my hand over hers, holding it to me for a moment. "I was worried I'd have to brush off my acting skills and tell you how great you sounded, and that it didn't at all remind me of cats fighting inside a bag."

She bursts out laughing, and her hand slides down. Damn. "That's the perfect descriptor. I'll have to remember that. I never thought I'd need another cat analogy, but you never know."

"Whatcha gonna sing?" I try again.

"Can't tell you. It's a surprise."

"Oh, c'mon. Tell me."

She leans in and taps me on the nose. "You're not very patient. You'll find out soon enough."

I've lost the ability to blink for a minute as her blue eyes twinkle at me. Finally I shake my head, if only to clear it. "Lemme get that drink. Be right back."

The crowd at the bar is thick. While I wait, I pull out my phone and find a text from Grayson.

Any progress?

Quickly, I text back that I'm working on it. I don't mention that we're in a karaoke bar so I can hear her sing before I offer her a part in our show. I don't mention that I haven't yet brought the idea up to her.

I also don't mention that I don't really want to.

I wouldn't mind spending the evening, or two even, with Tabitha, and that's not something I can do if she's in the show. I've seen too many in-house relationships blow up and explode, taking down entire shows in the process.

Hell, The Edison almost went under and out of business because of Grayson's ex-girlfriend.

You should never mix business with pleasure. Ever.

Not that I'd be in it for the long haul anyway. With anyone. I'm not cut out for it, nor do I want to even bother trying. Nothing but heartbreak and hurt.

Not to mention, the only people who could possibly understand my life are people living the theatre life, which brings me back to the beginning of not mixing business with pleasure.

On the other hand, she hasn't mentioned performing or show biz. I told her I worked for a theatre, and she didn't respond at all. She didn't even bite with the auditions bit. I mean, she started to nibble until she heard how far away it was. Perhaps she thinks this is all too beneath her. Maybe I shouldn't bring it up. I can tell Grayson she wasn't interested, and then if we continue to hit it off, maybe we can hang out while she's in town.

She'll leave in a few weeks, so there's no expectation of anything serious or long term.

There's a not-too-bad rendition of "Son of a Preacher Man," followed by a cringe-worthy version of "Killing Me Softly." Then it's Tabitha's turn.

I surely hope she can sing better than the last bloke. Ouch. I'm not drunk enough to listen to that. Odds are, I will never be drunk enough to hear that rendition again.

Right before Tabitha takes the center floor, as there is no real stage, I see her pause. She holds her hands out to either side, opening and flexing her fingers, as if she's squeezing something. She shuts her eyes tightly for a moment before adjusting her posture and walking to the mic.

She's put her performance face on.

And then the music starts. I'm trying to place it. Three words in, and I know it. "A Million Dreams" from *The Greatest Showman*. My heart quickens a beat. It's on our schedule for this summer. We were one of a handful of smaller theatres to be chosen to workshop it while they try to sell it to Broadway.

Tabitha has become radiant, belting out the song, intermittently closing her eyes and holding up her hand to the audience. It doesn't matter that we're in the basement of this small pub. She might as well be performing on the world's largest stage.

I don't know why her group didn't have more than one hit song with vocal talent like hers. I glance around and see more than one person with their phone out, recording her.

They should.

She's incredible.

I'd be nuts not to get her for The Edison. She could launch the theatre into the next stratosphere.

Dammit.

I try to see her impartially, just as I would do during an audition. I remind myself—this is an audition.

Stick with the plan.

But as Tabitha closes out the song, the place erupts in applause, and I find myself on my feet, cheering and whistling with the rest of them. Though she's probably only thirty feet away, suddenly there are scads of people keeping her from reaching our table. More than one person asks for—and receives—a selfie with her.

They must have placed her.

I'm a bit curious to see how she plays that off once she returns to the table.

Chapter 5: Tabitha

Singing may not have been the best idea, because, brown hair or not, I've been made. At least four people ask to take a selfie with me before I can make it back to Henderson.

I see more than one cat claw.

I'm going to have to tell him why people were taking my picture.

It was sort of nice that he seemed to be happy to spend the evening with just a single mom from California.

But no matter how hard I try, I'll never be just a single mom from California. I'm not sure I want to be either.

I smile and pose with one more person before I finally lock eyes on Henderson. He's sitting, relaxed in his chair, doing a slow clap as I approach. I take a quick little curtsey.

"*I sing a little*. That's complete and utter crap. You sing a lot, and you just sang the hell out of that." He takes me into his arms, crushing me in a big hug.

My cheeks grow flushed, though I don't know if it's from humility or the nearness of *him*. I was never quite as strong a vocalist as Mandy, but I could definitely hold my own. And I used to be able to own that. This feeling of modesty creeping over me is how I felt trying to wear Angie's shoes.

It doesn't fit me well at all.

"So, maybe I used to be a singer." I pull back, sliding into my chair and draining the rest of my wine. I could really use a water. And maybe another bottle of wine.

Or two.

"Maybe?"

"Okay, I was a singer. I had a career as a singer. But I don't do that anymore." I look around, this flushed feeling not going away. "Is it hot in here?"

"Girl, you are on fire!" The manager has appeared at our table. "We're so honored to have you here. Here's a bottle of champagne, on the house."

I stand up and shake his hand, thanking him. Henderson stands up too, also extending his gratitude.

I lean in and say to the manager, "I'm having a great time here with my friend. I'd love to continue this low-key night, if you don't mind. I'll be happy to give your place a shout out on my social media later, but I'd like to keep some privacy, if you don't mind." What's with all the "if you don't mind" crap? I sound like a bumbling idiot.

He nods profusely. "Of course. Is there anything else we can do for you?"

"I'd love some water. Flat. Cool, but no ice."

"Right away." The manager turns and is gone. I hope he comes back soon. I really need that water.

"Did you order your water cool, but with no ice?" Henderson raises an eyebrow at me as we slide back into our chairs.

I grin sheepishly. "It's how I like it, especially after singing. Plus it'll give him a story to tell of how demanding I was. It makes for better press that way."

And just like that, I'm falling back into my old ways.

Immediately, guilt washes over me. For a minute, up on that stage, I forgot myself. I forgot that I'm no longer Tabby Cat. I forgot that I'm just someone's mother.

Crap. Paisley.

I haven't heard from them all day. Not since our handoff at the Central Park Zoo, right before I was attacked by the goat. I should call her. Paisley. Not the goat. Or at the very least I should text Maria.

What kind of mother turns her child over to someone and walks away without looking back?

The bad kind.

Me.

"Hey, you okay? Your face changed there. You can't be nervous about having performed, can you? You're such a natural up there."

I want to hide my face in my hands, the shame overwhelming me. I can't, though, because all eyes—and cell phones—are on me. I straighten my shoulders, putting on my bravest performance face. I put my hand on his. "It's not that. I ... I can't say right now. I need to check my phone, but I don't want to do that right now." I glance around, and Henderson follows my gaze.

"Right. Got it. Hang on."

He waves to the manager, who is on his way back with my water. Henderson stands up, says something in his ear, and the manager waves me over. "You can use my office. It's a bit quieter in there."

Henderson walks me to the door, but stops before entering. "I'll wait for you here, unless you need me."

"Can you go sit at our table so we don't lose it? I'm not ready to go. I just ... I need to do this."

"No worries. I'll be holding your seat and trying not to judge the other singers who pale in comparison to you. You really were bloody brilliant up there." He gives my cheek a quick kiss.

My hands are shaking by the time I step into the office. It must be soundproofed in here because I only hear muffled thumps of the beat from the speakers. I text Maria, but when she doesn't respond immediately, I start to freak out. I call her. It goes to voicemail.

I am the worst mother in the world.

In a panic, I call Jonathan Spencer Maxwell.

"What?"

That's how this prince among men answers the phone. If his adoring fans only knew what he was really like in private. He gives Ellen DeGeneres a run for worst dark secrets.

I mean, obviously. He has a love child with me. He's certainly not the man he leads the media to think he is. No way, no how.

"I ... I couldn't get a hold of Maria. I wanted to know how Paisley is doing."

"Maria was giving her a bath last I know. I think. I dunno. They're in their apartment."

"Isn't she staying at your place? That was the whole point." I want to scream. He makes me uproot my daughter—and my life—for almost a month so they can bond, and he pawns her off on the nanny.

"I have an early meeting tomorrow, plus she liked Maria's place better. It's smaller, and she said it was more like her home."

Ouch. What a prick.

"She'll be here with me tomorrow night. I just had this last meeting that I couldn't get off the books. And it's my time with her, so you relax. I don't call you all the time about how she's doing. If we need you, which I doubt, we'll be in touch."

No, he doesn't call often, and if it weren't for his wife, I'm sure he never would.

I'm unsettled that I didn't get to talk to Paisley—or at least Maria—directly, but it is late. Knowing Maria, she's got Paisley settled in bed, and it would be too late to talk to her anyway. I should feel better that my daughter is with the only person I trust in the world, but I don't.

There's a soft knock on the door. Henderson pokes his head in. "Howzit going? You wanna leave?"

I start to nod, but then realize something. Now that I know Paisley is with Maria and therefore fine, I don't want to go. I want to stay in this moment and feel again how I did when I was on stage.

For the first time in a very long time, I felt like *me.*

I want to get up there and sing again. I want to be a star again. And I want to tell all that to Henderson, but it's not the sort of thing you say on a first date.

It's certainly not the kind of thing you tell someone who could then run and blab to any rag that will listen and publish. Let's face it, we all know that my "child support" includes a hefty implied "keep your mouth shut" bonus.

That's right. The world does not know that I, Tabitha Stetson, a member of the Sassy Cats, had a child with Jonathan Spencer Maxwell. Or that she was conceived in the back of a limo.

Or that Jonathan's wife, Anastasia Jerome, knows all about it.

I mean, it's one reason that I've tried to stay out of the public eye the past few years. Maybe not the *main* reason but … well, it is a big part of my motivation for privacy.

I didn't think I missed it, until now.

I stand up and take the glass of champagne that Henderson has so thoughtfully brought in here for me. I drain it before glamorously wiping my mouth with the back of my hand. "I wanna sing another song, and I want you to sing with me."

Before I give Henderson a chance to respond, I take him by the hand and drag him out to the bar.

It's time to get our song on.

Chapter 6: Henderson

Crikeys.

She wants me to sing.

Whatever she had to do in here, it visibly upset her. I guess there could be worse ways to deal with it. After all, she's not the one who will be humiliated.

Ah, but if she embarrasses me, maybe I can use it for leverage to guilt her into taking a role at The Edison. Though the more time I spend with her, the less that's actually on my mind.

"Right. What song?"

She scrolls through the duets list. "Um, how about 'Love is an Open Door?' It's from *Frozen.* My world sort of revolves around Elsa and Anna these days."

Ugh. No. "That's a pass." I scan for something that won't make me sound like a complete idiot. "What about 'You're the One That I Want?' from *Grease*?" I'd definitely be more comfortable with a show tune that I've heard and directed a million times. Plus, it's not like that song requires much range.

"That song is so tired. Oh! I've got it. It's perfect for us!" She selects an entry before I can see what it is. It'd better not be 'Shallow' or 'Come What May,' as I know those are both popular karaoke duets, and both out of my skill set.

Or at least out of my comfort zone.

But who'm I kidding? Everything about this night is outside my comfort zone.

Because Tabitha is Tabitha, we get the next slot. The manager's all too eager to have her back on the stage. I toss back the rest of my coldie and wish I had several pints more. She drains another glass of champagne.

I am not ready for this.

Then the title flashes on the monitor. "We've Got Tonight." I grin at her and she gives me a sly, seductive smile.

If I didn't know better, I'd think she maybe was coming on to me. I'm not sure though. It's not as if she started telling me about the time she went backpacking across Western Europe, hiking in the foothills of Mount Tibidabo.

"I thought it fit. And it was either this or 'Islands in the Stream.'" She leans in close and whispers, her breath hot and husky against my ear, "Don't tell anyone, but I'm a closet Kenny Rogers fan."

There's an unmistakable look in her eyes when she sings to me. If I didn't know she was a performer, I'd be falling for it hook, line, and sinker.

Maybe I still am.

We finish up and I pull her to me. It takes everything I have not to kiss her. But there are cell phones waving in the air.

"We need to go. I need to get out of here," she says. Once again, she takes my hand and pulls me from the stage area, heading toward the stairs. I pull her back quickly and grab our coats and her purse. Then, she's tugging me to leave again. The cold February air hits my face, but I can barely feel it. Tabitha continues leading me, stumbling as her heel catches in a sidewalk crack.

"Where are we going?" I ask.

She turns and pulls me into a small alley, pushing me against the brick wall. Instinctively, my hands go to her waist, pulling her body to mine. As she leans in, though, the reality of the situation hits me. "What are you doing?"

Tabitha pulls back, startled. "What does it look like I'm doing?"

I put my hands on her forearms to separate us, as well as to start backing her toward the street. "Tabitha, this isn't a movie set. This alley is probably filled with urine and feces and God knows what else. Not to mention it's a really good way to get mugged."

"Oh and yuck. Can we go somewhere?"

The neon lights of an overhead sign light up her blue eyes. Even though I've been looking at her all night, suddenly now she seems familiar. I can't place her, but it's like we've met before. Or is it just that something has changed between us?

Or maybe we're both drunk and horny.

The last option seems most likely.

"Let's go to my ..." I trail off, the earlier burst pipe returning to the forefront of my mind. "Crap. My place is flooded."

"It's fine. I'm staying with Angie and Sergei, but they're still out of town. Duh, obviously. So we have the place to ourselves. I mean, if you want to."

"Oh, I want to. Where do they live?" I've got my fingers crossed for somewhere close.

"Brooklyn." Her gaze darts to the side. "I honestly have no idea how to get there, though. I tried taking the subway earlier today and ended up in Chinatown. At least that's where I think I was."

I glance at my watch; it's pushing midnight. "Let's grab an Uber. Do you at least have their address?"

She nods. "I feel like such an idiot that I can't work the subway. I mean, like millions of people take it every day, but it's like reading Greek." Tabitha leans in close, her breath heavy with wine. "I don't speak Greek."

"I'll teach you how it works. By the time you go back to California, you'll be a pro at it."

"Is that a promise?" she asks coyly, holding my gaze for a beat before pulling out her phone and swiping away. "Uber will be here in seven minutes. I wonder what we could do to pass the time?"

"I've got a thought." I've got multiple thoughts, but many of them would have me arrested for public indecency and lewdness, so I try to keep it PG-rated.

"Me too," she says breathlessly, as her lips close in on mine. Oh good, we're on the same page.

This is a woman who knows how to kiss.

This is also not where I saw this night going. Not at all. Maybe schmoozing has an upside?

A car horn startles us apart and Tabitha giggles. "Oops, that's our Uber." She again takes my hand, pulling me toward the car. I don't even have a chance to open the door for her.

I may be thinking quite naughty thoughts, but that doesn't mean I'm not still a gentleman. Okay, maybe it does, but I can still open the door for her.

In the back of the car, Tabitha all but climbs me like a tree. It's all well and good until I notice the Uber driver watching in the rearview mirror. From the reaction at Oppa, Tabitha is at least somewhat recognizable to the general public. Photos of her and me in compromising positions don't need to surface.

Plus, the bloke is invading our privacy.

I put my hands on her hips and gently push her back onto the seat. Seriously, I didn't know I possessed this kind of restraint. I kiss her gently on the temple. "You're enough to tempt a man's willpower, but I don't think you want an audience for this." I nod toward the front of the car.

Tabitha rolls her eyes. "It's so annoying, never feeling like you can step out of the house without someone watching. Someone judging. And I know I'm supposed to lie low because of Paisley. Like, this could be a disaster." She motions between us.

Great. She called me a disaster. If that's not a blow to the ego, I don't know what is.

"Then maybe we should part ways," I say curtly.

She swings her leg over again, firmly placing herself on my lap. In the dark of the car, it's hard to make out her features. "I don't want to part ways. At least not yet."

The car lurches to a stop and Tabitha looks up. She opens the door and sort of slides out. It's not a graceful move, and I don't know how she doesn't topple arse over teakettle. She rights herself and holds out her hand to me. "You coming?"

Hell, yes.

Chapter 7: Tabitha

My head pounds. The throbbing is so bad, and this is before I've even opened my eyes. I think a slow death would feel better.

I am never drinking again.

I didn't think I'd had a lot to drink, but on the other hand, I haven't been out much in the past few years. I try to mentally count how many beverages I may have consumed. It started off with those delicious melon champagne things at dinner.

Dinner.

Henderson.

Henderson.

Yup, there he is, right beside me, lying face down on the bed. With the daylight streaming through the sheer curtains, Henderson's hair looks much more dark blond than the auburn I'd thought last night. He's still, breathing deeply.

I glance down and see that I'm in my bra and underwear. Huh.

He's fully dressed. Double huh.

The light is too strong and I have to close my eyes again. In my alcohol-addled brain, I try to piece together the rest of the night. I remember dinner. I remember the cool bar and karaoke. I remember calling and not being able to talk to Paisley. Then, things start to get fuzzy. I think there was more singing. I know there was kissing.

Lots of kissing.

And ... I don't know.

The last thing I really remember is being in the Uber.

Oh God. Please don't tell me I had another fling in a livery vehicle.

I was supposed to learn a lesson from the last time.

Of course, I've always been a slow learner.

Plus, who knows how clean those Ubers are? I shudder a little at the thought.

That slight movement sends a wave of nausea rippling through my body. There's a good chance I may vomit.

My former rock star self is so disappointed in this mellow, boring version of me who cannot handle a few cocktails and a few glasses of wine.

Okay, maybe more than a few, but still.

And a drawback to partying like a rock star when I am no longer one is that I don't have staff and crew available to help nurse me back to feeling human again. I'm missing the water and ibuprofen and B-12 and greasy eggs that would appear out of thin air the morning after a night out.

Jeez, even my hair hurts.

I get up, stumbling a bit and trying to navigate a strange apartment without actually opening my eyes. Of course I run into the dresser. And the door.

Ouch.

By the time I get to the bathroom, which seems about six blocks away, I'm covered in a cold sweat. Puke is most certainly going to happen.

Great. I can only imagine the story Henderson will sell to the tabloids. Though I can't really think of that right now. I lie down on the floor, the cool tile feeling like heaven against my head. I don't even have time to wonder if the floor is clean.

Frankly, it doesn't matter. I'd lie down on the floor in the bathrooms at Grand Central Station. I must doze off for a minute—or twenty—as I'm startled awake by the door opening.

And then closing.

I've never claimed to be that smart, but it doesn't take a rocket scientist to figure out that Henderson just snuck out.

Bastard.

He probably knew who I was all along. He probably has pictures of me in my bra and underwear, passed out on the bathroom floor. Or at least a lurid story to sell. At least Paisley wasn't around to be in it.

But what if he talks about how I talked about my daughter? There aren't that many Paisleys in the world—I know, I checked. If Paisley gets linked to Jonathan Spencer Maxwell through me, there will be hell to pay.

For me.

Secrets suck.

I want to smack myself, but I really don't think my head can take the pain. What was I thinking? Going out with a complete stranger. *Bringing him home.* God, I've learned nothing from my past mistakes.

Nothing.

I'm no better than my mother.

But ... Angie and Sergei set me up with him. He's one of Sergei's friends. Sergei should have known better. He should have vetted Henderson for me. Heck, they should have been here with me like they were supposed to be.

It's all their fault.

I mean, in reality, I know I'm a grown-ass woman who should know better than to drink too much and bring a perfect stranger home. It's easier not to take that on, though.

I should probably get up and make sure that Aussie scumbucket didn't steal money or any of my stuff. I bet the pervert stole my underwear to sell on eBay. I bet—

"Tabitha, are you still in the bathroom? I ran and got some Maccas for you. Well, for us really, but I bet you need 'em more."

I sit up way too quickly, causing the room to spin like a ride at Disneyland.

Whoa.

"Henderson, is that you?" I croak, managing to get to my feet. I grab a swig from the mouthwash bottle on the back of the sink, swishing it around in an attempt to rid my mouth of the taste of a thousand dumpsters lingering there.

"Yeah, Tabitha. Were you expecting some other bloke?" He pokes his head in the bathroom door, which is still open. "Where do you want the Maccas?"

"What's maccas?" I squint as I turn to face him, the light hurting my eyes. Nothing makes sense.

"McDonalds. There's one not too far. I got a bunch of different brekkies. Didn't know what you'd like."

I stand there for a minute, feeling like death warmed over. I don't expect my eyes to fill with tears, but they do.

He didn't leave me.

He brought me food.

There's probably a good chance he didn't even steal from me or sell naked pictures of me.

Maybe.

I hope.

"Let's sit on the couch. The bathroom doesn't seem like the right place to eat."

Henderson smiles. "After you." He steps aside and gallantly waves the hand not holding the McDonald's bag.

I start to walk by him, only to realize I'm still just wearing my bra and underwear. "Let me put some clothes on and I'll meet you out there."

Back in my room, I frantically begin tearing through my suitcases. I hadn't really started unpacking yesterday before I got ready to meet up with Henderson. God, that seems so long ago.

The effort of finding clothes quickly saps my energy. My tank is empty and now movement is hard, my arms feeling like they weigh nine hundred pounds each. Finally, I locate a pair of pajama bottoms and a tank top. I'm just about dressed when I hear a loud voice.

"Who the hell are you and why the hell are you in my apartment?" It's Sergei, and he does not sound happy.

"Oh my God, where's Tabby? Tabby, are you okay? Tabby?" Even from down the hall, I can hear the frantic note in Angie's voice.

I try to pull the shirt down over my head, only to get caught in the strap. I'm on the move, heading toward Angie as I do this, which promptly results in me tripping over the end of the bed and going down like a sack of bricks.

I'm going to be covered in bruises, not from being drunk, but from being hungover and clumsy.

"OWW!"

The shirt is still over my face as I flail around. Arms envelop me, and in an instant, I'm sitting on the bed. Sergei is pulling my shirt down. "Tabby, are you okay? What happened? Did he do this to you?"

"He? No, I couldn't get my shirt on right. I also couldn't walk and get dressed at the same time. I'm super hungover, so if you can stop yelling, I'd really love that. I want to eat my food and go back to sleep for ten years, okay?" I blink and then focus on my friends, who I haven't seen in over a year. "But give me a hug first. I've missed you two nuts."

I hold my arms out, and both Angie and Sergei melt into them. I can't stabilize myself against them, so I fall back onto the bed, pulling them with me. Then, because it's all so ridiculous, I start laughing. Angie joins in, and then soon the three of us are lying there, holding on to each other for dear life, laughing like hyenas.

It's nice to know that no matter what, there will always be a place for me in the arms of one of my fellow Sassy Cats.

Chapter 8: Henderson

This day keeps getting weirder, and it's only nine in the morning.

Tabitha certainly is in rough shape. I mean, it became quite apparent when she couldn't work the key in the lock last night. The downstairs neighbor didn't appreciate the ruckus, for sure.

Tabitha even took it quite well when I told her—despite her fervent, yet uncoordinated efforts—that I couldn't have sex with her while she was three sheets to the wind. I did acquiesce and agree to stay the night, at her insistence.

Weighing only slightly in on that decision was the fact that I had no place to go, as my apartment is still flooded.

Still, there was a good chance that she was going to be tossing her cookies, and it was only responsible to stay and make sure she was safe.

Obviously, I didn't expect her friends to return so soon. Just as I'm sure they didn't expect to find a strange man on their couch eating his brekkie. I'd have yelled too if I were in their shoes, but still, the bloke seems like a dick.

There's a lot of noise coming from the bedroom. I try to ignore it and pull out my phone. I'd turned it off last night to conserve the battery.

Apparently, that was a mistake, because the moment I power up, it begins blowing up with messages and notifications. I have six—*SIX*—voicemails from Grayson. There are at least ten text messages.

Any more progress?

Um, dude, what's going on?

H-what happened?

Are you OK? Call me man.

HENDERSON, CALL ME BACK. WERE YOU WITH HER?

I sigh, dialing Grayson without bothering to listen to the voicemails. I'm sure they're just more of him with his knickers in a twist.

I run my hand through my hair, unsure of how I'm going to tell him that we didn't really even talk about The Edison. He's so worked up already. He's going to flip his lid.

"Oh, man, Henderson, are you okay?"

"Yeah, fine. Why wouldn't I be?"

"Haven't you heard? What time did you leave her? Were you with her when it happened? Was it after you left? Did the police call you?"

"What in bloody hell are you rambling on about? Heard about what? Police?"

There's silence for a moment. "Then you don't know."

"I've no idea what you're talking about, mate."

"She's dead."

My mind immediately jumps to Grayson's mum, though I really don't know what that has to do with me. God, I am such a crap friend. I should have been there for him. Did he send the police to find me to tell me? Surely they have better things to do with their time. "Your mum? I'm so sorry, mate."

"My mom? No. What are you talking about?"

Maybe I'm a skosh hungover too, because I am not following this conversation at all. "What are you talking about?"

"Tawny Shane. She's dead."

The name means nothing to me.

"Okay, who's that?"

"*Tawny Shane*," Grayson repeats, like his saying it again is going to make a difference. "You know, the lead singer for Fate's Daughter."

Still means nothing.

Grayson continues, growing more agitated by the minute. "The woman you were out with last night. She was found dead at about two this morning. They think it was drugs. Did you know she was using? Was she high last night? Was she a mess when you left her? How did you part?"

Now I'm really confused. "I've no idea what you're talking about. I don't know who Tawny Shane is. Or was."

Grayson's yelling now, "SHE WAS THE GIRL YOU WERE WITH LAST NIGHT!"

"All right, simmer down, mate. No need to get all worked up." But even as I say it, I'm trying to process what possibly could have happened. "I didn't meet any Tawny Shane last night."

"Then who were you out with that you told me you were working on it? Were you lying to me? I thought you were better than that. Oh God, Henderson, are you messed up in this? Do you need a lawyer?"

I rest my forehead in my hand. It's starting to throb, probably because of all the yelling. Maybe a bit because of the beer. "I didn't lie to you, and no, I don't need a lawyer. Don't be daft. Gimme a minute to figure it out."

"Tell me what happened, from the beginning."

I recount the night. "I got to Jack's Wife Freda for an eight o'clock reservation. I gave my name to the hostess.

The minute I told her I was meeting someone, she was there, behind me. She said she was meeting me, and that they told her she'd love my accent."

"Did she ask you about shrimp on the barbie?"

I laugh, this joke going way back with Grayson and me. "No, but I thought she was going to. I owe you a shot."

"So Tawny was there?"

"No, it wasn't Tawny. It was Tabby. Tabitha."

"Tabitha?"

I lower my voice a bit, in case she can hear me. She's been in the bedroom with her friends for quite a while. I'm going to need her to come out so we can get to the bottom of this.

"Yeah. You couldn't remember her name, but said it was a T-something. She originally introduced herself as Tabby. And though she didn't mention it for a while, she was a singer. I took her to karaoke. She can actually sing. Quite well. She'll kill it at The Edison."

"So who is she then? What happened with Tawny?"

"No clue about the Tawny thing, and as to who she is, I'm going to find out. Call you back."

I stand up, determined to get to the bottom of this. As I approach the door, I hear raised voices.

"But I don't understand, Tabby. You were supposed to meet up with Dimitri. He's pissed that you stood him up. He was blowing up Sergei's phone all night. Sergei was so pissed at you. If we hadn't been on the red eye, we would have been blowing up your phone too. What were you thinking? How could you do this to us? I thought you were trying to be reliable. We told him you'd be there."

"I don't know what to tell you. I went to the restaurant like you told me. Henderson was there, and he said he was meeting someone. I heard the accent and figured it was him. I didn't see anyone else there alone."

Now that she mentions it, I didn't either. I wonder if this Tawny person, God rest her soul, even showed up last night. My money's on no.

I knock gently on the door. Two sets of accusing eyes swivel toward me. Tabitha looks like she's just completed an Ironman triathlon. "'Scuse me. I'd like to figure this out too. I just found out that you were not the person I was supposed to be meeting up with either."

"This doesn't concern you, you freeloading creep." The man stands up and steps toward me.

Is this really happening? Am I about to get in a fight over a case of mistaken identity? For Pete's sake, I didn't even sleep with her!

I take a breath and try to act like I'm calm. "Tabitha, can you please tell your guard dog to stand down?"

"Sergei, leave Henderson alone. He's nice."

"Nice, Tabby?" Now the other friend is on her feet, her brown eyes blazing with an intensity that's definitely scary. No doubt she could take me in a nanosecond. "How many times do you have to be swindled and taken advantage of? Hell, you have a kid because you're too trusting and gullible. He's just another one, trying to take advantage of your fame and fortune."

I knew she was fierce and ferocious—the heat in her eyes said so. This must be the Angie that Tabitha kept mentioning last night. My mind whirls as the pieces snap together. Holy crap. I spent the night in Angie Aliberti's apartment! My brush with Broadway royalty has not been the greatest.

"I swear, I was there to meet someone about business. Trust me, I was not hauling my ass from Long Island City to the West Village to try and take advantage of someone."

Angie looks at me for a beat before turning back to Tabitha. "The West Village? How did you end up in the West Village, Tabby? You were supposed to be in SoHo."

The silence in the room is so thick you could cut it.

Then, I start laughing. I can't help it. I know exactly what happened. I don't even know Tabitha well, but she was very upfront about her terrible sense of direction in New York City. "They're not that far apart. Easy mistake."

Tabitha looks at me, not following what's going on. "What mistake?"

"The restaurant—Jack's Wife Freda—has multiple locations. One in SoHo, which is apparently where you were supposed to be, and one in the West Village, which is where you ended up. It's where I was supposed to be meeting someone for an informal audition, but apparently she never showed."

Angie and Sergei look from Tabitha to me and then back to her. "How do you know this guy is legit? He could be feeding you a bunch of stories to take advantage of you. Audition my ass. You were probably trying to get her to your 'casting couch.'" Sergei sneers.

I need to put a stop to this before it gets nasty.

Nastier.

"Listen, mates, I'm not taking advantage of Tabitha. You can verify my story with Carson Reuben from *Backstage Magazine*. He set up the meeting on behalf of my partner, Grayson Keene. We're with The Edison Theater in Hicklam, New York. Grayson couldn't make it, so I stepped in at the last minute. I was supposed to be meeting Tawny Shane, but, well ..." I trail off, not knowing how to finish the sentence.

"Tawny Shane? Like from Fate's Daughter?" Tabitha cocks her head and looks at me, that puzzled expression back on her face. "I know her. God, what a small world. They tried to compete with us for so long, but they weren't that good. Tawny was the best of them, but she couldn't keep clean. Last I saw her she was high as a kite and a hot mess."

Tabitha knew Tawny Shane. Well, this is going to be swell news to break.

Chapter 9: Tabitha

I'm so confused.

The raging headache and lingering need to puke doesn't help. I know Angie and Sergei are only looking out for me, but Henderson doesn't deserve this abuse. I'm almost positive he was a perfect gentleman. Part of me also wants to get defensive that I can sleep with whomever I want to, but based on my track record, Angie and Sergei are being the friends I need them to be.

I also want to eat my Egg McMuffin, so I stand up and march out to the living room, brushing past an irate Angie and Sergei and an uncomfortable-looking Henderson.

Seriously, he looks like he might be the one to throw up.

They trail out after me. I look back over my shoulder and don't miss the exchange of wary glances, although they are mostly training their disappointment on me. "What? I need some food."

Henderson clears his throat. "Uh, Tabitha, I don't know how to say this, but, um, I believe Tawny Shane did not get clean and sober."

"Did not?" Angie zeroes in on Henderson.

He looks down at his hands. "Um, no. She was not able to kick drugs. I'm sure it's ... ah ... on the internet that she—"

"Tawny is trending? I've got to see what she did now. Angie, look it up." I talk with a mouth full, dropping a bite of egg out of my mouth. Super attractive.

Angie whips out her phone and begins scrolling. I don't even know where my phone is. Henderson's mouth opens and closes as he looks from me to Angie and back again.

"Oh my God. Oh my God. OH MY GOD. Tabitha!" Angie's on her feet, showing the phone to Sergei. Why is Angie yelling? It can't be good. Why did I ask her to look? I should know that curiosity killed the cat.

"What are you carrying on about over there?" I roll my eyes. Angie can be so dramatic sometimes.

"Go get your phone and see. I can't. I ..." Angie trails off.

I sigh, hauling myself up. My head hurts and I'm hungry and hung over, but my morbid curiosity about what Tawny's got herself into wins out.

The guest room looks like a bomb went off. I finally find my phone under my crumpled-up dress. I root around some more to find my charger. I plug it into the outlet on the bedside lamp and flop on the bed. I probably shouldn't leave Henderson out there with Angie and Sergei, but frankly I don't feel well enough to stay upright. Being hungover in your thirties sucks. I wish he'd come in here and lie down with me. After my phone powers up, I holler, "What site?"

Angie hollers back, "TMZ. No, E! Actually, go to Twitter."

Driven by a curiosity to find out why Tawny Shane is in the news and what horrible misstep she's made now, I select the Twitter icon.

But it's not Tawny that's trending. It's me.

Videos from the bar and karaoke, and even a picture of me giving that homeless guy money.

I'm all over Twitter.

"I'm trending!" Hangover temporarily pushed aside, I jump off the bed and run back out to the living area. Henderson is standing by the door, looking like he'd rather have a testicle removed than be here for one more second. "Henderson, I'm trending on Twitter! I haven't trended since I nursed Paisley on *Really Late Night with Dirk Diamond*. I didn't even have to whip out a boob this time!"

His head tilts slightly. "You've been on *Really Late Night with Dirk Diamond*?" If I'm not mistaken, his color lightens about ten shades, and he looks a little queasy. Maybe he should eat his Egg McMuffin.

"Yeah, it was right before our big reunion concert. What was that, Ang? Like three years ago? Almost four. Yeah, because Paisley was a newborn. I sang last night. I really missed it. You know, we should do another concert. The Sassy Cats are probably due for a reunion."

He staggers back a step, sagging into the door frame. "Yeah, so I ... um ... I should go."

"Why?" I take a step toward him. "I mean, I know they're being jerks, but their bark is worse than their bite. Trust me. They'll be fine. Eventually. Don't go."

I want Henderson to stay longer. I liked getting to know him and him getting to know me, without all the Sassy Cats stuff in the way. Plus, I have to make it up to him for getting so drunk last night. Not to mention, I need to make huge amends for Angie and Sergei's behavior. Seriously, where do they get off?

He looks from me to Angie, and then back to me again. "Look, I'm a little out of my league here. I was supposed to meet up with a washed-up former pop star to try to convince her to do a show this summer at my theatre in Upstate. I saw you last night; you're the furthest thing from washed-up that there could be. Obviously, we were both in the wrong place at the wrong time."

I take another step toward him, and then another, until I'm right in front of him. I reach out and tug his hands out of his jeans pockets. "But I thought we had a good time last night. I mean, what I can remember was fun."

His eyes crinkle slightly. "And what do you remember, exactly?"

Maybe because it's obvious he really didn't know who I was while we were on our date, so he may have been pure in his intentions. Maybe it's because I'm not used to being turned down. Maybe it's just because he's really cute. Whatever the reason, I don't want him to go.

"I remember you told me you would show me how to take the subway." I surprise myself when I say this. I didn't know I remembered it. "I have all this free time, and I want to spend some of it with you."

Sergei starts laughing. "Jesus, Tab, the man wants out. Look at him. You've got him cornered like a—"

Angie interrupts him. "Like a cat with a mouse."

I look at Angie and start laughing. Another cat joke. We've heard them all throughout the years. "Couldn't help yourself, could you?"

"You were in the Sassy Cats?" Henderson says finally. I can't believe it's taken him this long to put it all together. Especially since I just said it. "God, of course you were. I guess I knew Angie Aliberti was. I never put it together that you were friends with her because of it. Of course, I thought you were in Fate's Daughter, whom I've only vaguely heard of." He cocks his head, his brow furrowing slightly. "You're a big star."

I shrug in a fake-modesty-but-actually-thrilled-that-he-said-it kind of way.

I am a star.

And I hate trying to hide it.

But I have to. For Paisley.

But now I'm all over the internet, singing. I could go viral. "Oh crap, he's going to go ballistic when he sees this." I take a step back and reach for my phone. I need to look at the videos again. I need to see if I was doing anything embarrassing or anything that could be used against me. "Oh, God, Ang, this is bad." My knees give out as I plop to the couch.

How could I be so irresponsible?

Henderson takes a step toward me. "Tabitha, I'm sure it's fine. You didn't do anything wrong."

I smile weakly. I've done so much wrong. He has no idea.

Chapter 10: Henderson

I feel like I'm in The Twilight Zone.

It's all so surreal.

And I can't believe I was so slow on the uptake.

Tabitha is a member of the Sassy Cats. Hell, even I've heard of that group. You'd have to be dead not to.

That makes me think of Tawny Shane, may she rest in peace.

But at least Tawny Shane was probably more in my league. Or at least The Edison's league.

Tabitha is not.

And all I can do is hope she doesn't circle back to the whole secret audition bit before I can excuse myself and get the hell out of Dodge. I'd look like a bloody fool.

See? This is why it's no good mixing business with pleasure. It always comes back to bite you in the arse. And it's not like we even got to the pleasure part.

Not that I have any regrets on that—I did what needed to be done and was the responsible party. Still, I'd like to leave and put this all behind me.

Maybe it'll be an amusing party story one day.

Today is not that day.

As I take a step back, trying to make my way to the door again, I see Tabitha with her head in her hands. It doesn't take a rocket scientist to see how upset she is about the karaoke video.

I did this to her. My actions are directly responsible for her being upset.

Damn.

Although, I don't know why she's so upset. Her performance was far and above anything Oppa! has probably ever seen. Nevertheless, I can't leave her like this. I can't have her feeling bad because of me.

I move across the room. "You sounded great singing. Think about all the people there last night who got the treat of a lifetime. Seriously, you were fantastic. There's nothing to be upset about." I pat her awkwardly on the back, like you would do with a small child. Or your granny.

"You have no idea." Angie scoffs. "How could you let her do this? Do you know what it means for her?"

I'd like to say something biting and defensive back, but I don't want to piss Angie Aliberti off any further. She probably has the power to make or break me—and The Edison. We've already barely survived one Broadway star and her tantrums. I don't need to invite another.

"Actually, I don't know what it means. Until a few moments ago, I didn't really even know who you were." I address Tabitha and not Angie. "I don't understand why this is bad. Why would this make someone go ballistic? Isn't any publicity good publicity?"

"Not when the identity of your baby daddy is the biggest secret in Hollywood. And not when he's not supposed to have a child with a woman who is not his wife," Tabitha says dryly.

"Tabby!" Angie admonishes.

Tabitha looks from Angie to me and then back again. She shrugs. "Might as well tell him. I already let the—"

"Don't say it." Sergei rolls his eyes.

"—Cat outta the bag," she continues. Tabitha's speaking to Angie and Sergei, not me. It's as if I'm not even in the room. I hadn't pegged her for pretentious and condescending. Angie maybe, but not Tabitha. Not after last night.

"You should keep your mouth shut, Tabby," Angie warns.

Defiantly, Tabitha folds her arms across her chest. The two women stare at each other, volumes of conversation passing between them without a word spoken aloud. Finally, Tabitha turns to address me. She takes my hands in hers again. "Can I trust you?"

If nothing else, I'm at least trustworthy. "Yes, you can."

"Tabitha, you know you can't," Angie warns.

"I think I can." Tabitha looks from me to Angie and then back again before steadying herself with a deep breath. "Okay, what I'm about to say doesn't leave this room. Because if it does, I'll find out and there will be a passel of lawyers on you so fast your head will spin. Got it?"

I don't care for this aspect of Tabitha at all. I pull my hands out from under hers and nod.

"The 'he' is Jonathan Spencer Maxwell." Her lips form a tight line.

Angie shakes her head and folds her arms disapprovingly. I am definitely not supposed to know this. I don't think I *want* to know this.

"Like the big movie star, Jonathan Spencer Maxwell?"

"Like the father of my child, Jonathan Spencer Maxwell." Her gaze drops to the floor.

If I'd had any doubts about being out of my league and in over my head, they were just cemented. "Oscar winner and philanthropist, Jonathan Spencer Maxwell?"

"Seduced-me-in-the-backseat-of-a-limo-and-lied-that-he-had-had-a-vasectomy, Jonathan Spencer Maxwell."

I'm getting really sick of this bloke's name.

"Isn't he married to—"

"Yes, Anastasia Jerome. The biggest female producer of all time. She knows all about it. And she would like to keep this quiet."

I'm sure she would. The happy Hollywood marriage story of Anastasia Jerome and Jonathan Spencer Maxwell rivals that of Rita Wilson and Tom Hanks. Or even Paul Newman and Joanne Woodward. It's sort of disheartening to know that it's all a lie. Of course, I should have suspected nothing less. True love is a line of crap, fabricated for suckers. But like P.T. Barnum said, there's one born every minute. "Right. I'm guessing a love child is not in the script."

Tabitha finally looks at me again. "So you get it. There were already a few rounds of rumors and speculation that we managed to quash. I can't have any more. I can't be seen out and about too much. I can't let Paisley be seen with me, lest they see her with him and then everyone will know."

There are too many pronouns in that sentence to be totally clear, but I think I follow.

"But you weren't with her last night. You were with me. Why should it matter?"

"But I'm here in *New York*." She whispers the location, like it's some big secret.

"Yeah, you and eight million other people. I don't think it's a big deal."

"*He's* here in New York, and he's sure to be spotted out and about with Paisley. I'm sure he's going to be parading her about so he looks like father of the year."

"And whose daughter will he say she is?"

Tabitha looks down. "I don't know. I'm not sure if they'll try to play her off as their child."

"Um, wouldn't someone remember Anastasia Jerome having a baby? I'm pretty sure it made news the last time she did."

Angie sighs. "They'll say she's adopted. Or they used a surrogate. Surrogate my ass."

Tabitha's face is dark, her mouth downturned.

"Maybe he'll lie low to avoid such a conundrum, and you will be fine," I offer. It sounds stupid, even to me. Someone like Jonathan Spencer Maxwell will expect everyone to bend to his will.

It appears Tabitha already has.

"What if—"

"What if you mind your own business? Maybe it's time for you to leave." Sergei stands up.

This Sergei guy is a supreme jerk, and I've had enough of his crap. I shove my hands back in my pockets. "You're right. It's time for me to go. Tabitha, it was a lovely evening. I hope you get everything straightened out. Best of luck to you in your endeavors."

I pull the door open and then look back over my shoulder. "It was very nice meeting you. Good luck with the subway."

I don't look back again.

Speaking of which, I pull out my phone as soon as I'm outside to see what's the best way for me to get home. It's actually the bus, so I begin walking toward the stop on Rodney Street. The B24 will take me right up to Sunnyside.

Tabitha will never understand the subway system, let alone the buses. I let her down. Just as I let Grayson and The Edison down, though, truth be told, that one was probably not my fault.

I text Grayson.

So I guess Tawny Shane is out. Next choice?

I wish she had shown up last night. Then maybe she wouldn't have gone on a bender with irreversible consequences. Maybe I could have saved her.

Even as I think it, I know it's not true. I've known too many addicts to believe it.

But I wouldn't have met Tabitha.

As strange as this morning turned out to be, I actually had a good time last night.

A very good time.

Hell, if I'd known that I wasn't supposed to be getting her to audition, I probably would have had a better time.

I certainly would have been less grumpy to begin with.

I'd like a do-over.

I remember that look in her eyes when we were singing karaoke. I remember her mouth on mine, her body pressed firmly against me.

Yes, I'd definitely like a do-over.

Except I just walked away from her with no hope of contact again.

I'm an idiot.

Chapter 11: Tabitha

I don't hear from Jonathan Spencer Maxwell. I don't hear from Anastasia Jerome. I only receive a text from Maria, showing me a smiling Paisley, clutching what looks like a brand-new American Girl Doll.

This is good.

I check my phone again. I also haven't heard from Henderson. Not that I expected him to text me or anything. Things were so weird when he left, and Angie and Sergei were practically like rabid dogs.

Still, I thought we'd had fun. I'd definitely thought there was a connection between us. Maybe it was just the liquor.

Maybe it's just me being stupid, thinking that hooking up means more than it does. You'd think I'd have learned differently by now. I mean, I'm thirty-five. I've had sex with a lot of people. Though I'm pretty sure Henderson and I didn't actually have sex.

I can count on one hand the number of meaningful relationships I've had. Okay, two hands if you count my mother, my daughter, and my four bandmates. For the record, I've slept with none of them.

I should probably learn something from this one of these days.

So Henderson is just another meaningless notch in my lipstick case. Another quest for connection that leaves me feeling emptier than before.

I can't believe I told him about Paisley's father.

Seriously, I have no impulse control.

I go in and flop onto Angie's bed. "Why do I do this to myself?"

"Because you're looking for love in all the wrong places?" Angie knows me so well, I don't even have to explain.

"He's not going to text or call me. I know that. I just have to make myself believe it so it doesn't crush me."

Angie comes over and lies down next to me. "Tab, you know better. Not to mention, he lives here, and you live in California. I mean, what were you expecting to happen?"

"I was expecting to have a good time and be fine. But the problem is, I had a good time. Like a really good time. Like, he's funny and nice and sweet. He was all grumpy because he didn't want to be there—which makes like total sense now—but he was still nice to me."

"So, Tab, think about this. A person being nice and decent is enough for you to want to sleep with them?"

I sit up, pick up the pillow and whack Angie with it. "You know me. You know I don't know how to do like, real emotional stuff. I only know the physical."

"So, that's where you went with him, even though there was the possibility of a real connection?" she asks.

"Yeah ... no ... I don't know." I wrack my brain, trying to remember the end of last night. "I liked that he didn't know who I was, yet he was there anyway. Of course, this morning I acted like such a spaz that I doubt he'd ever consider texting me, no matter how big of a star I am. Or was."

"Why don't you text him?"

"Because that's desperate."

"And you aren't?"

I whack her again with the pillow. She snatches it from me. "All I know is that I nearly missed out on Sergei because I was too caught up in what I thought was going on to see what was really in front of me. Sometimes you need a different perspective. If you think this guy liked you for you, why don't you see if there's more there than just a hookup?" Then she bops me with the pillow.

"You're right. I'm going to text him." I pull out my phone and stare at it.

Crap.

"I can't."

"Oh, come on Tabitha. You can get up in front of millions of people and perform. Surely you can send a text message."

I look down at my phone again, scrolling through my contacts. "No, I literally can't. I didn't get his number. He didn't get mine. I'm never going to hear from him again because I'm an idiot."

Angie gives me an exasperated look. "Oh, Tabby, when will you ever learn?"

"It's fine. I don't need a man to occupy my time while I'm here. I don't need a man with a sexy smile and seductive accent. I certainly don't need a man who was willing to get up on stage and sing with me."

"He did what?"

I roll my eyes, thinking of the memory. "I made him do a duet with me."

"Is he a singer?"

I shake my head. "No, but he's a good sport. I mean, he's not a bad singer. With some vocal lessons, I think he could be quite strong."

"What'd you sing?"

I tell her, resulting in laughter.

"How drunk were you that you busted out the Kenny Rogers?"

"Don't go dissing my first love. Rest in peace, Kenny." I fold my hands in a prayer-like gesture.

"I'm surprised you didn't do 'Islands in the Stream.'"

"I thought about it, but I'm pretty sure I was trying to seduce him, so I thought 'We've Got Tonight' would be a better start." I put my hands over my face. "God, I'm desperate."

"You're not," Angie reassures. I look at her, arching my eyebrow. She continues. "Okay, you are. Totally. One of these days, you won't go searching for love in every single nook and cranny. It'll find you, and you'll know."

"I don't think it'll ever find me because I don't even know that love knows I'm out here."

Angie pulls me into her arms. "You know we love you. And Paisley loves you. Your mom loves you in her own way."

"My mom doesn't even love herself." And suddenly, we're talking about so much more than my inability to get Henderson's phone number.

"Then make sure you don't repeat that cycle."

I nod, the tears welling up. "I don't want to. But I don't know how to break it either. I ... I don't know anything right now."

"I do know one thing ..." Angie says gravely.

"What?"

"You aren't a brunette. What were you thinking?" Angie holds a section of my hair in her hand and shakes her head.

I laugh. "I wanted to see if brunettes had less fun."

"And?"

The memory of Henderson's body pressed into mine while we waited for the Uber flashes into my mind. "I think that's a lie used to sell hair dye." I know I can tell Angie the rest. "Also, I thought it might buy me some anonymity."

"If only you hadn't opened your big fat mouth."

In a whisper, I admit, "I miss singing. I miss being seen."

"Yes, but there's nothing you can do about that right now. You should probably sit down with Jonathan Spencer Maxwell and Anastasia Jerome and talk about this."

"We don't sit and talk. It's better that way."

"What are you going to do when Paisley is older? When she's in school and has plays and soccer games and all that? You either need to come up with a story, or it's going to come out. There really isn't any other option, you know. One of those things will happen."

It's not really my problem—it's his—yet it feels like I'm the only one dealing with the repercussions of our brief tryst. It's not my marriage that will blow up. Not that there's much of a marriage there to begin with. In fact, Anastasia herself has had many side pieces, including another member of the Sassy Cats, Callie Smalls.

That was certainly an interesting roller coaster to watch.

I don't know why Jonathan Spencer Maxwell and Anastasia Jerome insist on playing this happy couple when they're not. I don't know why they won't admit who they are and who they love, and that it's not each other.

All I know is I've lost everything because of it. I no longer circulate in Hollywood or the LA party scene. I don't turn up on talk shows or reality shows or quiz shows. I don't even have an agent anymore. I don't do anything, aside from Paisley. I need something else.

I love my daughter, but it's not enough.

And yes, I know that makes me a terrible person for admitting it, even if I haven't said it out loud. It's no wonder no one will stick around long enough to get my number. They know I have nothing to offer them if I don't have my fame. They can tell I'm not worth it.

We really do need to sit down and hash this out. I can't be expected to hide inside for the next fifteen years. Jonathan Spencer Maxwell is going to eventually have to fess up to his missteps. Dammit, I hate when Angie's right.

But enough of the heavy stuff. I've got more important matters to address.

"No offense, but I hate being a brunette. It works for you, but not so much for me."

"I think you being a brunette is like me trying to be a blonde. We are what we are. No use in trying to change that."

We are what we are.

Angie's right about that. "Can you get me in with your person?"

"I'm on it." She sits up, pulling out her phone and furiously texting away. She holds up her phone then, snaps a picture, and then resumes typing.

"What?"

"I had to show Cristian how desperate the situation is. He says come right over."

If this can't bring me back, I don't know what will.

Chapter 12: Henderson

T ell me again."

I sigh, knowing I will not ever live this down. "I met up with the wrong person."

"Who *also* happened to be in a girl band."

I nod, even though through the phone Grayson can't see me. The texting got too confusing, so he finally called.

I hate talking on the phone. If it can't be solved in a text, I don't want to deal with it.

"But you didn't know she was a legit star, so you played her like she was the D-list celeb that Tawny Shane was," Grayson continues. "And then you ..."

"Took her to karaoke so I could see if she really could sing. For the record, that answer is yes." I don't mention the duet.

"And then you ..."

"Went back to her place, where I proceeded to make sure she didn't injure herself in her extremely inebriated state."

"And then ..."

"A true gentleman never kisses and tells. But let's just say, she was in no condition for anything I may have had in mind."

"A true gentleman indeed," Grayson says dryly. "She's lucky she ended up with you instead of whomever she was supposed to be meeting."

I hadn't considered that. Tabitha was rather foolish to let herself get out of control like that. I think of her behavior in the alley. "I don't know that she's the best judge sometimes."

"Well, hell, she seemed to like you, so we know she's not," Grayson ribs. Normally I'd think he was funny. Right now, not so much.

I've a sinking feeling that I let a massive opportunity slip through my fingers.

For The Edison, of course.

I'm not thinking of that tightening in my stomach when she sang to me. I'm not thinking about what her lips felt like, pressed to mine. I'm not thinking about her in those pink panties and matching bra. I'm only thinking about how good she could have been for The Edison.

"Well, it's done now, mate, so we move on. Who else can Carson Reuben sweet talk into spending a few weeks with us this summer? Anyone else desperate and teetering on the edge that we can dangle the carrot in front of?"

Grayson laughs. "I doubt it. We'll have to really find some outstanding talent at auditions next week."

As he says it, I know I'll never be able to hear anyone sing "A Million Dreams" but Tabitha. One night that will haunt my brain forever.

Another reason—as if I needed one—why love is a waste of time. All it does is find new ways to torture you. "We need to move on and forget all about this misstep. At least it wasn't out there that we were actively scouting her. Can you imagine what fools we'd look like?"

I can almost hear Grayson shrugging this off through the phone. "It's fine. You know what they say—any publicity is good publicity. Just pick good people next week to make up for your colossal failure."

"She didn't even show up! She was probably dead already! What was I supposed to do?" I don't know why I'm yelling, but I am.

"Simmer down, man. I was talking about striking out with Tabitha Stetson."

"What would we do if she was interested in The Edison? We can't afford her. Not to mention, she's flighty and full of drama. You won't believe the situation with her baby da—"

Whoops.

I pull myself up short before divulging this private information. See? One date in and I'm already in a tangled mess. No thank you.

"What's that now?" Grayson's always been a nosy sort. He's perfect for the small town of Hicklam, where everybody is up in everybody else's business. Make no mistake, he has the talent for Broadway, even if his personality is more inclined to small town living.

It'd make so much more sense for him to live in the city, close to the action, where my personality would much prefer the sleepy pace of Hicklam. If there was work there year-round, I'd never come back to the city.

"Nothing. Just she's full of drama. Not my type."

"Who *is* your type, Henderson? I don't know that anyone can meet those standards. For all I know, you've taken a vow of celibacy. How many women—and men— from how many summers have tried to get with you? You turn them all down. And, if I'm reading between the lines, you turned Tabitha down too. If a hot celebrity like her isn't good enough, will anyone ever be?"

"It's easier this way. No headaches."

No heartbreaks.

"And one of us has to be able to focus on making this theatre successful. You're too busy out gallivanting around with Gloria."

"One of us needs to have a smile on his face, at least occasionally. See you next week."

As I disconnect, I can't help but feel like I messed up. Royally.

I wish I hadn't run out of there without getting her number.

Regret sucks.

Chapter 13: Tabitha

Two salon visits, more hours than I'd like to admit, and more money than I should admit, and I'm blonde again.

At least I recognize myself in the mirror again.

Yet somehow, I still don't feel right. Maybe it's because I'm not with Paisley. Maybe it's because I don't have anything to do. I still can't figure out the subway, and I'm really not a museum person.

Or maybe it's because I'm wishing I could go out with Henderson again.

I'm not used to people walking away from me.

That's it.

That's the attraction.

That's what I tell myself.

It's not the crinkles around his eyes when he finally smiles or the adorable accent or the fact that he took care of me. It also certainly was not because when he kissed me, I felt it to the tips of my toes.

At least I think I did.

I flop down on Angie's bed. I've taken up the habit of doing this daily. I'm pretty sure she's getting sick of it. Mostly because she rolls her eyes and says, "What now?

Let me guess: you're going to ask why you didn't get his number."

"Why didn't I get his number?"

"I told you what to do."

"But it's going to make me seem like a flighty airhead." I am *not* calling *Backstage Magazine* to ask Carson Reuben for Henderson's information. That's so high school.

And desperate.

I'm not there.

Okay, I'm almost there. But not quite yet.

"You're leaving in a few days. You're running out of time, and it's not like you've come up with a better plan."

I haven't. It's not like I can even casually wander the neighborhood where he lives because I have no idea where that might be. I'm lucky if I can find my way back to this place when I go to the nearest Starbucks. He mentioned an apartment that was flooded, but who knows where that even is. I remember that he said he had a theater about ninety miles away from here. Does he live there too? What was the name of the town?

Smallville.

No, that's from *Superman*.

Something equally diminutive. It gave me the impression of being a podunk town. Visions of tumbleweeds float through my brain. A place in the sticks for hicks. Hicksville? Hicktown?

"Hicklam!" I bolt upright. "His theater is in Hicklam." I beam, proud of myself for finally remembering this detail.

"Oh God, even the *name* sounds terrible. But is he there now? How does this information help you?"

"I don't know, but I feel like it does." I pick up my phone and immediately search for "theaters in Hicklam, NY."

A hit pops up.

The Edison.

I scan through the website, clicking on various items here and there until I find the page for the administration. There he is.

Henderson Quade.

The picture's a headshot, which shouldn't be surprising considering he mentioned that he was an actor at one time. His smile is small and tight, compared with that of the executive director, Grayson Keene.

It was the smile he wore through the first half of our dinner, though, it gradually disappeared throughout the night. I wonder what makes him hold back like this.

I continue scrolling through the website, looking at pictures of past shows and announcements for this year's up-and-coming season. It looks like they start in late May and run through Labor Day.

And then I see it.

"Oh my God, Ang. *Oh my God*." My hands start to shake, trembling with excitement. "I found him! He's holding auditions this week—today!—at some studio here. Eighth and Thirty-eighth. Where's that?"

"It's in Midtown." Angie doesn't look up from her phone.

"What's Midtown?"

"Midtown Manhattan."

"Right." I look back at my phone screen. "It says the auditions run from nine a.m. until seven p.m. all week. That's a super long time."

"Oh, poor guy. It's got to be hellacious for him."

The plan hatches in my head like a burst of light going off. As clear as day, I can see what I'm going to do in my mind. "Can you call Gayle? I want to talk to her for a minute."

I had a falling out with my own agent just after Paisley was born. Since I wasn't pursuing a career of any sorts, I never felt the need to replace her. Gayle has worked with us as the Sassy Cats, so I'm pretty sure she'll take my call. Hell, she'd probably even take me on as a client, if I ask.

This finally gets Angie's attention.

"Tab, what are you going to do?"

"I'm going to go see Henderson." I stand up and walk down to my room. I doubt I have the right clothing for this. Nope. Back to Angie's closet.

"What are you doing?" She's standing over my shoulder, like a protective parent.

Or as I imagine a protective parent would be.

"You know the reason he was out to dinner, right? He was there to convince Tawny Shane to audition for one of his shows. Well, he got me instead. I'm going to auditions."

I pull a pair of leggings and a leotard out from Angie's drawer. There are tights there too, so I grab them, just so I look legit. I find a warm-up wrap sweater, but then toss it back. I select an off-the-shoulder sweatshirt. "I'm borrowing these."

"What am I supposed to ask Gayle, exactly?"

"What do I need to have prepared for an audition? I guess I'm going to have to sing and stuff. The dancing will be hopeless, but maybe I won't need to do that. Do I have to prepare a monologue? I don't know if I know any."

I head into the bathroom to change. I haven't donned dance clothes in years, and I'm not sure what I'm supposed to do for shoes. I'll have to wear my little canvas sneakers. I'm sure everyone else will be wearing heels, but it's not like I'm serious about getting a part.

Just a date.

"Tabitha, you can't be serious," Angie says the minute I walk out of the bathroom. I'm scooping my hair up into a high bun. I hate to pull it back, now that it's finally restored to its proper glory, but this is what professionals do.

"I'm totally serious. How else am I going to get to see him? Hang around on a street corner and wait for him to come out? Um, stalker much?"

"How is this any different?" Angie throws up her hands in exasperation.

"Because he wanted me to audition. I'm giving him what he wants. And maybe he'll go out with me again. You know, he could have been pining away for me this whole time. I'm doing him a service, really. It's for the greater good. After all, I'm a giver."

"Un-huh," Angie says dryly. "This is nuts, you know. Why don't you just call the theater and leave a message? Surely they could pass it on to Henderson."

While Angie's argument is rational, it's boring.

"I don't want to play it safe. I want him to remember me doing this for him."

"Oh, I don't think there's any way he'll ever forget this."

"Ang, one last thing?"

She sighs. "What, Tabby?"

I crease my brow. "How the hell do I get to Midtown Manhattan?"

Chapter 14: Henderson

Audition days are either the best or the worst. One guess as to which this one is.

Grayson sits next to me and stifles a yawn. He's had about four energy drinks, so the fact that he's still tired speaks to the caliber of talent we've seen so far over the past two days.

Between us sits a computer with a spreadsheet open. I've got a notebook full of lists in front of me. It's easier for me to jot notes about the talent and then input the info into the spreadsheet later.

The logistics of this week are a nightmare. We're casting for seven shows for the upcoming season this summer. We're looking for the core of our company; women and men, eight of each, who will be in all the shows, in addition to leads and featured players for each of the seven shows.

It's a lot of bodies to place.

"Okay, next. What are you singing?" Grayson calls.

"Um, I'll be singing 'A Million Dreams' from *The Greatest Showman,*" the nervous actress says, twisting her hands into knots.

Great.

Another one.

She's easily the tenth person who's sung this today. Often, when the word gets out about what shows you're doing, the prospective cast comes in with those songs prepared. Sometimes it works.

Today is not one of those times.

Probably because all I can hear is Tabitha singing that song. No one will ever compare to her, so they shouldn't even try.

Two hours later, I want to stick a fork in my eye.

"Dude, what's up with you? I've never seen you this grumpy, and for you, that's saying a lot."

I shrug. "Dunno, mate. Just not feeling it today. I mean, have we seen *anyone* even remotely capable?"

Grayson lifts up his notebook, which has a lot more notes in it than mine does. I've got a lot of *no's* written down, but not much else.

"No, seriously, man, what gives?"

I'm going to sound like the biggest sap when I say this. Or the biggest sucker. "I can't get the way Tabitha sounded out of my head. Now everyone else who sings that infernal song just sounds like a cheap knockoff."

Morgan, our casting assistant, pokes her head into the studio. "You ready for the next one?"

Grayson holds up a finger without looking up from his phone. "Give me a minute. I need to watch something real quick."

I lean back in the chair, my arms behind my head. This is stupid. It was just dinner and some kissing. It wasn't anything else. I don't believe in anything else.

I don't want anything else.

Yet still ... her voice fills my head day and night, like a siren's call.

Even now, I hear it, as if she were in the room. It's—

It's not in my head. It's actually playing. Grayson has pulled up the video.

Dammit.

I've refrained from watching it because it would be pointless and futile and masochistic to do so. I'm not a masochist, which is why I avoid relationships altogether. Hence, no video watching.

Also, if I start watching it, chances are I won't stop. It'll go viral from my views alone.

"Yeah, she's good. I don't know that she's the be-all and end-all, but it would be great to have her in the show," Grayson concedes.

"Right. That's what I'm thinking about. Charity in *The Greatest Showman*. I can't see anyone else for the role."

That's it, and that's it alone.

"Oh, wait! Hold the phone! What do we have here?" Grayson's bouncing up and down in his seat like a toddler on a sugar high.

Apparently his caffeine has kicked in. I roll my eyes, in no mood for his energy level. "Henderson, you dog. Why didn't you tell me you were coming over to the dark side? Are you angling for a part this season?"

"What on Earth are you yapping on about now?"

Grayson flips his phone so I can see it. See us. Our duet.

"Don't watch that. It was late in the night, and we'd both had a lot to drink." I grab for his phone.

"There is no way in hell I'm not watching this." He pulls the phone out of my reach. After a split second, he puts the phone on the table, face down. "I'm sorry. I was only kidding. I won't watch if it makes you uncomfortable."

And now I feel like a shit because Grayson's girlfriend, Gloria, went through a lot of bad stuff when her ex-boyfriend released a sex tape of them and it went viral. She was super messed up for a long time from it.

"No, mate. It's not like a Gloria thing. I … well, you know me and singing." I shrug. "She wanted me to do a duet."

"I'm surprised you didn't tell her to take a flying leap. You're usually pretty adamant about not wanting to sing. At least with me you are."

"I don't want to sing around you because you never sound bad."

"But you just said you had already heard her sing."

I shrug lamely. "What was I going to do? You told me to do whatever I needed to do to get her to play a part at The Edison. I didn't want to piss her off. So really, this is all your fault."

"I suppose it's my fault that you've been mooning about like a lovesick teenager for almost two weeks now too?"

"Have not."

"Have too."

"Have not."

Luckily, Morgan interrupts our childish game. "Listen boys, enough of the tomfoolery. We've got someone who wants to squeeze in. Her agent called and begged me. She doesn't have a headshot and resume with her, but the agent is emailing one over."

I roll my eyes, sagging back into my chair, my singing video all but forgotten. I need to get my head in this game so we can be done with this part of the process. Tabitha will be flying back to California soon anyway.

That door has closed.

That ship has sailed.

Best to live in the moment, as I've been trying to do for the past thirty-five years anyway. I need to stick with my original philosophy of avoiding relationships. I'm much better off that way.

"Fine, Morgan. Send her in. She'd better be good." Grayson looks at me. It's his turn to roll his eyes. "What else do we have to lose?"

"Let me see what the agent is sending over." I pull the computer in front of me, minimizing our spreadsheet and opening up the email for The Edison.

Nothing in my account. I flip over to Grayson's. Nothing there either. Nothing in the main info. I repeat all three, refreshing constantly, growing ever more annoyed by the second.

"Welcome. Thank you for your interest in The Edison." I hear Grayson say for approximately the nine billionth time today. "What will you be singing today?"

Please not "A Million Dreams." I can't handle that again. I squeeze my eyes shut and hit the refresh button again. Still no email.

"I'm going to sing 'A Million Dreams' from *The Greatest Showman*."

Before I can even groan, "Shoot me now," she starts singing. My head snaps up so fast I may've given myself whiplash.

The blonde standing in front of us, clad in cropped leggings, a leotard, and sneakers, is the last person I ever expected to be standing in front of me during an audition.

Tabitha.

Chapter 15: Tabitha

He's not even paying attention.

He's sitting there, a scowl on his face, clicking away and staring at the computer screen as if it holds all of life's answers. I've seen that expression before; it's the same one he wore for the first hour of our date.

I'm gonna wipe that scowl right off of his face.

Initially, I'd planned on singing one of our Sassy Cats songs. Seeing that I don't even have his focus, I change my mind at the last second.

His head snaps up so quickly that it's got to hurt. Perhaps I'll offer to give him a neck rub later.

I wish I had my phone out because I would love to record his expression.

He rises from his seat, never breaking eye contact. I keep singing, praying I don't forget the words. I make it through my thirty-two bars, my voice trailing off at the end.

"I was looking for your headshot and resume. You're blonde. You're here," Henderson says quickly. The other man at the table looks from Henderson to me and back again. He's got a devilish grin on his face. That guy looks fun.

"I didn't feel like myself as a brunette. I was doing it to hide. I'm done hiding."

"You're here," he says again.

I shrug, looking down at my feet. "You said you wanted me to audition. Wasn't that the whole point to that evening? Wasn't that why you got me drunk and took me to karaoke?"

The other guy at the table chokes on the water he was drinking. He coughs, trying to clear his throat, obviously amused by our exchange.

"You got yourself drunk, but yes, I wanted to see if you could sing. Which, I think we established, you can." Henderson's still standing behind the chair, immobile. "What are you doing here?"

I expected a huge grin.

I expected him to run to me and sweep me up in his arms.

I expected anything but what he's giving me.

I blink slowly, trying to figure out what alternate universe I'm in. I know they say New York City is out of this world, but I didn't think they meant literally.

Henderson's companion clears his throat and stands. "I think what Henny old boy here means …"—he claps Henderson on the back—"what I think my ever-so-eloquent compadre from Down Under is trying to say is that you are a very talented singer, and we'd love to consider you for a featured role this summer at The Edison."

I finally tear my eyes away from Henderson to his partner. "I don't think we've officially been introduced. I'm Tabitha Stetson." I step forward, extending my hand. The man comes around the table, accepting my gesture.

"Grayson Keene. Very honored to meet you. I've heard lots about you." Grayson glances over his shoulder at Henderson. "How about it? We'd love to talk to you about a part."

Henderson stands there, saying nothing.

Grayson continues, "We were thinking Morticia in *The Addams Family* or even Christine in *Dirty Rotten Scoundrels*. We are getting to do a workshop performance of *The Greatest Showman*, so there is the possibility of Charity being available. We haven't fully discussed that yet." He glances over at Henderson.

"Um, Gray, I think we need to talk about this." Henderson looks at me nervously. "I don't know that this should be the plan. I'm not sure we want to go in this direction."

What the actual hell?

I came all the way here for him and he does *this*?

Maybe the whole line about Tawny Shane was bull, and he really was there for me. Like he planned this all along, getting me to come after him, seeking a part. I really thought ... I really expected ... God, I am so stupid. The guy left without even asking for my number. Why on earth would I think he might have felt something for me that one evening we spent together? Hell, he didn't even try to get into my pants. At least I don't think he did. And even if he did, he didn't follow through.

This is how I ended up getting knocked up in the back of a limo.

No, I will not be suckered again.

I take a step back. And then another. And then another.

Before I know it, I'm beating a hasty retreat out of the audition room. I barely stop long enough to grab my bag. My brand-new bag is big enough to fit my coat inside it, which I'm happy for because as soon as I run down the stairs and get out the door, I'm freezing.

If it were possible to die of embarrassment, I would certainly do it here and now.

I might just die of hypothermia though. I yank the coat out of my bag and pull it on. I had a sweatshirt at one point, but I've no idea where that is now, and I'm not going back to look for it.

What was I thinking?

I was thinking he'd jump up, thrilled to see me, and sweep me into his arms. He'd confess that he's been thinking about me as much as I've been thinking about him, and we should spend every waking—and sleeping—second together.

Desperate much?

God, I'm so stupid. You'd think I'd have learned by now. I can't trust other people. With the exception of the Sassy Cats, no one has ever consistently had my back. No one has been there for me. No one has wanted to be my ride or die.

Not that I'm saying Henderson was any of those things, but until a few moments ago, he had the *potential* to be that for me. To want to be with me. To want me for me and not because of my celebrity status.

Tabitha because she's Tabitha, not Tabby Cat.

No one wants Tabitha for Tabitha. They only want Tabby.

I should be used to this by now.

But hell, he doesn't want me at all, famous Tabby or regular Tabitha.

I will not cry over this. I will shrug it off and do what I normally do.

I will shop.

I will look at pretty things. Designer things. Expensive things. I will surround myself with things because they will never let me down.

I make a vow, not for the first time, to never let Paisley down. While I don't want to be one of those super clingy, overbearing moms that they make TV shows about, I don't ever want her to feel the way I do in this moment.

Used.

Utterly alone.

Oh God, and he knows my secret.

I am the stupidest person ever.

I step toward the curb, determined to hail a cab. I may not know how to get around this city underground, but I at least have the resourcefulness to find my way.

"Tabitha. Tabitha! Wait!"

Don't turn around. Just keep going. Whatever you do, don't look.

"Oh, Henderson, you caught me at a bad time. I need to leave." I wave for a taxi. I hope my gesture is natural and laidback. In reality, it probably looks like a poor imitation of Forrest Gump.

"Where do you think you're going?"

"Bergdorf's." Duh. Where else would I go at a time like this?

A lime green Prius pulls up. I take a step off the curb toward the car.

"Tabitha, wait."

"Sorry, I have very important shoe shopping to do. I took time out of my day to come here, and now I'm off schedule. See you ... never."

I start to get in the taxi when suddenly Henderson is there, his arm shooting out and blocking me. "Tabitha," he says quietly.

I don't want to turn and look at him. I'm not that good of an actress, and he'll see how crushed I am.

I guess crushes are aptly named.

God, what am I? A twelve-year-old schoolgirl?

"I'm sorry, Henderson, I've no intention of being in your show. I shouldn't have come. I'm sorry for wasting your time."

"You gettin' in?" the cabby yells.

"Sorry, mate. She's not," Henderson says as he pulls me back slightly so he can close the door. I have no choice but to turn around and look at him.

"What'd you do that for? I am going to Bergdorf's."

"Not before we talk. Tabitha, here, let's get outta the street."

He holds onto my elbow, guiding me gently back into the foyer of the building. Neither of us says anything. I pull my coat tighter around me, still freezing from the February air. Another reason to hate New York; it's too damn cold here. "What are we supposed to talk about?"

I don't take rejection well.

I never have, and I don't see that changing any time soon.

I turn to face Henderson, leveling him with my best Callie Smalls icy stare.

He stares back. Dammit, why does he have to be attractive? It's because he's rejected me. He's the cookie I can't have, which makes me want it all the more. It's because ...

All thoughts cease the moment his lips touch mine. Soft initially. Hesitant, then eager. Urgent. Despite my best intentions, I melt into him, returning his kiss with my own urgency. In this moment, I forget everything.

There is only him. There is only us.

"Oh my God, you're Tabby Cat! I thought you looked familiar!" A shrieking voice comes crashing down on us, breaking the magic of the moment. I feel Henderson smile against my lips before he pulls away.

"I should have stayed brunette," I mutter, turning to face my fan.

Henderson, still holding onto me, whispers in my ear, "The blonde looks good. Really good. It's you. Own it."

I greet the eager enthusiast, smiling and taking a selfie as he continues to gush. "I can't believe it's really you. I thought it was, but like, oh my God. Are you going to be in a show at The Edison? Oh my God, I would die if I could be in a show with you! I've been a fan of the Sassy Cats since I was a little kid."

Considering he looks like an adult, that statement stings a bit. "Thanks so much. I'm not sure about The Edison ..." I glance at Henderson who is cocking an eyebrow. "We're ... ah ... in negotiations about it currently."

The hopeful actor looks from me to Henderson and then back again. "I wish I could work on the negotiations process like you do. Especially with Grayson Keene."

Henderson barks out a laugh. "I believe Grayson's taken, but we'll consider your desire—for a part," he adds hastily.

As soon as the guy leaves, I lean back in to kiss Henderson again but pull up short. "This is not how I audition for a part."

Henderson closes the gap between us, saying against my lips, "I know."

I don't know that he does. And it may have been the way I operated in the past, but I want to be a better role model for my daughter. I pull back, my hands bracing on his forearm. "No, really, Henderson. You have to know, I don't want you to think that I'm kissing you and want to be with you because of a part in a stupid show."

He takes a step back. "Well, thank you for calling my life's work stupid. And thank you for assuring me that there is no way someone like *you* could ever be interested in someone like *me* without an ulterior motive."

Oh, he's pissed. Grumpy Henderson is definitely back.

"What's that supposed to mean? Someone like *me*? I'm saying exactly what I mean. That I'm interested in you with no ulterior motives. Just you. Although, I'm not so sure I'm interested in this side of you. I didn't want you to think this was about a part."

"Why would I think this was about a part?"

I throw my hands up in the air.

"Maybe because I just auditioned for your play? But no worries, since you made it clear that you aren't interested in me for me and definitely not interested in me for the play. So will you excuse me, please? I need to hail another taxi."

Time to drown my sorrows in the best Bergdorf Goodman has to offer. Helmut Lang and Jimmy Choo, here I come.

Chapter 16: Henderson

Well, I've gone and mucked things up already. I didn't even have to try.

She just ... she protested a little too much.

And it's certainly not reasonable that she would have come here simply for me. Why would she do that?

Why'd I kiss her?

Oh right, because I haven't been able to think about anything but her for the past two weeks. I can't be daft enough to let her slip away again. "Let's just make this clear. You're not interested in a part at The Edison, correct? Good. You are not getting a part. There is no part for you. Not even if you begged. Feel free to beg for other things, though, because I'd be willing to consider other favors."

She stares at me for a beat. Then two. Finally, she laughs.

Phew.

"I never really thought about an actual part. All I thought about was seeing you again. It's been such a long time since I felt like I could really be myself. And you seemed to like me for me. You even took care of me. You didn't have to, and you still did."

There's a weight behind her words, but now is not the time to process it. "I can't believe I walked out without asking to see you again."

"I can't believe I let them push you out the door. I've been thinking about you ever since."

I lean in and kiss her again. She tastes like a sweet fruit that I will never, ever tire of sampling. "And I still can't believe you're here."

"And I can't believe the two of you are standing down here, making out like teenagers, when we've still got nine bajillion people left to audition." Grayson's jovial voice is a reminder that I've got work to do.

I look at my watch. Grayson's right. We'll be here at least four more hours. "I'm so sorry. I ..." I trail off, not knowing what to say.

Tabitha's face falls for a second. "Of course you do. Silly me thinking I would waltz in there and you'd drop everything for me."

"He sort of did. You guys have been down here sucking face for at least fifteen minutes. Maybe more."

I roll my eyes at Grayson before turning back to Tabitha. "I'm here all night. After we're done with these infernal auditions, we've got to try and make heads or tails of it all. And it's going to be even worse. I wasn't focused before because of you, and now there's no way I can concentrate." An idea strikes. "Gray, what would you think if Tabitha sat in? She's got an ear for music, obviously, and with the way I've been, a third set of eyes wouldn't be a bad idea."

She looks at me, a small smile spreading on her face. "You'd trust me to make decisions?"

Grayson laughs. "God, no, but we'll allow you to voice an opinion. And then we'll ignore you and do what we want."

Tabitha frowns slightly.

I lift her chin gently. "Your time here is limited, and this may be the only way I can see you today."

She tries to pout, folding her arms over her chest, but I can see the smile breaking through. God, she's adorable.

"Please," I add, knowing that she needs the push.

Tabitha throws up her hands. "Okay, fine. But I'll have you know, I am a faithful watcher of all things reality TV, like *American Idol* and *The Voice*. Oh, and *Hollywood Dance Off!*, naturally. I want to be the evil judge. In the Sassy Cats, I was never the mean one. That was always Callie and sometimes Daphne. Angie was the driven one. Mandy was the super nice one, and I was the ditzy blonde. I want to go full-on Callie now. It's my turn to be smart and cunning. Well, at least to act like I'm smart." She shrugs helplessly.

I start laughing, pulling her into a hug. "We don't judge. We keep a neutral expression on our face and thank them for coming in, no matter how good—or bad—they are."

She leans back, wrinkling her nose. "Well, what fun is that?"

I tap her on her cute button nose. "And now you know why I want to stick a fork in my eye."

"Okay, lovebirds. Can we get back in there? The day isn't getting any shorter." With that, Grayson takes the stairs two at a time. That man should not have any more energy drinks today.

"Are ... are you okay with me staying here?" She drops her gaze.

"I wouldn't have asked if I didn't want you to. I—" I break off before I spill that I've been grumping about for days because of her. I'm not the type of bloke who moons about after a sheila he's only just met. Hell, I don't even moon about the ones I've known for a long time.

I don't do that. Just like I don't do relationships.

Yet here I am, grinning like a fool, unwilling to let go of her hand. I lead her up the stairs and back into the audition room. And now it's my turn to ask for reassurance. "Are you sure about this? About me?"

Tabitha leans in and kisses me, her lips a hint of so much more to come. "We've got tonight, babe."

I return her kiss. "Why don't you stay?"

She pulls back and grins. "Just try to get rid of me now. I'm yours until the moment I get on that plane."

"Promise?"

I take her hand in mine. Nothing has ever felt so right. I'm breaking my own cardinal rule here: don't get involved. But it's too late. This Sassy Cat has her claws in me.

And there's no place I'd rather be.

Chapter 17: Tabitha

I've never been known for my focus or attention to detail. This lands me squarely in hell right now. I mean, how am I supposed to concentrate on one singer after another after another—*and another*—with Henderson right here next to me?

I can't screw this up for him though.

I pull my hair out of its messy top knot and run my fingers through it, combing it out. Playing with my hair always helps me focus.

Okay, this guy singing sounds pretty good. I glance over at Henderson's notebook. I shouldn't be surprised that his handwriting is small and neat. He's not writing a lot down either. My paper is filled with my big, loopy scrawl. Phrases like "good tone," "pitchy," and "best friend material" march across my sheet. I'm not sure I'll even be able to make sense of what I meant later on.

I never was a good note taker in school.

There wasn't much I *was* good at back then, other than getting attention from others. That's another reason why the past few years, flying under the radar, have been challenging. I don't know how to function without calling attention to myself. I'm really only good at two things, and singing is the *other* one.

Yet here I am, in another situation where it's not about me. I'm here for Henderson. Quite literally, but to help him as well. I scribble some more indecipherable notes.

"Wow, you took this very seriously." Henderson nods at my stack of papers. The last actor has finally finished. I'm ready to crawl into bed.

In more ways than one.

"This is serious business. I didn't want to earn a reputation for distracting you today." I lean in and whisper in his ear, "Because I plan on doing that for the rest of my week here."

With my face so close to his, I can feel his cheek pull up into a smile. I'm glad we're finally on the same page.

"Okay, guys, we're in the home stretch. Now all we have to do is compare notes, argue for a while, have a cage match to the death, and we're good to go for callbacks ... when we get to go at it again. Let's start with perspectives for male leads. H—who do you like?" Grayson looks at Henderson expectantly.

I giggle at the thought of those two having a cage match to the death. I picture more of a dance duel.

Henderson turns and whispers to me, "Like I can actually answer Gray's question. Like I could focus with you and that hair. Why do you smell like vanilla? It's making me hungry."

The look in his eyes does not indicate a gastric hunger. I feel that look throughout my body. I'm hungry too.

I didn't mean to distract him by playing with my hair. But maybe, like me, just mere presence alone is enough to prevent his focus.

Without breaking his gaze with me, Henderson answers, "Uh ... I don't know. Who do you like, Gray? We can go with that."

Oh, good. He's going to wrap this up quickly so we can move on to bigger—and better—things.

"How about Number 36? Tony Garcia. I like him for Gomez Addams."

Henderson's head whips around to face Grayson. Damn it. I've lost him. "Are you kidding? Too skinny. Not the right presence. And if he can't bring it with his singing, I doubt he'll have it with dancing."

"Put him in a suit with shoulder pads and he'll be fine."

"Fine? We don't want fine. Don't be a bloody galah. Gomez Addams oozes sultriness and sex appeal. This guy looked like Morticia could snap him in half with her fingertips."

Maybe they weren't joking about the cage match to the death. You can cut the tension with a knife.

"How about that Todd guy—terrible name though, he should use a stage name—for Stacie Jaxx in *Rock of Ages*. I can see him much more as that part than Tom Cruise." I chime in, hoping to diffuse the situation. Henderson cocks his head in thought.

Grayson looks at his notes before nodding in agreement. "Thanks. That's one problem solved. But who are we going to get for Gomez if you don't like Tony Garcia?"

Before things get much more heated, the door opens, interrupting the onset of World War III. In glides a slim man with round tortoiseshell glasses and a crazy striped scarf. He looks like stock casting for Mark from *Rent*.

"How's my favorite Upstate, off-Broadway team doing?" His eyes lock on me, and he stops dead in his tracks, clutching his heart. "Tabby Cat."

I stand up, extending my hand. "Tabitha Stetson. And you are ...?"

"Carson Reuben, *Backstage Magazine*. It's you. What are you doing here? Are you with The Edison this season?

Please Say Yes." Then he laughs, obviously impressed with his reference to our last hit song.

I glance quickly at Henderson. "Carson Reuben? You're the reason I'm here. Thank you so much." I lean forward and give him a quick peck on the cheek.

Henderson stands abruptly. "Good to see you again, Carson. Um, Gray, Tabitha and I are gonna take off now. Sketch out some ideas, and I'll work on mine. We can compare notes tomorrow before you catch the train back north. You're not leaving until afternoon, right?"

Grayson laughs, looking from Henderson to me and back again. "Right. Your notes. Un-huh. I'll believe that when I see it. 'Night, you two. I'd tell you to have a good time, but I'm guessing that's exactly what you have planned." Grayson winks at me, and I can't help but laugh.

"Are we that obvious?"

"I think a billboard in Times Square might be more subtle. Now get outta here."

Henderson clears his throat. He's obviously uncomfortable talking about our evening plans with anyone. I can see why though. He's definitely not a limelight kind of guy.

This is a new one for me.

"Okay, we're going to go then. Carson, it's good to see you again. Gray, I'll catch ya tomorrow."

I scurry into my coat and grab my bag. Henderson shrugs into his coat and heads for the door. I have to rush to catch up with him. I'm out of breath by the time I'm finally close enough to grab his hand.

"Stop for a minute. Where are we going? What are we doing?"

He turns and looks at me, a tight-lipped smile dancing across his face before he leans in and whispers, "I'm going to make all your dreams come true."

Before I can ask what dreams, I know what he's referring to.

The one thing he promised was to teach me how to use the subway.

I couldn't care less about the damn subway right now.

All I can think about is his lips on mine and his hands on my body. I want more of that. Right now.

"This is an easy one. We take the 7 train toward Flushing."

He might as well be speaking another language. "Is this it?" I point to a sign with a purple circle and the number 7 in it.

"No, that's toward Hudson Yards. That's heading west. We need to cross the river to the east. I'm in Long Island City. It's Queens."

I blink slowly, trying to follow him. How can he be thinking of transportation at a time like this? Maybe figuring out the subway isn't really that important. "Maybe we could just take a car? It'd be faster."

"Not really. Maybe save us a couple minutes. That's it. And it's more expensive." He swipes his card once and pushes me through the turnstile. Down here, it feels like there's no air. Has anyone ever passed out from lack of oxygen? As soon as I'm through, Henderson swipes again and then enters. "Though I guess that's not an issue for you."

He doesn't say it accusingly; simply a fact.

"No one will ever accuse me of being overly frugal or practical, but it's also good to have life skills. I could use some more of those."

It's true. The life skills my mom pressed most were those that I could use to manipulate others. Mostly in a horizontal position. Well, vertical too because I'm good like that. But now that I'm a mother of my own child, I can see that Paisley is going to need a whole different set of life lessons.

Of course, I'm woefully unprepared to teach them to her. Good thing she has Maria.

As we're waiting for our train, I put my hand on his arm. "Henderson, what are we doing?" I don't want him to think I'm using him. I'm not. There's nothing I want from him. I'm here for the moment. That's it.

Ever so gently, he places his hand over mine. Smiling he says, "Going back to my place?" His smile drops. "Unless you don't wanna. Which is okay," he adds hastily.

"Of course I want to. I wouldn't have hunted you down like a deranged fan and sat through an endless afternoon of auditions if I didn't want to. I seriously can't believe you do that every year." I pause, trying to think of what to say so I don't sound like an idiot. "I … it's just … well, I live in California."

"And I live in New York."

"So we're just enjoying the last part of my week here and that's it." That needs to be it. I can't have him thinking I'd be moving here for him or anything crazy like that. I need Henderson to know that there are boundaries, and this is all in good fun.

It's all I can offer him.

"Obviously." He taps my nose. "I know you're used to people falling at your feet, but that's not who I am or how I roll. I don't do relationships. It doesn't mean I don't do other things. Things I'd very much like to do right now. But I don't do more."

A flood of relief washes over me. I'm not in a place to give to someone else. In four days, Paisley will be back with me and all of my efforts will return to raising her. That's what good moms do. They put aside their own needs for those of their kids. And I'm determined to be everything for Paisley that my own mom was not.

A large silver train rumbles in with a deafening roar. A voice announces something, but it's garbled and unintelligible. Yeah, without Henderson, I'd never be able to figure this out.

He pulls me onto the train and we find seats next to each other. There's a man at the opposite end of the car playing the guitar and singing. I lace my fingers through Henderson's and rest my head on his shoulder.

"This is crazy."

"Lots of people take the subway. Literally millions. Welcome to how the simple folk live."

I jab him with my elbow. "Not that, silly. This. You and me. I can't believe I came after you like a schoolgirl with a crush." Except that's exactly how I feel. Full of excitement and anticipation.

And the feeling that this will not end well.

Chapter 18: Henderson

She came to find me.

I still can't process this. Much like I can't process that I'm such a jackass that I took her on the subway instead of getting home as quickly as possible. When an attractive woman seeks you out to hook up, who—other than me, natch—is thinking about the cost of transportation home?

I'm also acting like we have all the time in the world, which we don't. "How long are you in town?"

"I leave Saturday, but I have to pick Paisley up on Friday."

It's Tuesday.

Tuesday night, to be exact.

Well, shit.

But it's not like this is anything serious. I don't want that. I don't do that. It's just ... well, she's intoxicating.

"How many shows are you casting for? There seemed like a lot of people in and out today."

"We run seven shows between Memorial Day and Labor Day. Each runs for two weekends, except one runs for three weekends. We're running one show while rehearsing the next."

"Holy crap, that seems like a lot. I remember what it was like to get ready for tours and to be adding new things right in the middle. It was a lot to process."

I laugh. "You could say that. We also run a three week children's program as a camp, and then they put on a production at the end. This year we're doing *Newsies*, which is a big one to stage. Gloria has her work cut out for her."

"Who's Gloria?"

I forget that Tabitha has not always been in my world. She just seems to fit. "Gray's girlfriend. She runs the camp. She does a lot with backstage and costumes and stuff. She also acts, but I don't think she's doing that anymore. Still, she's a great resource to have. Last year, she showed up in town and almost single-handedly saved The Edison. We owe a lot to her."

I don't want to think about the stress of last summer. The mere mention of it gives me heartburn. Hopefully Linda Keene makes better business decisions this year, so we don't end up getting through by the skin of our teeth again.

"Oh wow. I guess Grayson's lucky that his girlfriend has so many hidden talents. He picked well."

"Yeah, funny thing. They weren't together when she came to work for The Edison. But by the end of the season, they were inseparable."

"Aww, that's so sweet." Tabitha nestles into my shoulder again. "So romantic."

Ugh, no. I mean, Gray and Gloria are fine, but no. Just no. "For right now. We almost lost everything because Gray's ex is a vindictive bitch. It's really best not to mix business and pleasure, especially with the dramatic types."

Tabitha laughs. "Tell me about it. We had issues in our group. It's not why we broke up—not the full reason—but it contributed to it. Totally. And then, ten years later, the same who-slept-with-who thing came up and almost derailed our reunion concert. We made millions off that concert, so people screwing around could have really messed it up."

Millions.

She could probably buy and sell The Edison four times over. Another reminder that Tabitha is out of my league.

But that would imply that this is more than a casual thing. It's not, so we're equal. Still, I should warn her that my place is nothing special. As we walk down the stairs from the train station and cross Queens Boulevard, I start to worry.

She's gonna run the minute she lays eyes on the place. It's ugly brick, with people stacked on top of one another like a can of sardines. "Well, this's it." I shrug like I don't care.

"Oh, it's, um ..."

"Yeah. Welcome to Queens." I look around at the depressing neighborhood, even more dank in the artificial street light. "Not exactly fit for a queen though. I think it was misnamed."

Tabitha laughs, though I notice she's stepping a bit more gingerly, like she doesn't want to step in poverty. On the other hand, I watched her give a hundred bucks to a homeless man without blinking. Maybe I'm reading too much into this.

Maybe I'm looking for an excuse.

Maybe I need to pull my head out of my ass and kiss this woman.

Option C wins.

"Mmm," she says, her lips still pressed into mine. "Is that a sneak preview?"

"Consider it an appetizer." I plan to devour her, so it's not a lie. I hope the feeling's mutual. "I'm on the second floor, so it's not too bad."

"Except for when the person above you causes a flood."

I can't believe she remembers that. I'm glad she does, though, because there's still unpainted drywall on my ceiling and bathroom walls. At least it's been replaced already. I just won't turn on all the lights, and I'll keep her elsewise occupied.

I can live with that.

"Come on," I fiddle with the keys in the door. I practically run up the stairs. Mostly so she doesn't get too much time to look around, but also because I can't wait to get inside with her. I've been thinking about this since I walked away two weeks ago. Women are never on my mind for two weeks.

At least not like this.

We're barely through my door when Tabitha grabs my face, pressing her hands into my cheeks as she leans into me.

Nice to know I'm not the only one anxious for this. Her mouth is warm and inviting, as I suspect the rest of her will be. We're still wearing our coats, bags slung over our shoulders. Time to lighten the load a bit.

I slide the bag off her shoulder—good Lord, what's in here?—and toss it on the floor. My own rucksack hits with a thud. Tabitha is on the same page as she pushes my jacket off, never breaking contact with my mouth. I fumble a bit as I remove her coat. She shrugs out of it. My hands find her ribcage and slide south.

I caress her firm, tight backside and glide up, looking to free her of her shirt. Except I can't find the edge of it. I try to play it off as gentle stroking rather than the desperate fumble it truly is. Where the frick is the bottom of her shirt?

Tabitha starts to giggle. "What are you doing down there?"

Despite my previous resolve to stay in darkness, I flip on the lights and drop to my knees in front of her. "What are you wearing? How does this thing work?"

"It's a leotard. For the audition."

The audition—her walking in the room and belting out that song—feels like a lifetime ago. "Did you think you were auditioning for *A Chorus Line* or something?"

"I didn't know if I'd have to dance first. If that was the case, I'd never have made it to the singing round." She puts a finger under my chin and gently guides me to a standing position. "And I didn't know what to expect. Angie's a dancer, so I raided her closet."

"We do dancing at the callbacks. Depending on the part, we can work around a weaker dancer. We can't for the singers."

Her hand drops from my chin to the straps on her shoulders. She pushes them down, revealing a lacy black bra. "I'd think you'd know your way around a leotard."

Nice.

I bend over and kiss her shoulder, right next to her bra strap. "I told you, I don't mix business with pleasure. Plus, starlets aren't my type." I continue kissing up her neck and behind her ear. Tabitha goes rigid.

"I'm a starlet."

I pull back, looking at her. Her lips are swollen and full, absolutely delectable. The rest of her face, however, is pissed off. "Right. But that's not how I know you. You're not climbing up the ladder of success."

As soon as the words are out of my mouth, I wish I could grab them back and stuff them deep down in a pit and set them on fire so I never say anything so stupid again. Natch, I follow those words up with this gem: "I mean, you're not like a young ingenue just starting out."

For the record, telling the woman you're trying to seduce that she's old is never a smooth move, especially when you've already said she's no longer successful. I've got to make this better. Now.

"Tabitha, I'm saying this poorly. You obviously are quite successful. The most successful person I know, in fact. And you're not old. You're just not starting out right now either."

With her hands on my shoulders, she shoves me back slightly. "But I am starting over, so this is not what I need to hear."

I look at my feet. I don't know how I've bungled this so bloody quickly. "I know, and I'm sorry. I just don't want you to think that I'm some predator looking to seduce every young, nimble dancer who waltzes past. It's not how I work. In fact, quite the opposite. If I'm involved at all with someone, that automatically excludes them from being in my cast. It's a hard no for me. I'm not that kind of director."

Tabitha tilts her head, considering my words. "I wish the entertainment industry had more people like you in it. There'd be a whole lot less of the 'me too' movement going on. For sure."

My mind again flits back to Gloria and her trials with that nob, A.J. Michaels. She was disabled for over ten years while his career went on. I wonder how many more Glorias there are in his past. "There will be none of that here. If you're here, it's because you want to be, not because of what you can do for me. Or even what I can do for you."

Tabitha nods. "I think that's a good rule to have." She steps back again and looks down. Her leotard is hanging down, her leggings keeping it in place. "I haven't always had those clean lines. Maybe I should."

The anticipation of what she's going to do next is killing me. I'd understand if she pulls her top up and hightails it out of here. It's the last thing I want, though.

She looks at me for one more beat before bending forward. In one swift move, the leotard and leggings are down, and she's stepping out of them, standing before me in just her bra and panties.

Thank you, Jesus.

Chapter 19: Tabitha

That was worth the wait.

Henderson's been holding out, not only on me, but on the whole female species by not dating—or whatever this is—more. I've got three full days to relish in his skill set, and I plan to enjoy every single moment.

I roll over onto my stomach and prop up on my elbows. The sheet slides down over my bare back, but it's a little too late for modesty. Certainly not after the night we had.

"What's on the agenda for today, other than more of this?" I nudge him slightly with my elbow.

He rakes his hand over his face. "As much as I'd like to not leave this apartment until you have to pick up your tyke, I'm afraid I've another long work day ahead of me. Gray and I have to make decisions on who we want for call backs. Then I've got to contact them and set up their dance auditions. Gray heads back upstate this afternoon, so I'm on a bit of a time crunch."

Crap.

"I'd invite you along with me again today, but I don't want to bore you to death. It's a lot of talking and arguing, and there's not even singing to entertain us." He rolls over to face me. "Maybe if we can power through—and by power through I mean I just let Grayson do what he wants and not argue every point—I can probably be free by late afternoon. Can we grab a bite?"

It sounds fair. "I don't want you to compromise your artistic vision, though. Not for me."

He laughs. "I won't. I can just not drag it out as long. The Edison is what's important. We've all put in too much to let her down."

It's so cute how he refers to the theater as if it's a woman. There's a lot that's cute about Henderson Quade.

Too bad he lives three-thousand miles away from me.

"I—" my phone rings. I'm tempted to ignore it, but my lack of impulse control gets the best of me. It's Angie.

"Tabby, where are you?"

"With Henderson. At his place." I give him a small smile and a wink. "I texted you I wouldn't be home. What's up?"

"Oh my God, you don't know."

This is never a good thing to hear. My stomach drops in anticipation of the bad news that is surely coming my way.

"Tab, Jonathan Spencer Maxwell was in an accident."

Initially, I feel nothing. I don't like the man, but I don't want to relish in his unfortunate luck. Then, it hits me.

Paisley.

"What happened? Was Paisley with him? Is she okay? Why didn't he call me?"

"I don't know. All it says is his car was hit by a runaway SUV. There were two others in the vehicle with him. There's nothing on anyone's condition."

The edges of my vision narrow as my heart drops. "I have to go. I have to find her. I—" I look around Henderson's studio apartment, trying to get my bearings. Trying to figure out what to do next. Trying not to vomit.

I disconnect without saying anything, dialing Maria. No answer.

I try Jonathan Spencer Maxwell, but that call too goes unanswered.

Out of desperation, I try Anastasia Jerome. She doesn't answer, but texts. "Can't talk. We're at NYU Langone Long Island."

Henderson is out of bed, staring at me. "What's wrong? What happened?"

I relay my scarce information, finally springing to my feet. "I need to go. Where's NYU Long Island? Is that far away? Where are my pants?" I look around frantically. Clothing is strewn from one end of the small apartment to the other. I find my leggings and then my leotard. I think I had a sweatshirt at one point in the day, but I don't think I had it when I got here last night. I certainly wasn't wearing it when the rest of my clothes came off. "Crap. I don't have a shirt. How am I supposed to go to the hospital without a shirt?" My mind swirls with all the things that my baby could be facing right now without me.

I need to get to her.

I don't care if I have to walk in there buck naked.

"Here, take this." Henderson's tossing a pile of clothes at me. It's a soft, worn T-shirt, as well as a sweatshirt. Both have the name of his theater written across them. I pull them on quickly, and scan the area for anything else I may have tossed aside when we made ample use of every available surface throughout the night.

Pulling my hair up into a knot, I stop. He's sitting on the side of the bed, looking at his hands. He's pulled on a pair of jeans and looks like something out of the pages of *Vogue*.

"I ... I have to go."

"Of course you do. The Uber will be here in three minutes to take you to the hospital. NYU Long Island, right?"

I shrug. I should know this. A good mother should know where her three-year-old is.

Henderson stands and walks across the room to me. "Your car is a gray Toyota Corolla. BBG 6234."

I nod. The words have already escaped my mind. "What if she's not okay? I wasn't there for her."

He puts his hands on my arms, squeezing gently. "I'm sure she's okay. If she wasn't, someone would have been in touch."

His words make sense but in my mind, I keep screaming, *you should have been there.*

As I prepare to walk out the door, I glance back. I'd planned on days with Henderson. "I'm sorry."

"You have nothing to apologize for. Now go be with your ankle biter. If you want, let me know how she is."

The city streets buzz by the windows of the car. I'm trying to remember every little detail of Paisley's life, all while bargaining with a God I'm not sure I actually believe in.

Please let her be okay. Please let her be okay.

As soon as the Uber pulls up to the emergency department, I know I'm in the right place due to the crush of the crowd. So many photographers and fans. Holy hell, I'm never going to get through this.

I text Anastasia.

I'm outside. I need to get in.

There's extra security, trying to keep the crowd at bay. I put my sunglasses on and hope no one places me. Of all the times for me to be blonde again.

Go around to the Main Entrance loop. The staff door opposite the Women's and Children's Center. Tyree will be there.

Tyree is Jonathan Spencer Maxwell's second security guy. Angus is his first. I'm guessing Angus was in the car, as he usually is. Hell, I think Angus was in the front seat the night Paisley was conceived in the back.

I walk for about a mile before I finally find the door I'm looking for. Turns out, I should have made one left turn instead of making three rights. But finally I see Tyree, who opens the door quickly for me and pulls it shut before I'm barely over the threshold.

"It's a mob out front."

He nods, ever the strong silent type.

"Take me to Paisley. How is she?"

Another nod. Jesus, the silence is killing me. It's a void I cannot stand. "What happened?"

"Some old dude who shouldn't be driving was headed the wrong way on the Long Island Expressway. Plowed right into them. And they won't tell me how she is because I'm not a relative."

"What were they doing out here on Long Island?" Despite having just made the trip myself, I have no idea how far this is from Manhattan. Ten minutes? Three hours? Time no longer makes sense.

"Going to the children's museum out here. Thought it'd be less conspicuous."

I sigh. Jonathan Spencer Maxwell is all about appearing like he's avoiding the limelight while secretly doing things to be seen. Meanwhile, I've been banished forever.

"Who was in the car?" I need to fill the empty space with words, otherwise I'll start screaming. It seems as if we've been walking for three years.

"Phil was driving. Angus, Jon, and Paisley."

My stomach drops, and I'm instantly shaking, terror seizing me.

"Where was Maria?"

"She was in the second car with Ms. Jerome and me. We saw the whole thing." His voice breaks a bit at the end, betraying his composed façade. "The SUV came out of nowhere, I swear."

"Why didn't Maria call me? Why didn't anyone call me?"

"Ms. Jerome said to wait. She needed to plan first. I think she was about to call you when you texted her."

Plan.

On how to sneak me in without being seen.

Oh, this bullshit has got to end.

"Tabitha, it only happened about two hours ago."

I stop walking. "Tyree, a friend saw it on social media and contacted me. How is it that they knew, but I didn't?"

He shoves his hands in his pockets and looks at the ground. "We had a tail. A planned tail. Jon was hoping for a photo op."

I hate him. If I could take Paisley away and never have anything to do with Jonathan Spencer Maxwell again, I would. But he'll never let that happen. *She'll* never let that happen.

But I will not let them have this control over my daughter again.

As we round the corner, I'm prepared to see my daughter in the worst possible way. Images of beeping monitors and tubes dance through my head. Relief floods me like a tsunami wave when I see my little blonde moppet sitting up in bed, a cast on her right leg and bandages on the left side of her face. She's talking to Maria, as she always does. Tears of gratitude fill my eyes.

"Momma!" Her voice is strong and clear.

"I'm here, baby." While I want to run and scoop her up, I move gingerly. I don't know what else is hurt. "Maria, what'd the doctor say?"

"She broke her right shin bone. No surgery, just casting."

"What happened to her face?" I whisper this, so Paisley doesn't hear me.

"Flying glass. They stitched her up. She did great. They said she's the bravest three-year-old they've ever had."

"Was it the plastic surgeon or just the regular doctor?"

"Plastic, of course. I wouldn't let anyone else touch her face." She touches my child's shoulder gently.

"Why didn't you call me?"

Maria glances at Paisley in my arms. I'm probably smushing her. Heck, I haven't seen her in over two weeks. I'd be smushing her even if we weren't in a hospital. "I needed to stay with Paisley. He's not in great shape. Mrs. Anastasia is with him. It's …" She breaks off, looking at Paisley. "He wasn't wearing a seatbelt. Paisley was in her car seat."

Thank you, National Transportation and Safety Board for regulating those damn things.

"The other driver …" Maria's voice drops as she shakes her head. "This is going to be a media circus."

"It already is. I had to go around to a side entrance."

"What are we going to do?" She looks at me, her brown eyes wide with concern.

Maria's often the go between as we hand off Paisley. "As soon as the doctors tell me it's okay for her to travel, I'm going to book the first flight back to LA I've got to get her seen by a plastic surgeon out there. I can't let this scar her."

"What about Mr. Jon?"

It's funny to hear him referred to like that. I only ever call him by his three names, as if I'm an adoring fan. I'm not, but despite our shared offspring, we're not at a comfort level where I could call him Jon so casually.

"When we're back in California, we'll all sit down and figure this out. I can't go sneaking around anymore. It's too much. Too hard."

Maria doesn't say anything, only nods slightly. Since she worked for Jonathan Spencer Maxwell and Anastasia Jerome first, I'm never quite sure if her loyalty is to them or me. I know she loves Paisley as much as she loves Nico. They're like her own children.

"It's going to blow up one of these days, and we need to be out in front of it," I justify, in case she sees me as a threat to their perfect Hollywood image.

I'm not a threat, and I'm not the only one who should pay for our transgressions.

Still cradling Paisley, who has drifted off to sleep, I fish my phone out of my coat pocket so I can call my travel agent. I text Angie an update, and after a moment, text Henderson as well.

She's ok. Broken leg, some cuts on her face. Going back to LA.

I close my eyes for a brief moment, thinking about the night we spent together. A pang hits my heart when I realize I probably won't see him again.

We have no reason to.

I guess the song was right. We didn't need tomorrow.

Maybe I don't need it, but maybe I want it.

Chapter 20: Henderson

I'm relieved for Tabitha that her daughter is going to be alright, yet disappointment tugs within my chest.

See? This is why I don't get involved. I've only spent hours with this woman, yet here I am stewing in my negative feelings. I think of my mum, who lost herself—and eventually me—to similar feelings.

Bloody hell if I'm gonna let that happen to me.

Time to re-center. Re-focus. Re-fresh.

And rein in Grayson because he's totally going rogue with his choices here. He sees *her* playing *that* role? Un-uh. No way.

"Mate, stop for a sec. Really? You can't be serious. The character of Christine is young. Naive. Gullible. It's only at the end that we see her hard side when she lets you in on the con. Krystal is too hard. I don't think she can do soft. I like Marley for that part." I pull Marley's headshot out of the pile and toss it to him.

If I can only focus on work, then I don't have to think about Tabitha. As far as I'm concerned, she no longer exists to me. I mean, not in a *she's dead and I won't ever speak to her again* sort of way. More as in an *it's in the past and I don't need to waste energy on it* kind of way.

No matter that the past is only four hours ago.

What's past is past.

And it's not like she's dumping me because of me. It's her tyke, and I respect that. In fact, I wouldn't respect her if she didn't put her daughter first.

Mentally I revise my list of nevers.

Never sleep with a coworker.

Never sleep with an actress.

Never fall in love.

Never get involved with a woman who has a kid.

There isn't going to be anyone left in Manhattan to get involved with pretty soon. It's probably the universe telling me I'm not cut out for this. The universe often gives me signals that I don't pay attention to until it's too late.

What can I say, I'm a slow learner. I learn almost as slowly as the casting process is going. Three hours later and we're only about sixty-percent done. I don't want to admit that I'm being especially argumentative, but one of us is making recommendations from out of left field, and I'll be damned if I'll admit that it's me.

I'm not the only salty one today. Grayson was supposed to be on the three o'clock train back north, yet he's still here.

"Why is this taking so long?"

"Everyone sucks. We need better." Okay, maybe they don't suck, but no one's striking my fancy. I glower at Grayson. He glowers back.

"Hello, boys. How's it going today?" The voice breaks us out of our staring contest.

"Carson. Twice in two days. To what do we owe this pleasure?" Grayson stands to greet our visitor.

Carson looks around the room. It's easy to see the disappointment in his face. "No special guests today?"

It doesn't take a rocket scientist to figure out who he's sniffing around for. Carson Reuben may have helped save

The Edison, but that doesn't mean I trust him. He's an entertainment journalist, first and foremost. He's always going to go for the big story.

Also, I'm pretty sure he's in love with Gray, and since Gray is in love with Gloria, it has the possibility to end badly. For everyone. See previous note about entertainment journalism. And getting involved with theatre people.

"So, I need the dish. Like, all of it. Time to spill the tea. What's going on with you and Tabby Cat?"

Without meeting his gaze, I shrug. "Nothing."

Carson slams his hand down on the table, startling me. "What I saw yesterday was not nothing. I *love* the Sassy Cats. I wanted to be one when I was an impressionable young boy. And Tabby, oh, her style was *to die for*. Total California chic. I can't believe I was in the same room with her."

"Surely you must meet all sorts of celebrities in your line of work." I'm not impressed with his fan-girling routine. In fact, it's making me bloody crook. It's not like I've never lost my cool around a celeb, but Carson's just grating.

"But I *love* her." Carson stops and looks from me to Grayson and then back. "Oh, wait. Oh, God. This is too good. I cannot. I'm dying. Dead."

I have no idea what he's talking about, and don't have the inclination to find out either. I stand up. "It's been so nice of you to stop by, Carson, but Gray and I are way behind schedule. He was supposed to be on the three o'clock back up to The Edison. We're not close to finishing. Do you mind letting us get back to work?"

This was probably the wrong thing to say and do, but if Carson Reuben doesn't stop talking about Tabitha, I may explode.

I mean, it's nothing. Last night was nothing. Besides, it's not like she left because of me or anything I did.

It doesn't matter though. She's still gone.

Grayson picks up on my agitation. "Carson, thanks so much, but H is right. We're super bogged down. You know how complex this is. But I can tell you this—we're working on something totally fantastic for this season. I hope we can convince you to make the trek up to Hicklam to join us for a performance or two. Trust me, you're not going to want to miss this."

Carson looks at him for a moment before issuing a sly smile. He taps his nose. "I've got you, Grayson. I'm totally picking up what you're putting down. So I guess I'll see you soon then. Can't wait."

We sit in silence for a few minutes.

"That was weird," Gray finally offers.

"He's weird." He's not, but something about how he talked about Tabitha rubbed me the wrong way.

"Okay, before we go any further, are you going to tell me what happened?"

I shrug. It seems to be the best way to not have to talk about it. My two go-to gestures are eye rolls and shoulder shrugs. I guess I'm used to being in situations where either people are frustrating me, or I simply don't care.

The price and benefits of being perpetually alone.

"Come on, H. We're friends. You can talk to me."

What am I supposed to say? Yet another person bailed on me? No one, including my parents, think I'm worth sticking around for? It's pathetic. Totally pathetic. I'm just as bad as Carson Reuben, falling all over her and fawning about. I liked it better when I didn't know who she really was.

Actually, I liked it better when we were in my bedroom last night.

I can honestly say I was with Tabitha, not Tabby Cat. If I had to guess, I'd say that I saw Tabitha for her true self in ninety-percent of our interactions.

I doubt someone like Carson would ever stop to see the real her. It's got to be exhausting to deal with that all the time. No wonder she's lying low, trying to sneak around without people noticing her.

Perhaps it's for the best that this is over before it really began. I don't think I've got the chops to swim in her pond.

Gray is still looking at me, expecting me to talk or some shit like that. I sigh. "I do have something to say." He perks up like a puppy waiting for his treat.

Eye roll.

"We need to figure this out so you can get on the train and go back home. Where can we meet halfway?"

An exhausting two hours later, we've got enough for call backs. The dance audition will help us to figure out who's best suited for some of the more specialty parts. This season, we need a ballet dancer and aerialist, so those are auditions we definitely need to schedule.

The one thing we don't have is a big name star.

I mean, we've got Gray in at least two roles, but we should be looking for a female name to bring in some sales.

Sigh.

Tomorrow I'll be hitting my contact list, looking to see who I can scrounge up. I'm too tired to think about that now. Maybe Tabitha could put in a good word with Angie, and she'd be willing to slum it up in Hicklam for the summer.

Maybe if Angie was there, Tabitha would come for a visit.

Maybe I'm a pathetic drongo.

I know which of these scenarios is most likely, and I refuse to wallow. Not for a woman. Not for anyone.

All in all, it's a good thing Tabitha had to leave when she did. If this is how I'm feeling now, four more days together would've been the nail in my coffin.

No sir, I don't want that. I don't need that.

I'm lucky to have escaped when I did.

Yet, three days later, I'm acutely aware my luck, such as it is, has run out.

I awake to fourteen text messages from Gray. Most of them spewing profanities. Frankly I had no idea he could use such colorful language.

I don't even need to click on the link to put together what he's ranting about. Yet, I still do.

Is the Cat Out of the Bag? By Carson Reuben for *Backstage Magazine*

Gather 'round, you cool cats and kittens. Uncle Carson is here to scratch your ears with some of the hottest news. Last summer I had the pleasure of reviewing Chicago *at The Edison Theater in Hicklam, NY. In the months that have passed, I've wondered how Grayson Keene was going to top himself this season. This news is as high as the hair on a cat's back.*

When I dropped in on The Edison's auditions in Midtown, who should I find there but none other than Sassy Cat, Tabitha Stetson. Clearly dressed for performing, would it be hard not to guess that Tabby Cat will be parking her paws in Hicklam this summer? Grayson Keene was tight-lipped, and The Edison's managing director, Henderson Quade spirited Ms. Stetson away before I could get more details. The Edison is expected to announce their lineup, as well as cast, in a few weeks. One thing's for certain—you're going to want to get your tickets as soon as possible so you can catch Tabby Cat making her theatrical debut in Hicklam. Please visit their website for ticket information.

I dial Grayson. He doesn't waste time with a greeting. "Log in."

It only takes me a minute to see why Grayson is freaking out. There are over three hundred emails. On a normal day at this point in the season, we get two to three in our general email account. They're all asking for more information about Tabby Cat and what show she's going to be in.

"Oh shit."

"Right? How could Carson do this to us?"

A string of profanities runs through my mind. And maybe a few make their way out of my mouth.

"I mean, I think he was trying to help."

"Help? This is going to ruin us. We're going to be a laughingstock."

There's silence on the line. I can practically see Grayson running his hand through his hair, trying to figure this all out. I hear Gloria in the background. "It would be great if it were true."

"Yeah, but it's not. And it never will be. And we're going to lose our shirt on this. We barely made it through last year, and now we're going to tank."

Chapter 21: Tabitha

By the time Paisley was a year old, I'd turned off Google alerts. It was an unhealthy obsession for me. As I was making an effort to lie low, the lack of alerts depressed me. The lack of likes and comments and tags pulled me lower than I'd ever been. I deleted my Twitter, and my Instagram is private. I decided I'd rather not know that no one is talking about me.

The downside is now that I'm apparently in the news again, I have no idea. This is twice in the past month. I can't believe it.

This time, it's fake news, obviously, but I missed it nonetheless.

That reporter was really going out on a limb, thinking I'd be in a show at The Edison. I'm not actually an actress. Anyone who's seen *Sassy Catastrophe* knows that. Not to mention the fact that Henderson has a strict anti-fraternization policy at work.

And if I was going to be around Henderson again, there'd definitely be fraternization.

Lots of fraternization.

The last few days have been agony. They've been filled with worry and concern for Paisley. She's handling the cast like a champ, despite my stressing. The plastic surgeon thinks the scarring will be minimal. I probably didn't need to fly back to California so quickly, but I wasn't taking any chances with her sweet face.

Anastasia calls me daily to check in on Paisley, which is nice of her. I think she's secretly relieved that I got Paisley away from the hospital. The media is still camped out, waiting for news or a picture. The rumor is that Jonathan Spencer Maxwell's paralyzed or brain damaged. Anastasia hasn't said so, but I haven't asked either.

I probably should.

So when my phone rings this morning, I expect it to be Anastasia. I'm surprised to see Mandy's name marching across my screen.

"Tabby, is it true? Are you coming to New York? Hicklam isn't that far from where my home base is. I can make sure I'm around so I can see you." She's practically squealing. This is as close to giddy as Mandy gets.

Fake news travels fast.

"Yeah, sorry. I'm not sure where that story came from. That reporter must be smoking crack."

"Oh." Even three thousand miles away, and over the phone, I can hear the disappointment in her voice. "I got all excited. I started making all these plans in my head. I miss you."

"I miss you too. I didn't realize you were that close." Of course I didn't. If it's not right in New York City, I have no idea. And even then, I really don't know where I'm going. When you say New York to me, I think the city. I often forget that there's anything else.

"Yeah. Myles and I used to go down to The Edison before the twins were born. I haven't been back in … well, Colin and Madden are nine, so I'm way overdue. They always did a great job at that theater. How did you get connected with them?"

"I'm not. I mean, not really. I hung out with a guy who works for them. He's, like, a director or something." I've never had a good memory for details. Mostly because I don't pay attention. It's been my downfall on more than one occasion. "We were set up, like a date, kind of but not really, and I went to see him while he was running auditions."

"Is this the guy from the karaoke videos? He's cute. And also, I've missed talking to you. I love how you're all over the place, yet I still follow you."

I recount the date and then the quest to find him again, only to have our time cut short by the accident.

"Oh, right. I'd heard about that. I didn't realize Paisley was with him. Poor baby. How's she doing?"

That's a relief—Paisley's presence didn't make the news. Despite other people being reported in the car, no one seems concerned about who they were or how they're doing. I scoured the internet, looking for stories about it, and Mandy certainly would have picked up on it if it had been reported. It's like Paisley doesn't exist in Jonathan Spencer Maxwell's world.

I sit back on my couch, watching Paisley play on her iPad on the big oversized chair. She's stretched out, and at any moment, I expect her to ask me to feed her grapes from the bunch. In our video for "Anything is Paw-sable," we played different famous lovers throughout history. I was Cleopatra. Actually, I was Cleo-cat-ra, being wooed by Bark Antony.

Stupid cat puns.

Paisley's posture doesn't look far from the Queen of Egypt. She just needs heavy black eyeliner and some bangs.

And cat ears, of course.

"She's fine." I fill her in on the medical part. "Getting extra time on the iPad, so I'm sure she thinks it's the best thing ever."

"Right? My boys are practically feral until you put a screen in front of them, and then they can be quiet for hours. I feel guilty, but sometimes I need to get stuff done. It's hard trying to focus on writing when they're destroying the place."

"How is writing going? Are you almost done?"

"I've got about four songs totally done and recorded. Four more partially done, and two that don't exist yet. Ben's working on the music, but it's been … a delicate situation. Myles doesn't want Ben around when the kids are around, and Ben's still in Tennessee so … Yeah. Delicate. Complicated. Messy."

I don't envy Mandy and her asshole ex-husband at all. "Sheesh, that sucks. I mean, my situation is no walk in the park, but at least Jonathan Spencer Maxwell isn't openly hostile to me."

I'm always afraid he will be, but that's another story.

"Tab, it's been four years. When are you going to stop calling him Jonathan Spencer Maxwell? I'm sure not everyone calls him that all the time. What do the people in his real life call him?"

"Jon." Even as I say it, it sounds foreign and wrong. "But that's for the people close to him. The people important to him."

"You're the mother of his child. That's got to count for something."

I shrug, even though she can't see it through the phone. "Really, if I hadn't gotten pregnant, he would just be someone I slept with once." That is, if he hadn't lied to me about having had a vasectomy. I still don't know what his motivation for that was. It was almost like he wanted to get caught cheating. Why, I'll never know. With narcissists like him, you really don't want to ask why.

"Okay, so back to why I called. You're *not* going to The Edison? Are you sure?"

I laugh. "I'm sure, though I did audition, so technically I guess I could."

"Well, how did you leave things with them—and him?"

"I ran out on him. I mean, I left. I had to, to get to Paisley. We were only going to have a few days of fun together anyway. I live here and he lives there. You know I'm not cut out for a long distance thing, and I don't think he even does relationships. It is what it is. He's just another person I slept with."

Even though I said the same thing about Jonathan Spencer Maxwell, it doesn't feel the same. My time with Henderson is totally different. It's almost like it meant something.

Almost.

"Well, if you change your mind, let me know. Maybe Tenley can be like a mother's helper with Paisley or something. She's twelve and has matured a lot over the past four years."

"Tenley is my favorite. The way she put Callie Smalls in her place—she had bigger balls at eight than most people have in a lifetime."

"Yeah, but Callie and Asher are killing it in their design business. If Tenley hadn't spoken to her like she did, I don't think Callie would have accepted the role as stylist rather than designer."

"I saw some of their stuff in Bergdorf's. It's crazy. Callie's in Bergdorf's, you're writing an album for Sony Music, and I'm going to Gymboree and singing karaoke."

This is *not* where I saw my life going.

"I hear you. All the while you were jet setting and clubbing and walking the red carpet, I was changing diapers and pushing a grocery cart. I thought if I didn't talk about my past, it wouldn't matter. I was supposed to be happy being a wife and mother."

"Were you?" I know the answer to this, but I need to hear Mandy say it.

"No, of course not." She snorts. "Did you see me when we first reunited? I'd spent years eating my feelings—and the feelings of every neighbor on the block. I mean, I love being a mother. It's what I always wanted." She pauses. "At least it's what I thought I always wanted."

I get up and walk out to the kitchen so Paisley can't overhear. "But it's not enough, just being a mom."

Mandy's silence affirms my comment.

"So now what do I do?" I really need her to tell me this. I need someone to tell me what to do.

"I don't know what to tell you, Tab. You have to find that balance for yourself. You can't devote every single second of every single day for the next fifteen years to Paisley. It's okay to give up a lot for her, but you have to keep a little piece for yourself. Because when she's grown and flown, who will you be? You won't have yourself. You have to be true to who you really are."

"That's the kicker, Mandy. I don't even know. I'd say I want to be famous again, because you know how I love that attention."

Mandy laughs. "I know you do. But you also know that kind of attention is good and bad."

"Being alone is bad."

"And you know it's possible to be lonely in a crowd of people."

Isn't that the truth? That first day, when I'd said goodbye to Paisley and was wandering around, lost in Manhattan, I'd never felt more alone. Thinking about that makes me think about meeting Henderson, which brings me back full-circle to the reason why Mandy called in the first place. I stand at the kitchen island, watching my daughter across the open space.

"Wouldn't it be so funny if I ended up doing a show at The Edison? I mean, theater was always Angie's thing, but I could probably do it. Maybe." I've never been one to let unrealistic expectations get in my way. It's how I ended up being a Sassy Cat—as well as sleeping with the number one actor in Hollywood—in the first place. If I want something, I just do it.

"I'm being selfish, but I'd love it if you did. Just so I can see you some more."

My heart pangs, missing my friend who's always been like a sister—and mother—to me. "But really? I don't know if it's my thing. Hell, I don't even know what my thing is anymore." The truth of that hits me like a ton of bricks.

I have no thing. There's nothing I'm good at. Nothing I'm qualified to do.

Mandy can hear the desperation and sadness in my voice. "You're lost, Tabby. You need to find yourself."

Mandy's words are an arrow shooting straight at my heart. She's so wise. I wonder where she learned to be like this. "I seriously don't know how to be a good mother. I'm too afraid I'll end up being just like my mom." When I was younger, I thought my mom was so cool. She didn't make me do homework or care if I skipped school. It was acceptable to drink and smoke and have boys over.

I mean, I turned out fine, but I don't think that was because of her.

"Tab, would your mom have left a guy to come running to you? Would she have whisked you across the country to see the best plastic surgeon money can buy just so you didn't have a scar?"

"My mom couldn't even be bothered to attend parent-teacher conferences, so I don't think so."

"My mom neither."

I think her mother and my mother were cut from the same cloth, and yet Mandy went on to be Martha Stewart. I'm more like a reality TV show train wreck.

I think for a minute. "So how did you learn to be so good? I mean, I know the boys are hellions and all, but we'll just blame all those traits on your asshole ex."

Mandy laughs. "I don't know. I just tried to give them everything I always wanted as a kid. Stability. Love. Acceptance. Those aren't hard things for me to provide."

After we disconnect, Mandy's words echo in my head. She's still giving up things for her kids. She and Ben are meant to be together. Not just as a singer-songwriter-composer team, but like *together* together. Myles is still standing in the way of that. She still doesn't get to have what she wants, all because of her kids. I mean, it's because of her douchewaffle ex, but if she didn't have the kids, she'd be free to be with Ben.

"Mommy, can I have some more dragon fruit chips?" Paisley holds out her empty bowl.

"I guess, but make sure to say 'please.' No one likes a diva." I refill her bowl and hand it back to her. I will not have her acting like a spoiled brat just because I used to be someone famous. I slide onto the chair next to Paisley, gingerly pulling her onto my lap. Instinctively, she snuggles in. I want for her all the things Mandy wants for her kids. But I want to be happy too.

I'm not sure there's a way for me to have both.

Chapter 22: Henderson

C all her."

I look away, as if the voice on the other end of the phone can see my disinterest.

"H, man, you have to call her. You have to ask."

I still don't respond. I'm not having this conversation with Grayson. Again.

"She might say yes."

"She won't say yes, mate." I don't want her to say yes. I mean, I need her to. The Edison needs her to. Ever since Carson Reuben's damn article two weeks ago, we've been inundated with calls and emails, wanting to know when Tabby Cat would be appearing at The Edison, and can we please buy tickets. If the story wasn't totally false, Gray and I'd be jumping up and down with delight. It would mean we wouldn't have to be counting each seat sale, wondering if we were going to cover our costs for another season.

But if Tabitha came to The Edison, it'd be over between us. There's no way I could ... nope. Just no. It's a hard no.

"You don't know that she won't say yes. It's not like you even know her that well."

"I know her." I don't know her at all.

"Did you think she'd show up at auditions? I saw your face. You were stunned."

Gobsmacked was more like it.

"Okay, fine. If you're not going to call her, then I will."

I sit back and fold my hands across my chest, even though Grayson can't see my smug posture. "You can't. You don't have her number, and I'm not going to call her."

Grayson groans. "*Arrgh*. Why are you being so disagreeable?"

"I'm not being disagreeable, mate. It's ..." I'm being disagreeable. "I slept with her."

There's silence on the line. "Yeah, and?" Grayson says slowly. We came so close to losing The Edison last year. Grayson did everything he possibly could to save his family's theatre. This could be a huge boost.

But still, I can't get on board. "I don't do that. You know me. I'm not gonna be involved with anyone I work with. So I'm not calling her." As I say it, I know I sound like the world's biggest wanker. I probably am.

"Henderson, you know I wouldn't ask you if it wasn't important. Think about Gloria and what she did last year. How far that pushed her, just to keep The Edison going. This is small potatoes compared to that. You don't want to sleep with her, then don't. If you do, you do. That's not what it's about. It's about The Edison."

Gah. Gray's my best mate, and I'd do anything for him. I want to be that bloke who sticks by and digs deep, no matter what. You know, the bloke I never had in my life. I feel myself relenting. "I'll think about it."

We disconnect and nothing about this situation feels good. We're not even working together and being involved with Tabitha has already created more headaches than I want to deal with. I don't have time for this today. I've got to get to the studio for specialty dance auditions.

As I'm jostled onto the 7 train to Midtown, I curse Grayson. Curse him for deciding we *had* to do *An American in Paris*. That means it's not enough to have a lead who can dance, but she's got to be an actual ballerina. For this role, we're auditioning dancers first and then will have them sing. It's backward from our normal process, but because the dance is so integral to the role, we have to go this way.

This is in addition to the grueling two days of company auditions, plus another one of general dance. Too bad The Edison doesn't pay by the hour.

"Who's next?" I ask Morgan. I glance over to see her frowning at the paper.

"Weird. There's no name."

Eye roll.

"Call the number."

As Morgan crosses the floor to open the door, I'm not sure why we're bothering to audition this one. She's filled out her whole form, which is why I know she's a she, as she indicated she's auditioning for the role of Lise, but left the name blank. Whatever she has going on, I want no part of.

"Number seventy-two!" Morgan bellows.

While I wait, I pick up my phone and without thinking too much about it, I text Tabitha.

Hey. Howzit going?

Nothing earth-shattering. Hell, she probably won't even respond. I doubt she remembers me.

I hear a throat clearing, which forces me to drag my attention away from my phone and onto the clearer of the throat.

Number seventy-two.

On first look, she seems totally normal.

Except I know she's not normal because she *didn't put a name down on her application*. I don't know why this is bothering me so much, but here we are.

I sit and look at her. She stands, nervously clutching her resume and headshot. Her black leotard shows a body more curvy than a typical ballerina's. Her skin tone, too, is darker than the ballet world historically embraces. That doesn't matter for us at The Edison.

All that matters is if she can dance.

"Do you have a name?" Jesus, I sound like an asshole.

"Um, yes, but I'm considering starting to use a stage name. I can't decide."

I don't even bother to hide my eye roll. This is going to be a waste of my time. "Okay, are you ready?" The dancers have been in another studio learning the steps. Our choreographer, Kori, has sent on the ones she likes best. I've already seen these steps about ten times. Ironically, there's a ballet audition scene in the show, so the dancers are doing that combo.

As the music rises for the Lise's audition dance, my phone pings. Almost involuntarily, my eyes dart down.

It's a text from Tabitha.

How'd you know I was thinking about you?

Huh. She was thinking about me.

She remembers me.

Is that so?

She quickly responds.

Yeah. I keep going back to that article. About me. In your show.

Shit. I hope she's not mad.

Don't know why he did that. Sorry.

I add in the shoulder shrugging, I-don't-know emoji. As soon as it sends, I regret it. Did I really just send an emoji to Tabitha Stetson?

I'm lame. Movement catches my eye and I glance up. Okay, she is at least a competent ballerina. Her extension is high and her fouetté arabesque is sharp. Number seventy-two is finishing with a well-executed piqué turn, stepping through to en dehors rond de jambe à terre, finishing in a kneeling courtesy, just as Kori taught.

"That's great. Thanks." Sure, she was good, but unless she was Misty Copeland or Julie Kent, I'm not sure I'd cast her. Her application, sans name, tells me she's got issues, and we're choc a bloc with them already.

My phone pings again.

So, like, what if I wanted to do a show. Can I?

The words float across my screen. Yes! No! Holy hell! Anyway you slice it, I'm screwed.

As if my fingers are not connected to my brain, they type, *Why?*

I stare at my phone in disbelief. Why did I type that? What was I thinking? Why isn't there an undo feature on texts?

This time, she sends back the shrugging, I-don't-know emoji.

"HENDERSON!" Morgan's tone is sharp.

I look up at my irate assistant, totally clueless as to what's crawled up her bum. "Yeah?"

"That was the last one. You need to pick. You need to choose. We have to get this done. Put your damn phone away and tell me who is playing Jerry and who is playing Lise."

"Don't go all crook on me. Give me a second. I might be working on something big here. I'm about to land Tabitha Stetson for a role." Apparently my mouth is also working independently from my brain right now.

"Shut the front door. No way! She's really gonna do it? Are you really that good in bed? I bet you have secret moves."

I nearly drop my phone, shocked by Morgan's brazen words. I shouldn't be shocked. She's got a mouth—and mind—like a sailor. Usually, my behavior is above reproach. I make it my business to be nobody else's business. My phone pings again.

I know, stupid idea. Every year I vow I'll stop being so impulsive ...

Shit. Shit. Shit. What do I say?

Not stupid at all. It'd be ...

My finger hovers over the screen, unsure of what to type. Fun? Good? A big, huge, horrible mistake?

Before I can finish my thought, another text from Tabitha pops up.

I don't know what I'd do with Paisley anyway.

Right. She's got a tyke. That's a complication.

Don't you have a nanny? If not, I'm sure we can hire someone local to help you out. It's a great place for kids.

It's like my dick has taken over and is typing these answers. He's obviously sure that if we can convince Tabitha to come to Hicklam, he'd get a lot more action. Dumb fool.

Do you have an apartment there too?

There too. Like I'm made of money and can afford two places. On the other hand, she probably has multiple residences. She is made of money.

No, I sublet my place in the city. I stay in the cast dorms.

Dorms?

Christ, I sound like a child. Better for her to know now. *Yep, like college. Or summer camp is more like it. It's a lot of fun and some nights I actually get three whole hours of sleep.*

The older I get, the more this bothers me. The young kids in the cast like to party and fraternize. I'm the crotchety old man living at the end of the hall. Like an R.A. who never graduated.

Never went to camp or college. Went on tour instead. Maybe it'd be fun?

I try to picture Tabitha Stetson in the dorms. My first thought is thank God Grayson and Gloria renovated them last year. But no amount of paint and flooring will make up for the fact that it's still a low-end dormitory compared to the five-star digs Tabitha is used to.

You'd be better off in a house in town.

I wonder if Malachi Andrews would be able to set her up in something nice. His brother and sister own a lot of property in town. They've been working on rehabbing and renovating Hicklam, one old mill building at a time. Hopefully they have something suitable for pop music royalty. I quickly add to my text.

I can work on something, if you want me to. I know a realtor.

I look like a nice, thoughtful guy. It's not at all because the idea of her staying in the dorms, so close to me, would drive me crazy. It's going to be hard enough to be around her and not resume right where we left off.

It's almost as if I'm imagining her sneaking into my twin bed.

Everything about this conversation goes against my rules. I'm happy to be texting this, so I can measure my words. I don't know what would come flying out of my mouth if we were speaking.

Um, I guess?

I see three dots waving on the screen. I don't know what to say. Lucky for me, she continues texting.

Is this crazy? It feels crazy.

It's totally crazy, for both of us. She has no stage experience. I'd be a fool to cast her, practically unseen. On the other hand, with her name recognition—and what it's already doing for The Edison—I'd be a fool not to cast her.

A little crazy is good every now and again.

I'm in.

As those two words dance across the screen, a pit forms in my stomach. I have a strict policy, and I'm breaking it. I'm going to need every ounce of control and restraint to stick to my guns. If this is going to work, I need to be cool and aloof.

That's all there is to it.

Cool and aloof.

Chapter 23: Tabitha

Cool and aloof.

He's been so cool and aloof the past two months that I could practically get frostbite. Maybe he doesn't do the distance thing well. Maybe once we're not three thousand miles apart, he won't seem so distant.

Distant isn't even the word.

Once I'd texted him, that was it. Everything came from Grayson, or it went through Gayle, who took me on officially as a client. She worked on the contracts and negotiated everything. She's also made the travel reservations and figured out where I'm going to live for the six weeks I'll be spending in the rinky-dink town of Hicklam.

I mean, seriously, it even has hick in the name.

Gayle swears she found me a good place to stay. She's always taken good care of Angie, so I hope she does the same for me. I'm probably pretty stupid to trust this whole process. Angie and Mandy keep telling me it will be great.

And maybe I could get more excited if only Henderson wasn't being so cool and aloof. I've had six texts from him in two freakin' months, not that I'm counting.

Who does he think he is, blowing me off like that? I sort of wish I hadn't agreed to do his stupid theater in the first place. Maybe I wouldn't have if I'd known he was going to drop me so completely.

Yet now, here I am, landing in Albany of all places. Paisley, Maria, and I still have almost an hour car ride ahead of us, once we get our bags.

It's already been a long day and one of us is whining excessively.

The other is only four and is handling this in stride.

Maria, of course, is the consummate professional. Thank God she had the forethought to suggest I ship things out ahead of time. I can't imagine trying to haul all that luggage, plus Paisley. It's especially stressful because— shocker—I have no idea where I'm going or what I'm doing. Grayson told me he'd have a driver waiting for me in baggage claim, and sure enough, as I descend the escalator, I see the sign with "Stetson" on it.

Not that many people think of my last name right off the bat, so we get through this arduous process without being stopped. I mean, who would think I'd be flying into Albany? This airport seems small and empty compared to some of the other places I've been. There's only one terminal!

"Hello Ms. Stetson. I'm Kyle. Grayson Keene sent me." He's overly stiff and awkward, and if I'm not mistaken, he curtsies a little. I start to laugh, but quickly rein it in when I see the serious expression on his face.

I look around for a cart to put our luggage on, including Paisley's booster seat that I'm losing my grip on. Seriously, traveling with a little kid is not all it's cracked up to be.

Henderson better'd be worth it.

Yet I know he's probably not.

I see one lone baggage cart in a corral next to a far brick wall. "Stay with Paisley," I say to Maria. "I'll be right back."

The machine tells me to insert four dollars and doesn't take credit cards. What a crock! Who carries ones these days? Do I look like a stripper? I trudge back over, taking Paisley's hand. "Maria, do you have any money? We need to get a cart."

She shakes her head. "Who has cash?"

"Right?"

I turn to Kyle. "What are we going to do? We don't have cash for the baggage cart."

"Okay." He blinks slowly.

There's no way we can carry everything. Kyle just stands there. Is he going to make me beg him for the money? Screw that. I'm not begging. "How close can you get the car?"

His head slowly cocks to the side. "Well, I think they'd frown upon me driving through the building to get right up to the conveyor belt, if that's what you mean. It'd really mess up the Hertz rental counter there. Otherwise, I'm right outside."

It's about a hundred feet or so. I feel like an idiot. "Oh. Well, I think we can manage."

He looks at me, and I think I see an ever-so-slight head shake.

"I'm used to larger airports."

"Of course you are." His tone is dry. People don't interact with me with a dry tone. I don't know what to do with this.

"And I don't have any ones on me." I try to justify this situation. I'm also not used to justifying.

"So I shouldn't expect a tip then."

I may be a lot of things, but a tightwad is not one of them. "I didn't say I don't have any cash. I don't have any ones. I tip well. I'm not one of those a-hole celebrity types who expects everyone to do everything for them. I mean I do, but I pay for it."

If I'm not mistaken, I see the edge of his mouth twitch so very slightly. "Don't get your panties in a wad. Oh, this has got to be you."

He nods to the matching Louis Vuitton bags, their pale pink handles on traditional brown monogrammed leather. Both Paisley and I have two bags checked, in addition to my carry-on bag. And purse. And Paisley's backpack. And stroller. And booster seat.

Not to mention Maria's bags.

I let out a nervous laugh. "I hope you have a decent-sized car."

"No worries. It'll all fit in the back of the pickup."

My head spins to the large glass doors and windows that make up the front of the building, searching for his truck. I'm sure my eyes are the size of saucers. "You can't be serious! Do you know what the bags alone cost? Not to mention the contents. What if it flies out all over the freeway?"

Kyle laughs, pulling one bag and then another off the conveyor belt. "First of all, you need to learn to take a joke. Second of all, we don't have freeways here in New York. Third of all, unless it washes, folds, and irons your clothes for you, who cares how much it costs? A bag is a bag."

My mouth opens and then quickly closes. He's got me.

Then he mutters something that sounds like, "No wonder stars go broke and have to do things like go on reality TV shows."

I could respond. I *should* respond. But I don't, considering I need his help. If my mom taught me anything, it's don't bite the hand that feeds you. At least not until you've got the bone all to yourself.

She didn't give me a lot of life skills other than using my sex appeal to get what I want, but that one's come in handy over the years.

Kyle's driving a clean—but not new—Toyota Sequoia. "Will this do?" Considering he curtsied at me a few moments ago, he's certainly gotten quite uppity. Somehow, we quickly got off on the wrong foot.

"Sure. I just ... well, this isn't what I'm used to. It's good. I was just worried about losing all my stuff. I don't know when my other things will arrive, so I need the things in these bags."

"You have *more* stuff coming?" Now it's his eyes that look like saucers.

"I'll be here for six weeks." I can't believe I have to say something so obvious.

"Most of the cast brings less than this for the entire summer."

"I'm not most of the cast."

He looks me up and down. "No, you're not. I just hope you're worth it. Grayson has been one of my best friends since we were five. The Edison means everything to him. I hope you're here for them and not for you."

Maria glances at me, raising an eyebrow. I don't respond. Even as we load all the luggage into the back of the SUV and I buckle Paisley in, I still don't say anything.

Mostly because I don't know what to say.

I don't know why I'm here.

I mean, I do.

I'm here for a guy. But it's too pitiful and sad to admit that I have to chase someone—who's barely said three words to me since we slept together—across the country. Have I ever mentioned I'm a slow learner? Have I also mentioned that I can't handle rejection?

At first I was attracted to Henderson because he didn't fawn all over me. Now I'm desperate to make him fawn all over me. Well, desperate is a strong word. I mean, it's not the only reason I'm doing this.

I've got to do something. In truth, I have no idea what. But without an agent pounding the pavement for me, I was at a loss for what to do next. Since the accident, the press has been all over Jonathan Spencer Maxwell, looking for a scoop and a story. Paisley would be the scoop of the year. I want to keep her far, far away from the media circus surrounding him. He's back in LA, so moving Paisley to the other side of the country seems like the best way to separate the two of them.

I don't know how he's doing—not really any more details than what's been reported; that the recovery has been, and will be, long. Maybe I should have reached out or something. I don't know. I haven't heard from him at all. It's all been from Anastasia. She didn't even bat an eye when I told her I'd be in New York for six weeks. Normally she's the stickler for the visits.

But if she's not going to put up a fight, then I should run with this. I'm not going to beg them to see my daughter. I'm done begging.

I think she really loves my kid, which is more than most women can say of their baby daddy's wife. Especially considering she was his wife when he became my baby daddy. Still, there's something I don't trust. Like maybe she's being nice in order to control what I say and do.

It's not like she can be nice just because she's nice. No one in Hollywood is like that. Everyone wants something. The only currency I have is sex and my child. I'm not willing to give either to Anastasia Jerome, so I do my best to stay on her good side.

It's why I took the past four years off from being a celebrity. I just didn't think the world would forget about me so soon.

It's a terrible feeling.

Maybe that's another reason why I'm so desperate—er, eager—for Henderson to want me. I used to think Angie was crazy for going to extremes to stay in front of an audience. With her Broadway shows and *Hollywood Dance Off!* she ran herself ragged trying to be relevant.

At the time, post-Sassy Cats, I didn't understand where that need came from. On the other hand, I was doing television appearances and out on the social scene, so my face was never far from the spotlight. And now, I just feel … invisible. The only person who sees me is Paisley.

We're on a highway that is practically deserted. I mean, there are cars, but the traffic's moving at a clip unheard of in LA. Then suddenly, the road narrows to three small lanes as we cross a river. And now there's green. There are tree-covered mountains in front of us and fewer and fewer cars.

"Is traffic always like this?"

"Nah," Kyle throws over his shoulder. "It's the busy time. All the state workers are getting out."

"*That* was traffic?"

I see him shrug. "I mean, sometimes there's an accident that causes it to really pile up, but yeah. Oh, that's right. You're from California. I guess this is a little different."

We're, like, in the middle of nowhere already. We only left the airport twenty minutes ago and now we're in … farmland? The roads twist and turn and there are honest-to-God red barns and cows.

"Look! Paisley! Look at the cows. Moo! Moo!"

I'm mooing.

Paisley squeals and stretches her neck, practically standing up on her booster in order to get a better view. "Horses too, Mommy!"

And now I'm making neighing noises.

If they could see me now.

"So, Kyle, tell me about Hick-lam." I don't mean to emphasize the 'hick' part, but as we're driving through nowhere, it seems to fit.

"I think you mean Hick-lame. That's what we like to call it. I can never figure out why people want to come here. I've spent my whole life trying to get out."

"Why didn't you?"

He shrugs. "My two best friends are Grayson and Drew. Not to mention Joe." He says those names like they're supposed to mean something to me.

"And?"

"Well, Grayson's got the theater. He left for a while, sort of, but was always coming back. I think I knew he'd never leave The Edison. Joe's family owns the autobody shop in town. And Drew's dad is the police chief, so you know he's never going to go anywhere. Plus Drew and Tina are getting married at the end of summer. Ain't never gonna leave now."

"And?" I'm still failing to make the connection.

"Where would I go? What would I do? Who would I do it with? Us four have been together since we were little. I can't split up the band."

Though I realize he's talking in metaphors, I know what happens when the actual band—who are the only family you've ever really had—splits up. "Yeah, I get it. How do you think I ended up with her?" I catch Kyle's eyes in the rearview mirror as I nod toward Paisley. "The band breaks up, and suddenly you're mooing at cows in the middle of nowhere."

His ears turn bright red as his gaze drops back to the road.

I decide to let him off the hook. "The theater's good, though. Right?"

Please say right.

He shrugs again. "I guess some people like that sort of thing. It keeps the town afloat. Plus, there's always new faces floating through. It's the only thing that makes Hicklam bearable. Every summer, there's a hot new cast, as well as people in town for the shows. Keeps me busy." He looks at me in the rearview mirror and waggles his eyebrows.

Is he coming on to me? Um, he's so not my type. Or what used to be my type. Do I even have a type anymore? *Australian.*

"Oh, uh, yeah. So, tell me everything you know about Henderson. I mean I know he's Australian and ..." I trail off before I can add something mortifying like "a generous lover" to that statement.

"Yeah, he doesn't really like me. I try to steer clear."

"Why doesn't he like you?" I wonder if Kyle swooped in and stole his woman or something interesting like that.

Kyle lets out a long sigh. "The man is all work and no play."

I wouldn't say *no* play.

"You think?" I try to keep my face even. Never too early to work on those acting skills I'm gonna need soon.

"Totally. He eats, sleeps, and breathes The Edison when he's here. He never has any fun. And he certainly doesn't appreciate that I do, if you know what I mean."

If Kyle were any more blunt, he'd be a Mack truck.

"I think he's jealous that the ladies like me."

"I thought Henderson didn't date people he works with."

"Yeah, that's what he says, but he's just afraid of striking out. The man has a complex or something. So he plays it off. Truth is, he probably couldn't land any of the cast if he tried. He's got no game. Not that it matters anyway. Henderson has laser-like focus. And he'll never stray away from his position that work and play don't mix."

We'll see about that.

Chapter 24: Henderson

You sent *Kyle* to pick her up?" Bloody hell.

"Yeah." Grayson doesn't look up from the pile of books he's sorting.

"But *Kyle*? Wasn't there anyone else? Why didn't you go?"

That gets Grayson's attention. "Because I'm busy as hell in here. And if you were so concerned, why didn't *you* offer to go?" He cocks an eyebrow at me.

"You know I'm in the weeds here, mate."

"So then what's your problem?"

"You know how Kyle is. He's probably hitting on her right this very moment," I say nonchalantly.

"And do you think she'd go for him?"

"Hell, no. Not a chance."

Grayson smirks. "Then what's the big deal?"

I don't dignify him with a response. Not responding is my specialty. I have a string of text messages from Tabitha that I didn't answer. In any other setting, it'd be ghosting. But no, not for me. I'm bringing the woman I'm blowing off across the country to work with me.

Against my better judgment.

"What's the update?" I've asked Grayson this question at least three times a day for the past eight weeks. Once the announcement went out that Tabitha "Tabby Cat" Stetson would be in our production of *The Greatest Showman*, ticket sales exploded. We added an additional show on Thursday night to accommodate all of those interested. So we've just ratcheted up the ante by opening a day earlier. Swell.

"We've had three tickets open up on Sunday."

"Okay, I'll contact the wait list. Want me to offer them to the next party or the next party of three?"

Grayson gazes off into space, as if he's doing long division in his head. "If there's a party of two and one ahead of a party of three, do that. Otherwise skip down to the party of three."

Our ticket sales for the entire season are up. This is a massive contrast to last summer. Now we have a waitlist!

Grayson knocks me off cloud nine with his next statement. "I hope she can do it."

That's the elephant in the room. Once Tabitha connected with Grayson, the train barreled out of the station at full speed. No one bothered to make sure all the wheels were intact.

"You sent her the book and music, right?"

Grayson nods. "For the millionth time, yes."

"Did she have questions? Has she asked for guidance?"

"Nope. Nothing."

The pit in my stomach deepens. It's been growing by the day. "Gray, what—"

"Don't say it." He holds his hand up, cutting me off. "It's going to be swell. It'll be great. We're gonna have the whole world on the plate."

I stand up and walk toward the door. "This is not the time to channel your inner Ethel Merman. If she can't pull it off, The Edison could go up in smoke."

I head outside, the sun bright on this mid-June day. Thoughts, mostly ones I don't want to think about, flood my brain.

Can she do this part?

Were we stupid to cast her?

Will she be mad at me for blowing her off?

Will she be happy to see me?

I have no answers to the first two questions. As for the last two, my guess is the former will be affirmative, while the latter will be negative.

Good. That's how it needs to be. I need her mad at me so she doesn't want to pick up where we left off. There will be none of that. She's just like any other cast member.

Off limits.

It'll be fine. It wasn't even anything to begin with. I wasn't supposed to have more than a few days with her. I simply need to keep my head down and focus on The Edison. It shouldn't be too hard. There are only about a million things to do.

It's a transition week, which means we're finishing up one production while getting ready to launch the next. We'll perform *Dirty Rotten Scoundrels* tonight and twice tomorrow. Then on Monday we'll strike that set, shifting into tech rehearsals for *Kiss Me, Kate* which will open on Friday night. Additionally, we'll start music and dance for *The Greatest Showman*. Just explaining the process exhausts me, and I'm not in any of the shows.

Grayson's sitting out *Kiss Me, Kate* to get ready for *The Greatest Showman*. There's a lot riding on those three weeks of shows.

I don't need to worry about Tabitha. Even if I wanted to, there's no time for anything but rehearsals and shows.

"Is she here yet? Is she coming to the show tonight? You know, I just had a brilliant idea. Like totally brilliant." Grayson's voice startles me. I hadn't heard him sneak up behind me. He's half-dressed already for his role as Freddy, in wrinkled khaki pants and a loud Hawaiian shirt.

I glance at my watch.

"Thirty-minutes 'til curtain. I gotta go call it." I'd rather have something to do than wait for a car that may or may not show up anyway.

"What about my idea?"

"Let's talk after the show. I need to get backstage."

The last performances of a show are the easiest for me. The kinks have been worked out and the cast knows what they're doing. There's very little for me to fix or nitpick. In other words, I wish I were busier right now. Still, before I know it, Grayson and Bobby Benson are singing the closing song, "Dirty Rotten Number."

I never fail to be amazed at the magic that happens on that stage every night. For a long time, I wanted to be up there as well. I don't feel that tug anymore, mostly because I've convinced myself that I don't need to act. Directing, managing, and doing everything else behind the scenes is equally as important. The show couldn't go on without someone like me.

I don't need the spotlight. I'm totally fine with this.

As the cast and audience settle into the after-hours cabaret, Grayson catches up with me in the business office. He's still on a performance high and has more energy than a pot of coffee. I feel like my nerves have been stretched so thin they're about to snap.

Sometimes Grayson reminds me of a big, slobbering puppy dog. This is one of those moments.

I look up at him, not saying anything. He's practically reverberating with excitement. Finally, I cave. "What's your brilliant idea?"

He slides onto the corner of the desk. "I don't think Tabitha should play Charity."

"What? We brought her out here for that role. Our whole season is built upon it. *Selling the show* is built on it. You can't do that to her. I mean, to The Edison."

"No, listen." He shakes his hand, as if he's trying to frantically clean something. "She's not Charity. She's not right for the role."

"Well, you know, you could have told me that before I hauled my ass all the way across the country." The voice coming from the doorway surprises both of us. Grayson jumps up and envelops her in one of his trademark bear hugs.

"Tabby Cat! You're here!"

He releases her and she stumbles back. As soon as she gains her footing, she tilts her head, cocking her eyebrow. It's her pissed-off look. "Should I be? Or did I make this God-awful trek for nothing?" She glances at me. There is no warmth in her blue eyes.

I shrug. "I don't know anything here."

"I'm sure you don't. Or at least if you do, you can't be bothered to text it."

Grayson's still reverberating with enthusiasm. "No, we still want you. *Need you*. But I have a great idea. I know we cast you as Charity, and I'm sure you'd be good in that part, but I think you'd be *great* as Jenny Lind."

Good God, if it had been any more obvious, it would have bitten my nose off. Of course, Tabitha should play Jenny. The opera star, so luminous and effervescent that she makes P.T. Barnum almost forget about his wife. I'd been so short-sighted, only seeing Tabitha as Charity because of that night at Oppa's.

This woman clouds my professional judgment. I shake my head slightly, as if to clear it.

Tabitha relaxes her eyebrow. "It's a great song."

Grayson grins. "It is."

"And I wouldn't have to dance. I can dance, but it's hard for me to pick up. That's the part I've been most worried about."

Grayson shakes his head. "Nope, no dancing. Just singing and acting like a big star."

Tabitha laughs. "I wouldn't even have to tap too deeply for that. I'm game."

I shake my head one more time, trying to snap back into reality. "Wait, Gray, what are you doing? What about Marcelina?"

"Marcelina would be great as Charity. This is her third season with us. She was smashing as Velma in *Chicago* last year. She can totally handle it. I'll go tell her."

And with that Grayson's off and running. "I can't believe he's doing this to me."

"To you? I'm the one who's been studying the wrong part for a week."

I look at her. "You have?"

"Of course I have. You sent the materials." She pauses. The head tilt is back. "Actually, it wasn't you who sent them. It was Grayson, wasn't it?"

"Yes." Better to say as little as possible. I'm in enough trouble.

Though, I remind myself, I want her mad at me. I don't want her to rush in and throw herself into my arms. That would make it harder. This is for the best.

"Okay, then. Well, I have my work cut out for me. I'll see you at rehearsal." She turns and begins to walk out.

I let out my breath that I'd been struggling to hold onto. I sink back into my chair, devoid of all energy.

"Wait!" Tabitha sticks her head back into the room. "When is rehearsal?"

"Monday, nine a.m."

"Okay, so I guess I'll see you then?" She hesitates, waiting for me to say something. I can't give her that.

Oh, but how I wish I could.

Chapter 25: Tabitha

That was good, yet bad all at the same time.

I mean, I should have guessed that Henderson wouldn't be waiting for me with two dozen roses and a bottle of champagne, but would a hug have been too much to ask?

At least Grayson gave me a hug.

I don't want hugs from Grayson.

Stupid, stupid, stupid Tabby. When will you learn that men want you for one thing and one thing only, and as soon as they have it, they're done with you?

I can't think about that now. I have to focus on the part change.

It's a lesser role for certain, but I know without a doubt, it's a smart move. I've been freaking out about my ability to do this. Jenny Lind, I can do.

I can be the starlet.

I can be the home-wrecker.

Hell, I don't even have to act.

I can sing about being unfulfilled.

I walk around the house I'm renting. It's older than anything I've ever lived in. There's an attached house made out of stone, and there's a carriage house too. It's tons of space. I could bring an entourage out for the summer and we'd all be comfortable.

There are dark hardwood floors that match the molding and built-in bookshelves. There are so many rooms. On the first floor alone, there is a dining room, a library, a kitchen, a small powder room, a living room, and an additional room the real estate agent called a parlor. It's like they've never heard of open concept.

How am I supposed to see what Paisley is doing if I'm in another room?

On the other hand, I sort of want to put on a regency style dress and lounge in the parlor like one of the Bridgertons. The house gives me that sort of vibe.

I should totally have a party here.

I have to forget about Henderson and focus on this.

Instead, I pick up my phone and call Mandy. She answers without saying hello.

"Tabitha, you know I love you dearly, but for the love of God, can you please remember about the time difference? It's after eleven here."

"It's after eleven here too. My body just doesn't realize that."

I have to pull the phone away as Mandy shrieks. "You're here!"

I laugh. "I am and I already got fired." I tell her about the role change.

"Yeah, but 'Never Enough' is the best song. I mean, there are so many great songs, but that song gives me chills. I love to sing it."

And I bet Mandy would be better at it than me. I almost say that to her, but instead ask, "Do you have a vocal coach you work with? I might need some help with some of the belts. I don't want to kill my voice."

"Oh my God, yes. I can't believe Chester never had anyone in to work with us. I'm surprised we didn't hurt ourselves more than we did."

"I'm not sure which suffered more, my vocal cords or my liver."

Mandy laughs. "Isn't that the truth! I have someone I work with. I can get in contact with him in the morning. Do you have any idea what your schedule is going to be like?"

"Um, I know there's a lot of rehearsals, like every day, but I don't really know the times yet." I pause for a moment before saying, "Though Jenny Lind is a much smaller role, so maybe I won't have to be there as much."

My words hang in the air for a minute before Mandy responds. "Are you okay with that?"

Suddenly, I'm not. I'm pissed off. They drag me all the way out here and then do a bait and switch on me? I bet this was Henderson. He's probably been regretting casting me ever since I texted him, but didn't know how to get out of it.

Okay, well I know it was Grayson's idea, but did Henderson subliminally plant the seed to make them demote me? Could he even be that devious?

Even though the conversation I heard definitely sounded like it was Grayson's idea. Still, I bet Henderson somehow manipulated the situation.

"You know, it's kind of insulting, actually. Who do they think they are?"

"I mean, Tabby, I'm sure they think this is for the best. You were sort of made for that part."

Even though I usually trust Mandy to be a sane, sage source of advice and guidance, this time, I don't buy what she's saying. "You know, I'm gonna go back up there and give him a piece of my mind, once and for all. Who does he think he is?"

I run upstairs and check that Paisley is sleeping soundly in her temporary room. Maria's in the next room, monitor on. I motion to her that I'm going out, still while ranting to Mandy.

"You know, this is why I never look for more than a quick fling with someone. You can't put expectations on people. It makes you hope, and hope makes you hurt."

"I thought you two just had a quick fling."

"Yeah, because I live in California and he lives in New York. But now I'm *here*, because of him."

"Oh Tabby, you didn't come just for him, did you?"

Her words halt my feet in their tracks mid-step. "No, of course not. I need to do something with my life. Let's face it, it's not like anyone out on the West Coast is banging on my door. I figured this would be a good way to get my feet wet again. Plus, Henderson would be here. And now I look like a fool. Nobody makes me look like a fool." I run down the stairs and to the front door. "I'm going to go and give Henderson a piece of my—"

As I pull open the heavy oak door, I catch Henderson, fist raised in preparation to knock.

"Tabby, are you okay?"

"Mandy, gotta run." I disconnect and drop the phone down from my ear. "Yes?"

I don't move. He doesn't move.

This is going to get old real fast.

"What do you want?" It's almost as if I've forgotten that I was on my way to see him. "Why are you here?"

His gaze drops, and I follow it down. Nothing remarkable about his Adidas sneakers. His feet shuffle slightly as he shifts weight from side to side. "I, um, wanted to make sure you were settled."

I fold my arms over my chest. "I am, no thanks to you."

He looks up at the door and then from one side of the porch to another. "Did you get this through Andrews Realty?"

"Yeah."

"The people I put you in contact with? Right. I'm glad I was of no help." I'm gifted a trademark eye roll.

Dammit.

"I mean, it's not like you met me at the airport or got me settled in."

"We had two shows today. I couldn't leave. I believe Grayson suggested you come in during the week? I asked him to ask you."

"Why didn't you just ask me?"

He shrugs, but at least he's now looking at my eyes.

"Would you have come to pick us up?"

He doesn't have to say anything, because his suddenly dropped gaze tells me it all.

"I see. Well, Henderson, I can be a professional if you can. But you owe me one thing."

His jaw clenches as he meets my gaze. "What's that?"

"An explanation for why you want me to change parts. Why you demoted me."

He shrugs. He's going to sprain his shoulders shrugging that much. "It makes sense. Really, it does. When I suggested you play Charity … I wasn't thinking clearly. Because of that night … I was letting my personal life cloud my judgment. Otherwise, I'd've seen this option sooner. And truly, it'll be for the best. We've got a lot riding on this show. It's totally sold out, even with the additional performance added in."

They're using me for my name. They don't care about me. I can't stop the thoughts from flooding my mind.

"Yes, I'm aware of what I'm bringing to the table."

"No, I don't think you are." He puts his hands on my arms, trying to make me focus on what he's saying. Except all I want to focus on is the fact that he's touching me.

It's been a long three months.

"We're doing this show as a workshop. It's a special thing, and if the powers that be like it, it'll hopefully be on track to go to Broadway. So it needs to be perfect. And now that Grayson's brought it up, I see that you're not perfect for Charity. No matter how much I want you to sing 'A Million Dreams.' I was stupid for letting my personal feelings get in the way. I could have ruined everything for The Edison."

"Instead you'd rather ruin everything between us?"

His hands drop from my arms. I feel cold where his touch had been. "There is no 'us,' Tabitha. There can't be. I thought you understood that. I almost mucked things up enough. It's why we shouldn't be involved. I'm sorry, but I can't let the theatre down."

I feel as if he's punched me in the gut.

It's not the first time someone's wanted me for my talent or name recognition. It won't be the last. You think I'd stop being surprised by it.

"Of course not. You can't let people down." *Except me.*

"I have a job to do here."

"Apparently. And so do I. I've had a long day so if you don't mind, I want to go to bed." I turn to go back inside when I feel his fingers on my arm again. I glance back over my shoulder to look at where he's touching me, then shift my gaze to his face. "Yes?"

My arm feels like it's on fire with the spark of a thousand volts of electricity. Does he feel it too?

He must, because he's staring at his own hand on my arm. Neither of us move. Then finally, he drops his hand without saying a word. Henderson shoves his fists in his jeans pockets and turns toward the stairs.

I walk in the house and shut the door without looking back.

It's a skill I've perfected.

I lift my phone, prepared to call Mandy back, but then I remember the time. I wander around the downstairs, turning off one light and then another until the unfamiliar surroundings are dark. Lighting my path with my cellphone, I carefully walk to the stairs. A soft glow comes from under Maria's door.

I knock gently before opening. "Maria? Do you have a minute?"

She's propped up in bed, reading on her Kindle. She lowers her glasses and smiles. "Everything okay?"

"I got demoted. They switched my part to a smaller one. I think they think I can't do the role, but they still want my name."

"Can you do the role?"

Maria is wise. She knows so much about babies and kids. I've never asked her about my personal life because, well, she's here for Paisley. But I need to talk to someone.

That need is crushing and overwhelming. I take a deep breath and open up. "I think I can. The new role will be a slam dunk. Less dancing."

"Well, that's a relief."

My difficulty in picking up steps is legendary.

"But they're using me for my name."

"Yeah, and? Aren't you using them?"

I put my hands on my hips. "How could I be using them?"

Maria lifts her brow. "Did you audition? Did you have to work to get the part like everyone else did?"

"Well, no. I mean that reporter wrote that article, and I thought it would be nice if I did it."

She folds her arms over her chest. "Why?"

I match her gesture. "I don't know."

"You do know."

The air is thick as she waits for my admission. Finally I say the words that we both know are true. "I want to get back into the spotlight, but I need to do it away from Jonathan Spencer Maxwell. But really, I just want people to clap for me again."

"You're using them for the applause. For the validation."

I only lift my shoulders in response. What else is there to say?

"Maybe don't look at it like they're using you or you're using them. Consider that you each have needs the other can meet."

Her words make sense, but sit uncomfortably in my chest. I don't deal in symbiotic relationships. I'm used to more parasitic ones.

"So, like, I've been thinking," I say, quickly changing the subject. "I'm thinking we could have a cocktail party or something here one night. This house is so cool. I'd love to make it a Roaring 20s theme. You know, to give something to the cast and all. What do you think?"

"I think you have a four-year-old who has no other place to go in the evenings, and a busy schedule. Maybe after the show is done?"

Maria's no fun. She's also not wrong. I may not listen to her, but she's probably right.

"Fine. But don't you think people are going to want to hang out with me?"

She smiles. "I think you're missing hanging out with people. Don't force it. Let people like you for you, not for what you give them."

I don't need a therapist—not that I've been going to one anyway—when I have Maria. I start to walk out of her room, thinking about her wise advice when something occurs to me. I turn back. "Thanks for the help, Maria."

As I lie in bed, I keep mulling over what Maria said. People should like me for me. People can meet each others' needs and not just be using each other. *People should like me for me.*

You know what? She's right. And if Henderson doesn't want me for me, I'll find someone who does.

Chapter 26: Henderson

Day one of rehearsal for *The Greatest Showman* is off to an auspicious beginning.

It's pouring, which is never fun. The dorms are just far enough away from the theatre to ensure we get soaked while dashing over, yet too close to warrant driving. There's no heat on, and the cool sixty-degree temperature makes for a chill on soaking wet clothes.

It's not like I need any help with my grumpy mood.

But then Tabitha walks in, her smile beaming with the wattage of the sun. Instantaneously, my mood lifts.

Dammit, no. It cannot lift. She cannot brighten my day just by being.

That whole notion is foolish.

I make myself stay in place, midstage, when she comes in. I'm fighting every urge I have to approach her. No, focus. Grayson's late, as usual, so I turn my attention toward that.

"Anyone seen Grayson? It's hard to start working on music if he's not here. Screw him. Let's jump right in with 'This is Me.' Josh, you got this? Where's Azalea? You ready?"

Azalea, who will crush this song, springs to her feet. She's one casting decision with which I have no doubts.

I start to read through the cast that will be in this number but skirt around. "Okay, Marcelina, Jasmine, Levi, and Tabitha, you're not in this. Jasmine and Levi, why don't you start working on your aerial stuff?" Jasmine is a skilled aerialist and teacher. I trust her inherently to choreograph their number.

My mind begins to whirl, thinking about the choreography and staging. It's going to be a circus in here—quite literally—and we still only have the two weeks we normally would.

What were we thinking?

But there's no time to analyze or lament. We have thirty hours of work to fit into a twenty-four hour day.

In the blink of an eye, it's time to shift gears to rehearsing for *Kiss Me, Kate*, which opens on Friday. "All right, that's a wrap for today. If you aren't in *Kate*, and want to continue working on your own, have at it. Josh will be tied up with us, but maybe can float over for questions. Otherwise see you at eight."

This week is a beast. Normally, the complexity makes the days go by with a rush of adrenaline. This time it's different. I can't make up my mind about how things should go. I can't figure out transitions, which are normally my specialty. During The Edison's off-season, I've often worked as a play doctor, going in and figuring those out for others.

Now I'm the one that needs the help.

"No, no, NO!" I yell as the cast fades out singing. "It's not right."

Grayson elbows me. "It's fine."

"It's not fine. It's not working and I—"

"H, man, take a break. You have this vein that looks like it's going to rupture. We can't afford for you to have a stroke."

I look at him as if he's got three heads. "Grayson, I—"

"Unless the next words out of your mouth are 'need to take a break,' I don't want to hear them. The scene is fine. You are not. Now go." He points toward the door.

Begrudgingly, I head out. The rain has finally let up, leaving the air heavy with moisture. It's not quite night yet, the sunset normally occurring around eight these days. On the other hand, it's not light either. I just start walking.

As a child and teenager, walking was my solace. It was the only way I could escape my house and the chaos my mum brought to it. After, when I'd moved to the U.S. with my dad, it was how I dealt with missing home and the crushing loneliness I felt. Putting the earth underneath my feet and taking in the scenery grounded me.

Sure, sometimes it took walking for an hour—or two ... or three—before I felt better, but it usually helped. Though I choose to be on my own now, I generally don't feel the loneliness that plagued me as a child. Back then, all I wanted was connection.

Now that I have the choice, I choose to be self-sufficient and self-reliant. At least I know I won't let myself down.

Yet right now, those old feelings of want and desire rise up, filling my chest with a tightness I don't want. I keep walking. I walk until it's pitch black and I'm too knackered to keep going. I manage to slide into my dorm room without anyone noticing me, and slip off to a quick sleep.

But in the morning, that tightness and unease is still there. It's got to be the stress of this show. I thought last season was bad, but it's in our hands if this show makes it to Broadway. If it does, there's a good chance that some of our cast may have an advantage with getting parts. And maybe, just maybe, it'll solidify business for The Edison so Grayson and I won't have to stress over each and every ticket sale.

Some security'd be nice.

And if The Edison were more successful, we could do it year round. I could give up my dump of an overpriced apartment and live here permanently.

I wish I felt confident enough in The Edison to do that. I wish she were that successful.

Maybe if I had that assurance of success here, I wouldn't feel empty.

As I think it, I realize that's what's wrong. That's the feeling inside my chest. Emptiness.

Which is daft because I have a full life. I have the theatre, which keeps me busier than possible during the season. I have some friends. I ...

I have an empty life.

Better to be empty than to try and pour endlessly and futilely into a broken vessel. That's what Mum did. One man after another. Men she met through work. Bad men. Terrible people who used her up and spat her out. Men who hit her. Men who demeaned her. Men who made her think she was so useless until she was.

I'd rather be alone than give someone that power over me.

I will fill my life with work. Lord knows there's enough to keep me busy.

"Good morning everyone. Let's start with choreo today. We'll do 'This is Me.' Jasmine and Levi, you keep working on your stuff. Josh will be available to go over the song in a little while with you if you want. Marcelina, go with Grayson and Josh to work on 'A Million Dreams.' The kids will be here at nine to rehearse. Okay everyone, we've lots to do and little time."

I pour over my notes, writing down ideas for staging. I used to be able to do it all in my head, but now my mind is a swirling vortex.

"What are you doing?" Grayson nudges me.

"You're supposed to be working. Leave me alone."

"No, man, what are you doing? Tabitha's the only one not doing anything. Again," he whispers. "This is her second day and you've yet to run anything with her in it."

I shrug. "She's not in much of the show. I can't help it. You're the one who switched her. Her number isn't until the finale of act one. We're not there yet." I glance over, but she's absorbed in her phone. Something catches my attention up on the stage and my focus shifts. An hour later, I look out into the audience, but Tabitha's seat is empty.

Great. She's probably flaked off.

I don't blame her. I'd flake out on me too.

I'll talk to her about it later. I've too much to do. This show is too big. I'm not sure how we're going to pull it together. We only have one more hour of this rehearsal before we have to switch to *Kiss Me, Kate*. Three more days of double rehearsals and then I can re-focus on this show.

Who am I kidding? Knowing that I can see her anytime, I'll never be able to focus with Tabitha around. Every time I close my eyes, I see her naked beneath me. I hear her voice in my head. Her laughter wakes me from dreams during those precious few times that I can sleep.

That laughter is what permeates my ears now. I snap to attention like a dog that's heard an intruder.

What's she laughing at? Who is making her laugh? Why isn't it me?

I walk—okay, I run—out to the lobby to see Tabitha in a crowd of people, none of whom I recognize. There's a rugged-looking man, wearing faded jeans and cowboy boots next to a non-descript brunette wearing an oversized floral shirt. A girl—maybe a teenager—is engrossed in her phone. She looks like the non-descript brunette. Additionally, there's a bald bloke in skinny jeans.

My groin chafes just thinking about those tight pants.

Who are these people and why are they here? Is this one of the kids for the show? Why isn't she in rehearsal with Josh?

"Can I help you with something?" I don't know why I lead with this. Idiot.

When Tabitha looks over to me, the grin quickly falls from her face.

Dammit. I want to be the one to put the smile there, not take it away.

Wait—no. I can't be thinking like that. It's good that she doesn't want me around. It's how it needs to be. "We're ready for you. It's time to run through your song." I hadn't actually planned on this, but I need her to come with me instead of being out here with others.

What the hell am I doing?

"Josh is waiting for you in the music room. You can warm up there."

"I don't need to warm up. I'm good."

"You have to warm up. You'll strain your voice," I admonish her, as if she's never sung before.

"Henderson, I've got this." Her tone is cool and clipped. "C'mon." She motions to the people with her. "Ben, would you?"

It's only then I notice Mr. Cowboy is holding a guitar.

Tabitha and her entourage march past me and down through the theatre. She doesn't stop until she's midstage. The cowboy sits down at the piano in the pit. The bloke in the tight pants says, "Remember to bounce the sound. Play with the cry."

Who is this dipstick?

Before I can figure it out, the cowboy is playing the opening notes, and Tabitha starts singing. She's in the middle of the stage, commanding all attention with her soulful voice. Silence descends over the theatre, with the exception of the piano and her voice. As she approaches the chorus and her first belt, I realize I'm holding my breath. As much as I try, I cannot get my lungs to work. The only thing my body can do is devote everything to absorbing what Tabitha is giving.

I cannot look away.

As her voice, purposefully breathless, trails out on the last two words, I gasp for oxygen. The spell breaks as applause erupts from various locations in the theatre. A hand claps my shoulder.

"Dammit, Henderson. We cast this wrong. You should be playing P.T. Barnum. You've nailed the smitten look perfectly."

I want to growl, to turn away, to ... something, but I can't. She has me transfixed.

Grayson continues. "This is so cool. I can't believe Mandy Calhoun and Ben Reynolds are here. Word on the street is they are collaborating on an album."

The names finally permeate my brain with some recognition. Mandy was a Sassy Cat—the lead one, if there was one. Her vocals are phenomenal. Ben Reynolds started off with the group as one of their musicians but has gone on to have a Grammy-winning career as a songwriter. We are in the presence of greatness, all because of Tabitha.

"Who's the guy in the excessively tight pants?"

"That's Daniel Vasquez. Vocal coach. He's worked with everyone who's anyone. Tabby brought him in to work with her. I guess she's pretty serious about being here."

I look at the cast, now surrounding Tabitha and her guests. They all look like starstruck fans backstage at a concert. I want to join in, to be part of the crowd, but instead I stay back.

I watch Tabitha, though I try not to. If I thought she lit up when doing karaoke, that was a dim bulb compared to how brightly she's shining now. I don't know what she's been doing with her life, but she was made to be in the spotlight.

Now I need to figure out how to get her there.

Chapter 27: Tabitha

This.

This is what I've been missing.

Performing. The stage. The applause. The love.

Centerstage, belting out the notes. In this moment, I am reborn.

I steal a glance at Henderson, but he's busy looking at his notes. Did he even listen to me sing? Does he even notice me?

Okay, maybe I'm the same old me.

Why does it matter? He's just someone I slept with once. Nothing more.

But I want more.

And he doesn't want me.

Why doesn't he want me?

I blink back the tears that have suddenly filled my eyes. Damn him. How dare he take this moment away from me.

My voice was shaky in some parts and a little pitchy in others. But for my first time, it wasn't half bad. Who knew under the cheese of the Sassy Cats' songs that I had actual vocal talent?

I'm a long way from "Meow and You."

I try to focus on the notes that Daniel and Ben have helped me craft and hone over the past few hours. Mandy worked her magic, getting Daniel to help me work on vocals. Ben was an added bonus, as he flew in last night to see Mandy.

Oh, sure, it's under the guise of working on their album, but the look in his eye says he has anything but work on his mind. He's totally head-over-heels in love with her.

I have no idea how that must feel, but I want it.

Tenley's along for the ride, which is great. The plan is for her to play with Paisley for a bit. I pulled Paisley out of preschool a few weeks early to come out here, so at least she'll sort of have some kid interaction. As soon as I'm done here, we're going to the playground.

Mandy pulls me into a hug. "Oh, Tabby, that was beautiful." As she releases me, I notice her eyes are sparkling with tears as well. "Why couldn't we have sung beautiful, meaningful songs like this when we were together?"

It was like she read my mind. The Sassy Cats were a novelty act. No one took us seriously, including the writers. Though I was impressed with the number of cat-related puns they were able to come up with. On the other hand, it limited the amount of music we could do.

There are only so many feline-related jokes one can tell.

The cast is crowding around us, offering praise and hoping to rub elbows with my guests. The one person I wanted to rub anything with remains on the other side of the theater.

What a jerk.

I need to move on. To stay grounded.

I take a long drink of water from the bottle Daniel hands me. I've no idea where Mandy found him, but his coaching was exactly what I needed. "Don't live in your head. You're switching to your head voice. It can work, but I don't want you to live there. Bounce the sound and play with that before you commit to your head voice. Call me if you need me." He gives me a hug and kisses both cheeks. "Ciou, darling."

"Who was that and why are his pants so tight?" Henderson's voice growls behind me.

I hadn't noticed him cross the room.

"That was my vocal coach, Daniel. And I wasn't paying attention to his pants. Why were you?" It's of course a lie. His pants are obscenely tight. I don't know how he sits down in them. Maybe I should try a pair to see if it helps me get up to those higher notes easier. "I think I'm done here for the day, right? I'm going to play with my daughter. Why don't you text me when you need me again?"

With that, I grab my bag and walk out. Mandy links her arm in mine, and I feel as if I can take on the world. It's not until I get outside that I realize we're missing Ben and Tenley.

I cannot walk back in there. No way, no how.

"Ben's got her, right?" I keep walking, though Mandy's frozen in her spot.

"No, Ben barely knows Tenley."

"Really? It's been like four years."

"We're not dating!" Mandy wails. "Why doesn't anyone believe me? My divorce only went through last week."

"Holy shit. What took so long?" I can't believe Mandy's had to be tied to that douchewaffle all this time. He left her right before our reunion concert.

She folds her arms over her chest. "Money. Of course, money. He wanted half of everything I've ever made, plus half the royalties from 'Please Say Yes,' not to mention alimony and child support."

"Child support? The kids live with you!"

"You see why it took so long."

"Plus, he didn't earn that money. How did you even explain it to him in the first place?"

Mandy shrugs, keeping an eye on the theater door for her daughter to come out. "It was in a trust, so he actually couldn't get any of it. The kids are the beneficiaries, which explains the custody thing. He thought if he was their guardian, he could have it."

"Yeah, but didn't he ever ask where it came from?"

"I told him I came into it. He thought I meant from like my grandparents, and I didn't correct him. I had my accountant do the taxes and everything, so he never really looked. Honestly, he had no idea. I mean, not until Angie announced it during that performance."

"I still can't believe he never knew you were famous."

She laughs. "Yeah, well, have you noticed that people don't recognize us like they once did? Or that if we're not wearing stupid ears and tails, they don't see us?"

"I've been using that to my advantage since right after the reunion."

Mandy cocks her head. "Yeah, but is that really you, Tabby?"

"You did it. You totally disappeared from fame. If it weren't for Callie, you'd still be flying under the radar."

"But that was me. And you're not me. And, if I'm honest, I wasn't truly happy like that either."

"Are you happy now?" I look my friend up and down. She looks happy. Her weight is healthy. Her hair has shiny highlights. Her clothes are neat. Her cheeks have a glow to them.

I attribute the glow to Ben, who has just walked out with Tenley.

Whether Mandy wants to admit it or not, she and Ben are head over heels for each other. I mean, who waits like this?

I can't even get Henderson to look my way.

No, I will not give him any more room in my brain.

It's so much easier when I know I'm just using people for sex. At least I have no expectations.

I was stupid to have expectations.

But at least I'm back to performing.

God, I'm going to perform again. My name will be in lights.

Okay, not really, because The Edison doesn't have a marquee or anything, and I'm not even the star. I'd be like eighth or ninth billing.

Maybe I should buy them a marquee.

Maybe it's time to get active on social media again.

Should I call my publicist? Sure, I'd let Rachel go years ago, but she could always come back. Maybe Gayle knows someone better. An assistant at least to handle postings and whatnot. And then ...

I derail my own train of thought.

Nothing's changed.

I can't be out there, because of Paisley.

Well, Paisley's sperm donor.

"This sucks," I say out loud, as if everyone has been in my head and knows what I'm thinking about.

"You were a little pitchy in places, but you didn't totally suck. You have time to get better," Tenley offers.

Balls of steel on that one.

I stop walking and roll my eyes. "Thanks. Everyone's a critic, aren't they?"

"Just trying to help."

"Tenley, don't be rude. I'm sure Tabby was talking about something else. Her singing was beautiful."

"I was just thinking that this show is what I need to relaunch my career, but the reason my career stalled in the first place hasn't changed."

Mandy nods in understanding. "Tabby, you know what you have to do. You need to tell the people in your life what you want from them and what you need. That goes for your career *and* your love life."

Like when I told Henderson three days ago that I wanted to be with him?

There is no us.

Screw him and Jonathan Spencer Maxwell and every other man who broke my trust. I don't need any of them.

And maybe, just maybe, if I keep telling myself that, someday I'll actually believe it.

Chapter 28: Henderson

If I walk any farther, I'll be in Massachusetts. I'm skipping out on the *Kate* run-through, even though I should be there. Gray can handle it. I need to walk.

I need to think.

I need to get Tabitha out of my mind.

I'm like my own worst self-fulfilling prophecy. I got involved with someone at work, and it's mucking things up. Like right now. I'm leaving the theatre in a lurch because I need to clear my head.

I turn down a road that leads to an old cemetery. God, I love it up here. The lane is uneven, tires leaving large dips and ruts in the dirt. The entire place is a series of rolling hills. From a distance, it looks picturesque, but up close, it's a mess. Tombstones lie toppled over, tops split from their bases. Some gravestones are angled forward or back. Yet others stand as straight and erect as the day they were installed.

It's the perfect metaphor for life. Some of us handle the changes in terrain. Some of us topple.

Mum toppled.

And I've been so afraid of toppling too that I forgot to try to stand on my own. I lay right down, figuring if I was already there, it wouldn't hurt to fall.

But what if ... what if I tried standing up straight?

Is Tabitha worth standing for?

I don't know, but perhaps it's time I find out.

I begin the walk across Hicklam. Toward Tabitha. Toward maybe something more.

And more is what I find when I finally reach the house Tabitha is renting on the edge of town. Cars and people everywhere. Not just people. The entire bloody cast and crew from The Edison.

I stop Josh, who's walking by with a plate full of food and a beverage. "What's going on here?"

"Tabitha invited us over for a bite to eat. With Mandy Calhoun and Ben Reynolds here, we'd be stupid not to take her up on it. When else am I going to get a chance to hang out with a Grammy-winning musician? I mean, until I am one myself. I'm working up the courage to pitch them the idea for the show I've been writing. Maybe they'll listen to a song."

He seems almost giddy. Josh is never giddy.

"But why aren't you in rehearsal?" My question falls on deaf ears, as Josh has already moved on to delivering the drink to the aforementioned Ben Reynolds. I make my way through the crowd, no one paying much mind to me. Finally, I find Grayson sitting in one of the Adirondack chairs sprinkled about the lawn.

"Gray, mate, what's going on? Why aren't you all in rehearsal?"

"We ran through it once, and it was good to go. We've got two more days. With the amount of work coming up getting *Showman* ready, I figured everyone could use a minute to relax and breathe."

"We'll breathe after Labor Day."

"Henderson, we've got something special here. You know it as well as I do. The next few weeks are going to be insane. Think of this—these few hours—as the calm before the storm. We're going to have eighteen-hour days. You know we'll be running on fumes soon. Let's fill up the tanks first. I only called rehearsal about an hour early anyway. We were in final costume and wig fittings tonight. Erica and Gloria assured me they could get it done, even with this. Plus, it's super nice of Tabitha to do this. I don't know how she pulled it together so quickly."

The spread is certainly more lavish than anything Hicklam is used to seeing. Charcuterie boards and tapas line the table. There's another table with oysters and shrimp. A raw bar?

Once again, I'm reminded how out of my league I really am here.

"Henderson, you're here! This is amazing," Jasmine says, whirling around, her ebony curls bouncing with her movement. "Get yourself a drink."

It sounds like good advice. I find a large tub of coldies over ice and grab a bottle. Looking at the label, I see they're microbrews from an Upstate brewery. Naturally. Nothing bottom shelf here.

As I wander around sipping my beer, I notice how relaxed everyone looks. Happy. These are some of the hardest working people I know. They're my friends. I want them to be happy.

I want to be happy.

With purpose, I set off to find Tabitha. Weaving in and out of the crowd, I don't see her outside. I check one room and then another, before I find her in the kitchen, along with two chefs clad in long white aprons. Her bright smile falls when she sees me standing in the doorway.

"You're here," she says flatly.

"Was I not invited?"

She shrugs. "I've got to tend to my guests." With that, she starts to walk out of the room.

"Tabitha, wait." I reach forward, gently grasping her arm. "I ... can we talk?"

"Oh, are you talking to me now? I thought you were still ignoring me. Or wait, is now when you tell me you don't want to be with me? Or are you going to ghost me again? Or we could go right back to the beginning when you were just sullen and surly. I mean, it's always the same upshot—you don't want me. I get it. Message received." She tries to pull away.

I hold on. "No, don't. I don't want to topple over. I want to stay upright."

She blinks, looking at me blankly.

Right. She wasn't with me in the cemetery for my big epiphany. "I ... I don't want to be with you."

"As you've indicated," she says dryly.

I put my finger on her lips. "I'm bad at this. I need to explain." I look around and notice that there are people milling about everywhere. "Can we go for a walk?" My finger lingers a moment longer on her lips. She nods gently.

"Let me go check on Paisley and see if Maria can keep an eye on her. And I've got to make sure Mandy and Ben are set. I don't know if they're staying here or getting on the road."

Now it's my turn to nod.

People are talking to me, but I don't hear what they're saying. Instead, my mind is abuzz with what I'm going to say to Tabitha.

I haven't the foggiest.

This goes against everything I stand for. Everything I believe in. Because, let's face it, I don't believe in love. I don't believe that it heals all or can move mountains or anything like that. From what I've seen, it tears you down and destroys everything you've built up.

I don't want that.

Yet I want Tabitha.

Christ, I'm a mess.

Jasmine bumps me as she twirls into the kitchen. I swear, she's always moving. "Sorry Henny, gotta get me some more oysters. God, I *love* them. They're an aphrodisiac, you know. Levi'd better watch out."

Then everyone laughs, myself included, because Levi has no more interest in Jasmine than I do in Grayson. Now, if Zak had made that same statement, I'm sure Levi would be all over that. And him.

I wander out into the backyard. It's quiet out here, dark finally settling in on this June night. There's a chill to the air. Nights don't stay hot yet. They won't up here for another month or so. Even after living in the states for over twenty years now, it still seems odd that I'm waiting for it to get warmer in June. As a child, June was a month of new snow and cold.

Funny, if you'd've asked me when I left Australia if I'd ever feel at home anywhere else, I'd have sworn you were bongo. But here in Hicklam, I do feel at home. Linda and Grayson have been much more of a family to me than my own flesh and blood ever were. If we could make the theatre a year-round thing, I could see myself in a little house on Chapel Street, coming home to Tabitha and Paisley, the perfect family—

Whoa.

Where did that come from?

I'm not some starry-eyed sheila, dreaming about houses and picket fences.

Except I just was.

Like my mum always was. She always thought the next bloke would be the one to take her—us—away from the poverty and squalor. Except every bloke was like the last.

At least I can say Tabitha is nothing like the women I usually date. Mostly because I don't date.

And let's face it, Tabitha is like no one I've ever met. Not to mention, she comes as a package deal, giving me the family I've never had.

Still, I'm not ready to be talking about a commitment and a house and the whole gamut.

Christ, I'm more confused than ever.

That is until I see her coming out of the bright house into the dark summer night, illuminated like an angel. Her hair hangs down over one shoulder in a careless braid. Short jean cut-offs, oversized sweater. She's effortless in her style that was most likely crafted with extreme effort. Even at her most casual, her star shines through.

Yet, that's not why I'm drawn to her.

It's the real her that is most appealing. The Tabitha who is worried about being a mother and a good human being. The vulnerable Tabitha.

I extend my hand, hoping she'll take it. I see her pause and consider before slipping her hand into mine. When I touch her, the empty feeling that inhabited most of my chest since I was a small child starts to dissipate.

One person shouldn't have this effect on me.

Yet, here I am. Beginning to sweat like a stuffed pig, despite the temperate night air.

"Mandy and Ben are taking off, and Paisley is with Maria. Where are we going?"

I lift my shoulder and let it drop, but Tabitha can't see the gesture in the dark. "I like to walk when I have a lot on my mind. I started doing it as a kid."

She's silent for a minute before saying, "I'm confused, Henderson. I don't know what I'm doing here."

"That makes two of us. I ... I shouldn't have asked you out here with me, but I couldn't take it anymore."

"Take what?" She stops and I feel her turn toward me. I face her as well.

"Take being near you but not being with you."

She stares at me, not saying anything. It's too dark for me to read her expression, but her hand dropping from mine tells me all I need to know.

"Look, Henderson, I don't play games, and I don't like people who do. If we were having a casual, non-committal type fling, that's one thing. And I know that's how it started off, but ... I don't know. It seemed like it grew into something more. I know I wanted something more. You obviously didn't. Don't. Which is fine. But I can't do this back and forth. I can't be your little side piece when you're in the mood and nothing to you when you're not. I've done all that before, and I'm too old for that crap. I—"

I silence her by kissing her. It's obvious I'm not good at telling her what I'm thinking, so perhaps if I show her, she'll understand. I take her mouth in mine. At first, her lips seem eager to join mine. But then suddenly, she stops moving with me. I pull back.

"Tabitha, I—"

"Henderson, I just told you I don't want a casual fling, and you respond by kissing me."

"I ... I..." I falter, looking for the words. "I don't date."

She sighs. "Yes, I know. You don't mix business and pleasure. Actresses are too much trouble. Too much drama. Blah, blah, blah."

"No, it's not just that I don't date people I work with, it's that in all honesty, I don't date. I don't do relationships at all. I've seen how they destroy people, and I never wanted to go through that."

My admission hangs in the night air.

"So you're telling me you've never dated? Been in a relationship? Been in love? Was I your first?" She makes it sound as if I've just admitted to eating babies or something equally as sordid.

"No. I've had sex, obviously. I am human. But no, I've never done the dinner and flowers and romantic walks. Honestly, I'm not sure I've even held hands with anyone besides you."

"Why?"

"Why or why not?" It's time to be honest with her. She needs to know the mess before she signs on. I tell her about Mum. "And Dad wasn't much better. I mean, they had a stupid fling when they were high school students and Dad came to Australia on exchange. He left before he knew about me. He came back a few years later, and they vacillated between hooking up and hating each other. When he realized that Mum was beyond saving, he came back to the U.S. with me in tow. He could at least hold down a job and keep a roof over our head, which is more than Mum could do. He'd have women around for a while, but nothing ever worked out for him. He wasn't really interested in me, that's for sure. I was more like a roommate, even though I was only twelve. He didn't care if I came or went, as long as my chores got done and my grades were solid. I thought if I did that, he'd like me more."

I kick the gravel at my feet. I haven't ever opened up to anyone about the pain of my childhood. And while I like to blame Mum for how messed up I am, it's not like Dad won any prizes for loving—or even wanting—me. "He certainly didn't come to my plays or school events. He was too busy looking for something. I'm not sure what it was exactly, but he never found it. And all that trying made him bitter and hard. Well, more bitter. He was never a jolly sort to begin with. I guess getting stuck with a totally unplanned kid will do that."

As soon as the words leave my mouth, I want to stick my foot in.

Well, this certainly isn't the way to win over the girl.

Chapter 29: Tabitha

I'm used to smooth talkers trying to get in my pants.

Henderson is not this.

In fact, he's the opposite. Maybe that means he's being genuine, or maybe he's that good at playing the game.

I hate players.

But, and maybe this makes me stupid, I don't think Henderson is playing me. I can see the anguish on his face. Well, not really, because it's pretty dark out here, but his voice sounds sincere.

At least I want it to be sincere.

Yet, on the other hand, he just told me that he's carrying massive baggage because his mom was a single mother who was a hot mess express, and his dad got stuck with a kid he didn't want and it ruined his life. That one hits a little too close to home.

"Do you really think *I'm* the person you should be with then? You've already said you don't want to want me, but yet you do. I mean, it doesn't take a shrink to see all the mommy issues here."

"No, it's not like that. I want to be with you *in spite of* the mummy issues."

Part of me wants to make a joke about mummies and vampires, but something tells me it wouldn't be well received. At least not right now.

"Tabitha, please." The vulnerability in his voice makes my heart flutter and my stomach clench. Isn't this what I've wanted to hear from him? Especially over the last few days when he practically pretended I didn't exist.

Forget few days; try few months.

"Henderson, you've done nothing but jerk me around since I left you that morning. It's like you're holding it against me. Like I had a choice, and I chose Paisley over you. I mean, you know there is no choice, right? I'll always choose Paisley."

He hangs his head. I wish I could see his face better. I put my hand underneath his chin, tilting it upward. "It's not about you. It's not against you. It's because I'm her mom and I have to choose her."

Even if I don't want to.

The thought that races through my head startles me. Why would I think that? God, his issues are rubbing off on me.

Fantastic.

Like I need help being any more messed up than I already am.

"I know you have to. I wouldn't respect you if you didn't."

He wouldn't respect me if he knew the real me.

"But Tabitha, I can't get you out of my mind. I'm transfixed by you. I can't stop thinking about you, no matter what I do. No matter how far I walk or how hard I try not to, all I do is hear you in my head. It's like you've imprinted on me, and I can't erase you. I don't even want to. I just want you. All of you."

This.

This is what I've been waiting my whole life to hear. Someone who wants me for me and that's it.

This time, it's my turn to bring my mouth to his. I find it easily, and his eagerness matches my own. Our bodies press together, hungry for each other. Starved from being apart so long. A longing I didn't know I was capable of possessing rises up. If he doesn't take me right here, right now, I may die.

That tingling and zipping sensation spreads everywhere, including to my legs. Except what I'm feeling *there* isn't exactly what's going on with my lower limbs.

"Ouch." *Ouch ouch ouch*. What in the hell? I slap at the stinging just below my knee. And on my ankle. And my other foot. And my thigh. I slap at my leg. Henderson's doing the same.

"Bloody mozzies. We must be near some water. This is almost as bad as in Australia. Nasty bloodsuckers." Henderson's waving his arms, trying to dissipate the swarm that's descending upon us. "Let's go." He takes my hand and pulls me along, walking fast at first before breaking into a jog. While I enjoy a good run as much as the next person, my Tory Burch sandals are not up for the task.

"Can we slow down? I'm not sure we can outrun a cloud of vicious mosquitoes anyway."

He slows his pace, not letting go of me.

"Let's head back to my place," I suggest.

"There's lots of people at your place."

"There's lots of rooms there too. The house is like over five-thousand square feet for just Maria, Paisley, and me. Then, there's a carriage house. I'm sure we can find a nook in which to hide away."

He laughs. "I guess considering my room is a single dormer with a twin bed, you win."

But as we approach the long driveway leading up to my rental house, we're greeted by flashing red lights breaking up the dark summer night.

My first thought is Paisley. Shoes be damned, I break out in a run to close the distance between the ambulance and me. I reach the back of the vehicle to see Jasmine sitting there, holding her hand amidst a pile of bloody bandages. My knees go weak with relief that it's not my daughter, but I know I won't be satisfied until I see her with my own eyes.

I continue running into the house and up the stairs until I reach her door. Quietly, I open it, the creak barely audible. I scan the room to find Paisley sitting straight up in bed, staring at me.

My heart seizes, as it sort of reminds me of something you'd see in a horror movie. I only allow myself a moment before I move across the room to her, taking her in my arms.

"What's wrong, baby?"

"It's so loud. It hurts my ears. I don't want it to be here."

"I think someone hurt their hand. It looks like she's going to be okay though."

Paisley's eyes are still wide. "Are they going to take me to the hospital? I don't want to go."

"No, you're not going to the hospital." I don't know why she would think such a thing.

"Are they going to take you away? I don't want you to go away and never see you again. I never get to see Daddy since the ambulance took him away. I think he's dead, but you just didn't want to tell me. I don't want you to be dead too. But if you were dead, I'd want to know."

That's a lot to digest.

"Baby, Daddy's not dead. He was hurt, like you were hurt. You're still alive."

She tilts her head to the side. "So he broke his leg too? What color cast did he get?"

"No, baby, he didn't break his leg. He broke ... his head." I don't know how else to put it. Also, it never occurred to me to tell her before now. It's not like I have too many other details myself.

"He wouldn't talk to me. His eyes were funny and there was a lot of blood."

I pull her in tight so she can't see the tears forming in my eyes. I was so worried about her body that I didn't think to ask what she'd seen or what her four-year-old brain had processed. This is what she's been dealing with while I was planning to sneak off with Henderson.

Shit. Henderson.

Well, as much as I want to run off and hide with him, I can't. Paisley needs me. "Paisley, baby, I've got to go give someone a message. I'll be right back. Will you be okay until then? Why don't you go snuggle in my bed and I'll be right in?"

She nods, looking so little. More fragile than when she was in the hospital after the accident.

I steal out of her room, looking for Henderson. He'll understand.

When I find him, sitting on a stool in the kitchen, it's obvious I'm the last thing on his mind. His head is in his hands, his shoulders slumped, and he looks dejected.

No, defeated, is a better description.

Is this because I was with my daughter? I'll be the first to admit that I don't know how to balance dating and motherhood—obviously—but get a grip, man. I wasn't even gone that long. And I just told him I'd always pick my daughter first.

"The ambulance scared Paisley. Because of the accident, you know. She never really told me what happened. But now she's afraid that I'm going to be carted away and never come back."

He doesn't say anything.

"So I need to stay with her tonight."

Henderson just nods, almost imperceptibly. I stand there for a minute, a bit stunned by his indifference. Where is the man who wants to be with me, who is willing to throw his own personal issues to the side because he can't stop thinking about me? Where is the man who just pursued me?

But when I step back, all I see is a sad little boy who just wants someone to love him. To pick him.

And I didn't choose him.

I wish I could, but Paisley is more important than a man.

I wish Henderson's mom had felt the same way.

Chapter 30: Henderson

I cannot believe this. The ambo—Jasmine—this can't be happening.

I don't need to wait for the report from the hospital to know how bad this is. All because I was off with Tabitha.

Okay, well, maybe not, but I can't help but feel the universe is sending me a message. If it were any clearer, it'd be in big, flashing neon letters that say, "You don't belong with anyone!"

Apparently Jasmine decided she needed more oysters. Very drunk people and sharp knives don't mix.

If she were in literally any other role in the show, we'd be able to work around this injury. But she's playing Anne, the trapeze artist. Jasmine's quite good, but not good enough to do all her tricks on the silks and lyra with one hand.

And it's not like there are dozens of Black aerial artists who can also act and sing floating about out there, ready to step in on a moment's notice.

Normally we don't cast based on something like race, except when it's integral to the story line. For example, you can't talk about race prejudice without casting actors of different races.

I mean, theatres do it, but they really shouldn't.

And The Edison isn't going to start now.

I pull out my phone to see if there's been any update from Grayson, who followed the ambo to the hospital. I'm not sure who was sober enough to drive him. I look around. The place has pretty much emptied out, with the exception of waitstaff—were they here the whole night?—cleaning up.

How's Jas?

I wait for Grayson to respond. I don't need to be waiting here in Tabitha's house. She already told me she has to be with her tyke.

As it should be.

I wish Mum had been a little more like that.

Mum would have let me—did let me—lie awake in my bed while she was entertaining a guest in the next room.

I stand up, prepared to slide out unnoticed; an act I'd perfected in my early years. Then I stop. I need to tell her good-bye. To say good night. To close the evening without just slipping away as I'd done before.

Tentatively, I walk upstairs. To the right is a sitting area lined with bookcases and a door. To the left is a short hallway with more doors. Prolly two bedrooms and a loo, if I had to guess. I try the door to the right, knocking softly.

"Yes?" Tabitha's voice is soft and faint.

Slowly I open the door, peeking in. Tabitha's sitting up in a large oak four-poster bed, her daughter curled in tight to her side. "It's just me. I ... I'm leaving, and I wanted to say a proper good-bye instead of sliding out like I normally do."

She smiles, squinting a little. Her voice is barely audible. "I think we're both good at sliding out, and both terrible at a proper good-bye. I'd get up but ..." She looks down at her child, nestled and still. "I think she just dozed back off."

"Right. Jas's wound is bad, and she's out of the show. So, well, things are a disaster now and ... well, I don't know what's going to happen. " I shrug uselessly. That's how I feel right now. Useless. For Tabitha. For The Edison. For it all.

"I don't either. I'm sorry I can't help. That I can't be there for you." She tilts her head toward Paisley. "I don't know how to balance this. I don't know how to do anything."

I give her a tight smile. "That makes two of us. Maybe we just ... see. Things are going to be bonkers for a bit. I'm not sure how we're even going to pull this off now but ..." I shrug again. I'm going to pull a muscle in my shoulders if I keep doing that. "It's like the universe is conspiring to keep us apart. I'm not sure if we should listen or fight."

I've never wanted to fight for a relationship before. Mostly because I've never had one worth fighting for.

It's not until I'm outside that I realize I walked here. The last thing I want to do is walk back to The Edison now. It's got to be at least five miles. My arms are covered in mozzie bites, and I'm knackered.

I wish I hadn't told Tabitha I was leaving. I could have asked to crash on the sofa. I'm sure she would have said yes. It's too late, so I trudge along the dark road until I reach The Edison. Why does it have to be located on a bloody hill?

Still, the walking's given me some time to think about what to do with the show. Wasn't there someone else who indicated some aerial skills on their application? There weren't many who checked that box, but I seem to remember that someone else did. Jasmine was a natural choice, having been with us for the past two seasons. In the winter months, she teaches aerial classes. Grayson and I never considered anyone else for the role of Annie. Nor did we consider needing an understudy.

Obviously foolish.

As I shuffle the last few steps into my dorm room, I briefly consider going over to the office to look at the applications. The odds of this working out in our favor are slimmer than a 90s fashion model.

Our imminent failure can wait a few more hours.

Chapter 31: Tabitha

I need to call him, but I don't want to.

I hate calling Jonathan Spencer Maxwell on a good day, and I don't think he has too many good days these days. It's been hard to discern what kind of shape he's in, but when I hear 'brain injury,' I tend to think the worst.

But I need to find out. For Paisley.

At the last minute, I chicken out and dial Anastasia instead. I don't mind going through her. In fact, I'd rather her know everything that's going on so she doesn't think I'm up to no good. I don't want her to think that I'm trying to carry on behind her back or anything.

Damn it. Voicemail.

"Hi, Anastasia. It's Tabitha Stetson." Duh. Like she doesn't know me. "I, um, well, I was calling to check in on Jon—" I force myself to stop and not say his full name. "Um, Paisley was asking for him. She's missing him and is still a little freaked out from the accident. So, yeah, just checking in. 'K, bye!"

I certainly live up to the reputation of the ditzy blonde. I can practically see Anastasia Jerome rolling her eyes as she listens to the message.

The thought of eye rolls makes me think about Henderson, who could win an Olympic medal for eye rolling. I wonder how he's doing. Should I call him? No, he said he's going to be busy with theater stuff. I should let him call me when he has the chance.

I mean, I'll see him in an hour at rehearsal anyway. Surely I can wait.

Almost immediately, my phone rings. Anastasia.

"Hello Tabitha. How nice to hear from you. I've been thinking about Paisley."

"Um, yeah. Well we're back in New York for a few weeks. Upstate. Not the city," I quickly add in at the end. "You remember I'm doing a show out here."

"Right, you told me. It's exciting to take on a new venture."

I'm such an idiot. Of course we had this conversation. It's not like I could just whisk my daughter away without prior approval.

"It's okay, isn't it?" I can't believe I have to ask for permission to have a job. What if she says no? If she wanted to, she could crush me like a flea.

Speaking of which, my legs itch like crazy. I lean over, scratching one bite and then another. It looks like I had a wrestling match with a cactus—and lost.

"Tabitha, I have enough to do with babysitting Jon here. I can't tell you what to do as well." Her voice is clipped.

"So I take it he's not great?"

She sighs. "I know I can trust you with this information. You'll keep our secret. No, he's not. He has virtually no short term memory anymore, and he's quite impulsive. As if he wasn't impulsive before."

Paisley is proof of that.

"Oh." I don't know what else to say.

"I have to tell him about the accident every day. He doesn't remember it. He thinks it's about five years ago."

If the last five years have been wiped from his memory... "Does he ... does he know who Paisley is?"

The silence on the line tells me all I need to know. Oh, my poor little girl.

"We'll continue the child support, obviously. But until he's had some more healing, I don't know if he should see her. It'll confuse both of them, I'm afraid."

My heart is breaking for my little girl who loves her occasional father.

On the other hand, is this my get-out-of-jail-free card? Can I move on and be done with them? Life can't really be that easy, can it?

How would this impact Paisley? I mean, I never knew my dad and I'm fin—

Okay, maybe not the best example.

Any way you shake it, Paisley is probably going to have parent issues. At the end of the day, don't we all? I'll do my best to alleviate them. Her dad was in an accident and has a brain injury. Sucky things happen.

"I guess it's a good thing I came to New York for the summer then," I say lamely.

I think I hear a sniffle on the other end of the line. It must be static, though. I can't picture Anastasia Jerome crying. "Will you still send me updates on Paisley? Pictures and everything? I ... I miss her. It's best not to have her around, but it doesn't mean Nico and I don't miss her."

The pain in her voice makes me wonder if I've been judging this situation all wrong. "Anastasia, um, I need to ask you something. About Paisley."

"Okay," she says slowly.

Here goes nothing. "So, after our reunion and everything, once you and I'd connected, I tried to stay out of the public eye, especially with Paisley. I basically gave up my entire career. I didn't want to be out trotting about with Paisley and have someone connect the dots between me and you guys."

"We've always tried to portray a certain image, whether it was the truth or not. You know how it is. You create a public persona, and then you get stuck living it, no matter how far from reality it becomes."

I do know. We all had our roles as the Sassy Cats that had very little to do with who we actually were. Hell, it's hard to develop a public image of yourself when you don't even know *who* you are.

"I never wanted to be one of *those* Hollywood couples with torrid affairs and scandals, yet that's exactly who we became."

"Can I be totally honest?"

"Please, Tabitha. I expect honesty from my friends." *Friends.* She considers me her friend.

"I was afraid to have a public presence. I thought that if anyone ever figured out Paisley's paternity, you'd ruin me."

Anastasia laughs. "Oh, come on. I dated Callie for a while. You know I'm not *that* evil."

"Evil?" I think about how she's treated Paisley—like her own child. "Evil, no. But scary. Intimidating. And I didn't want to upset you by pursuing a career."

"Tabitha, you're a fool if you don't pursue a career, if that's what you want to do. If you're content staying at home, then stay at home. But don't let fear hold you back. Even fear of me. I'd love to see this show, but I don't see me traveling any time soon. But maybe I can video chat with Paisley, when you get a chance."

After we sign off, my mind is totally abuzz. *Don't let fear hold you back.*

Those six words should lift a tremendous weight off my shoulders, but somehow, I'm just as paralyzed as ever. So

I have Anastasia Jerome's blessing. What does that mean? What do I do with that?

Good God, I'm just as lost as ever. Too bad there's no Google Maps to help me figure out my life.

Chapter 32: Henderson

Last season we nearly hit a catastrophic roadblock when our star walked out the week of *Chicago* opening. She was a big name for Broadway, and we were expecting to lose everything when we lost her.

Thanks to Gloria and Carson Reuben, The Edison was saved.

But those once in a lifetime, buzzer-beater passes wouldn't be so phenomenal if they occurred all the time. There's no way we might be so lucky as to escape this massive mess.

Grayson and I have been at this for an hour already when Tabitha walks in. We look at her morosely and go back to not having any answers.

"I guess we could fudge the tricks. Like have whoever we cast just hold onto the silks and hoops, but not actually do anything?"

Grayson's provided the only real solution, but I feel as if we're copping out. We had a vision for this show, which included an aerial act. That would have sold it to Broadway. I mentally cross my fingers as I shift through the stack of applications, looking for the one other person besides Jasmine who'd checked aerial experience.

Terrence Masters.

"Well, that's not going to help."

"What's not going to help?" Tabitha's voice rings in bright and chipper.

"The only other bloke who auditioned and listed aerial experience is, well, a bloke. He's not right for the part of Anne."

"Not unless you make it Andrew." Tabitha quips.

You know, that *could* work. It certainly fits the taboo love story for the time period. "It's a thought."

She shrugs. "I know, a stupid one. Let's face it, no one ever accused me of being the brains of the operation here, and if you're listening to me for ideas, you're probably pretty screwed."

Grayson laughs. "We're pretty screwed, so what else you got?"

Tabitha starts shuffling through the resumes and headshots. "Anne is Black, right? You need that, I'm guessing."

I nod, watching her as she tucks a lock of blonde hair behind her ear. "Okay, I'll sort these. Then you guys go from there."

I look at Grayson who nods in agreement. Normally we'd never make casting decisions on something so superficial. In a minute, Tabitha hands me a pile. A very small pile. The pickings are slim.

"I put this one on top because she's a ballerina, so would probably look the part of a trapeze artist at least. She could like, do bendy stuff."

I glance down. "Ugh, no. It's number seventy-two." I look up to see both Grayson and Tabitha staring at me. "She couldn't even figure out what name to put on her application. We don't need someone who brings that kind of baggage here."

Tabitha shrugs. "I'm pretty sure we all come with our own baggage, Henderson. I have lots of it. But since it's mostly Louis Vuitton, no one seems to mind. Give this woman a chance. You never know what she'll do."

I want to believe in her words. I want to take her advice. "I need whoever steps up to be able to do this without thinking. This one," I wave her headshot, "couldn't make up her mind between her stage name and her real name."

"Could she dance?" Grayson asks.

I think back. I was distracted by Tabitha texting me, but she did all the steps properly. Quite well, actually. "Yes, Morgan liked her. She's the alternate for Lise. I would have considered her strongly in the running for the actual part if she'd been more together personally."

"I'm not together personally, and you casted me," Tabitha offers.

"Gloria certainly wasn't together personally, and she saved our asses," Grayson adds.

I shake my head. "I can't fight you both. Gray, are you going to call her or shall I?" The cast for *An American in Paris* isn't set to arrive for five more weeks, so she might not even be available.

"Can you call, H? I've got to get back to rehearsal. Tabby, we're probably not going to get to your number for a few hours. I don't want you wasting your time here if there's something else you want to do. We can always call you when we need you."

Tabitha smiles at Grayson before turning to me. "I think I'll hang around and see if there's some way I can make myself useful."

"Shouldn't you spend this time with your daughter?" The words are out of my mouth before I can stop them.

The smile drops from her face like a curtain falling. "I … I can go." She turns to leave.

I stand quickly, needing to rectify my mistake. "No, Tabitha, don't." I grab her arm. "I … it didn't come out how I meant it. What I meant to ask was is Paisley doing better this morning?"

She nods without turning around. I release her, sinking back into my chair. "Good. Don't want her to be too upset. Now, I've got to call this ..." I rifle through the papers on the desk, looking for her name, "right. Leslie Ann Moose."

I see Tabitha tighten through the shoulders, cringing at the name. I mean, I guess I can sort of see why she was stuck on it, trying to decide whether a stage name would be better. It's horrible, especially for a ballerina. But still, we have enough drama without looking for it with someone who's having an identity crisis.

And she totally needs a stage name.

"So maybe I was a tad harsh on her. It's your fault, really. I was in a bad mood because you'd left me."

Tabitha turns around. "Henderson, you've been in a bad mood since I met you, and it rarely has anything to do with me. You need to own your shit for once."

I blink, processing her words. She's right, of course. "I am in a bad mood. I generally am around members of the opposite sex who are potential dating material. It's like as soon as I register that someone could be interesting or whatev, my brain short circuits, and I become a huge wanker."

She tightens up one side of her face, almost in a sneer. "That is the lamest excuse I've ever heard."

I shrug. "I don't know how to date." I don't think I've ever admitted it out loud. "Maybe because I've never wanted to date. I ... don't believe in love."

I catch Tabitha's barely perceptible wince, those blue eyes wounded.

At least I didn't before I met her.

Oh no.

Chapter 33: Tabitha

Leave it to me to fall for a guy who doesn't believe in love. I'm practically a cliché.

There's no practically about it.

I'm not smart about a lot of things, but there is one thing I do know—people don't change. They are who they are. And if Henderson doesn't want to believe in love—to believe in the possibility of *us*—then I can't change that.

I can't waste the effort on it.

And we don't have the time to waste. There's a show that's going to open, regardless of our personal drama. We should probably focus on that. You know, maybe Henderson was onto something with his 'no dating at work' policy. We've already lost a lot of valuable time.

"Okay, well, let's get back to this. Are you calling this Leslie Ann Moose? I'll help you out by telling you the answer is yes." I don't wait for him to respond. "She's your Obi Wan Kanobe."

"How so?"

"Your only hope." I smile.

He returns the gesture for a brief moment before the seriousness returns to his face. "Well then, we're screwed."

"She could be great. I mean, the name thing can't be your only gripe."

Henderson doesn't answer. Holy hell, he's basing all of this on her own confusion about her name? Okay, even to me it sounds flighty, but maybe she's got a good reason.

"Henderson, don't be stupid. Call her. You need her here, like, yesterday as it is. This show has to come together."

Without saying another word, he picks up the phone and dials. I wander out of the office while he's pitching this deal. God, I hope she says yes. There's already been a lot of press about this show, and there's bound to be more in the coming week.

My name means a lot.

Actually, I take that back. Tabitha Stetson isn't even that recognizable. They still have to put "Tabby Cat from the Sassy Cats" on most of the publicity so people can place me. The name no longer sits well with me. It's like pants that I outgrew but kept in the back of my closet for that time when they *might fit* again. I mean, four years ago, I did squeeze back into them when we did that reunion performance. But there are no plans to get back together, which is fine with me.

That realization makes my heart rate rush. I don't want to be a Sassy Cat, but I don't know what to do without that safety net.

This.

A voice rushes through my head. *Do this.*

Maybe? I could look at doing more theater. I've had fun so far, and it's not nearly as intimidating as I thought. Even the dancing I've seen them teach seems manageable. I could pick and choose what shows I do—surely my name would afford me that luxury—so I could work when it works for Paisley and me.

I could be her mom *and* an actress.

My heart begins to slow and my muscles relax. I could do both.

My phone sounds, the telltale theme of the Wicked Witch of the West letting me know my mother is calling. Without thinking, I rush to share my epiphany with her.

"Mom, I figured it out. I can do this theater thing and still be there for Paisley. I can just do it during the summer or at a time when it's convenient for her. I've got Maria, so I think this could really work!"

"Theater? Really? Tabby, is that really who you are? Theater people are deep and intelligent. You're … more California."

Leave it to my mother to rain on my parade. "What's that supposed to mean?"

"You know, the LA beach Instagram scene. Like Khloe Kardashian. But older. New York theater people are more intellectual. Like well-read and stuff."

Khloe Kardashian and I are the same age, for the record.

"Mom, it's not like I'm illiterate. I graduated from high school."

"Barely, and only because you slept with one of your teachers. Tabby, you need to know what you're good at. Have realistic expectations. That's all I'm saying."

She might be three-thousand miles away, but for all intents and purposes, she may as well have been standing right here, taking a stiletto to my gut. Shame burns my face as if I opened a pizza oven. Normally, I own my sex life. Right now, I feel like the lowest of low.

I will *never* make my daughter feel the way she makes me feel.

"So Mom, tell me then, what do you think I can do?"

"You should see if Callie will get the group back together again. You're not getting any younger, and if you don't start getting work done, you won't be able to cash in on your sex appeal. You have a very small window of time left to use that."

"Do you think I can do anything without the group?"

"If you could have, wouldn't you have by now? Callie's a megastar. Angie too. I hear Mandy's coming out with new music. You and Daphne are the weak links. And we all know how Daphne got into the group."

She doesn't say it, but I know she thinks I slept my way in. It was, perhaps, the one time that I used my talent—my vocal talent, that is—to get ahead. Well, then and now.

But what if she's right? What if I'm not smart enough to make it here? Hell, if I can't succeed in this rinky dink place, I can't succeed anywhere. But I'll never get to prove myself either way if this show doesn't go on. I disconnect the call and rush back into Henderson's office.

"Did you get in contact with her? What did she say? Is she coming? Does she live in the city? Do you want me to drive down and get her?"

This is when you know I'm desperate—me, offering to drive to New York City. I can barely find my way from my rental house to The Edison. With a GPS.

Okay, fine. Maria drives me and drops me off every day. I'm hopeless.

"I'm gonna see if Kyle can pick her up from the train station tonight."

"So she's in?"

Henderson lifts one shoulder before casually dropping it. "She said she'd see. She wasn't sure if the part was something blabbidy blah. Either way, she wouldn't commit. The only thing I could get her to commit to was coming up and checking us out."

"You have to convince her. Turn on your charm."

"Charm is more Grayson's game." Henderson rolls his eyes. "If you're bringing me in as the schmoozing closer, you know you're already screwed."

Grayson does have tons more overt charm than Henderson does. Henderson is more subtle in what makes him endearing and engaging. "So then why did they send you in to meet with me?"

"I wasn't meeting with you. I was meeting with Tawny Shane, who was much less valuable. But also, we were screwed. Trust me, I'm no one's first choice." He's looking down at his computer, barely paying attention to me. My mom is probably right. I'm only good at two things, and singing is the distant second.

"Yet somehow, we're both the ones who screwed."

Henderson's head whips up, his eyes blazing. "Shhh! You can't say that here." He's up on his feet, meeting me in front of his desk.

"What, about us screwing? How else should I say it? That we had a raucous and energetic night of acrobatic lovemaking?"

His finger presses against my lips, trying to silence the words coming out. "Tabitha," he hisses, his voice low and feral. "Stop saying that. I don't want anyone to hear."

Never one to follow directions, I lean in, whispering in his ear, "What? You don't want them to know that behind this grumpy exterior, how very skilled you are in the bedroom? That you had me screaming in ecstasy, and that every night I dream about the next time you touch me?" I lean back so I can look him in the eye.

His hands are clamped on my arms, as if holding me tightly will stop me from saying these things. "Every night?"

I give him a slow nod with a sly grin to match. "Every night."

Henderson closes his eyes, his body sagging into mine. "What've you done to me? I need to be focused on this show. On pulling our fat out of the fire, and all I can think about is how to spend time with you. To see you again. To touch you again. You can't say things like that to me because I'll never get my job done now."

"Why not?" I tease.

"Because if I'm not actually carrying you off into the bedroom, I'll be thinking about what I will do to you once we're in there."

I whisper softly in his ear, "That sounds promising."

That's all it takes to bring his lips crashing to mine. His grip releases on my arms as his hands slide around my back and down my bottom. He lifts me up, and I oblige, wrapping my legs around his waist.

In this moment, this is what I need. To feel whole. To feel accomplished. To feel ... something. I need him.

Chapter 34: Henderson

I need her. I need all of her. Right here. Right now. In my office.

It doesn't matter. I can't go one single minute longer without tasting her, feeling her, consuming her. I break away for only as long as it takes me to lock the door. There's a good chance I've absolutely lost my mind. Not only am I about to have sex with someone at work, but it's literally *at work*.

No. I need to stop this. But I don't think I can. I don't want to.

"Henderson, wait—" Tabitha puts her hand on my chest, pushing me away slightly. Her hair is messy from my hands, and neither of us is wearing a shirt.

"Right. I don't have anything with me." Of course not. There's never been a need for me to have a condom on me at work.

"No, it's ... I don't think we should do this. Not here."

It's like she's dumping a bucket of ice cold water over me. Ice cold water that I'm in desperate need of.

"I want to," she continues. "Trust me, I *really* want to. And I can't promise that I won't jump your bones a little later. It's just ... well, my mom."

If that's not a boner killer, I don't know what is. "What's your mum got to do with us having sex?"

I'm not even sure I want to know the answer to that question. *Shudder.*

Tabitha pulls her shirt on and perches on the edge of my desk. I think I'm going to need her to drop another bucket of cold water on me. Hastily, I yank my shirt over my head.

"I'm trying to figure out what I want in life. What I want to do with my life. I'm done with being a Sassy Cat. But my mom basically told me all I'm good at is sex."

"You are very good at it." I mean it as a compliment. Her face falls though.

"I want to be able to do something else, you know? Surely I'm good at something else. Anything else. And as much as I want to be with you right now, I think I need to stop using sex as my default. It's my go-to when I don't know what else to do. And right now, I don't know what else to do."

I should feel relieved that she's taking the temptation away. Her being here has already led me astray from my work. I should have called Kyle to make sure he'll be able to fetch Leslie Ann Moose from the train station. I'm losing focus—no, I've lost focus—because of Tabitha. I should feel relieved.

But I don't.

I feel like I did when I was a kid and I wasn't enough for my mum. I'm not enough for Tabitha. My love—or whatever this is—isn't enough to make her feel whole.

I'm not enough.

And while I fear that I'll never be enough, looking at Tabitha, disheveled and vulnerable, I know I want to try. I need to be enough for her so she feels like she is enough.

"Right then. Let's put a pin in this," I motion between the two of us, "and we'll figure out what you're good at. It's better for me really, because, well, you know my rule."

"What if you broke your rule?"

"I almost did."

"Yeah, and what if there was no almost?"

I plop back into my desk chair, running my fingers through my hair. "We're putting a pin in it, remember?" If we change the subject, then I don't have to think about the almosts. I pick up my phone to see a string of texts from Grayson. Kyle's not available to pick up Leslie Ann.

Shit.

Tabitha smooths down her hair. "Don't panic. We can figure this out. But also, I don't think you should send just anyone. You need her, so this isn't a warm body job. Who would have more charm than you and is as invested in The Edison succeeding as you and Grayson are? That's who you need to send."

My God, she's brilliant. There's only one answer. Josh, the musical director.

"I'm going to send Josh. Believe it or not, he's got some game. And do you mean to tell me that smooth-talking Kyle didn't sweep you off your feet?" I jest.

"I'm sure he would have if I'd let him. But I'm not interested in Kyle. Or anyone else for that matter."

"Pin," I remind her. It's actually a reminder to myself because I'm not thinking about anything that I should be thinking about right now.

"Right. Consider me pinned. Now, what else do we need to do? I'm sure this show needs something. Do you have a list? What's next?"

I stand up. "What's next is I need to talk to Josh, and then get into rehearsal. You need to be learning your lines. And everyone here pitches in with sets and props and whatever else, so another set of hands would be appreciated."

Tabitha looks at her hands, flipping them over and examining them. Finally she looks up at me. "You know I can't really do anything, right? I've got no skills, other than singing and well," she shrugs, "that thing that we're not talking about."

I take a step toward her, taking those hands in my own. "Tabitha, you've accomplished more in your life than most people ever dream possible. You're supremely talented on stage, and you've got your hands full being a single mum. At some point, you need to give yourself credit for some of it."

Her big blue eyes hold a vulnerability I'm sure her adoring fans have never seen. I should feel privileged that I get to witness it. Instead, the desire to flee consumes me. It's too much.

I can't be this for her.

Chapter 35: Tabitha

Mommy, can I come with you today?" Her little voice turns me to mush.

"Of course, baby girl. It might be boring, but you can bring your iPad." My answer is automatic. Rehearsals have been running so long at The Edison that I feel like I barely get to see Paisley. We have breakfast together in the morning, and once Maria drops me off, I don't see her for the rest of the day. I'm never back before she goes to bed.

These are some mighty long days.

They're not unlike the grueling rehearsals I put in during my Sassy Cat days, but I never had a kid at home waiting for me then. But I was also twenty years younger then, so my well of energy never seemed to run dry.

Now it's like the Sahara in there.

And then add a four-year-old.

When this is done, I'm sleeping for a month. Maybe two.

I don't know how the rest of the cast and crew here do it. I've been in rehearsals for eight days now, and every inch of my body hurts. And I don't even really dance. I do stand around in heels for most of the day, and by the time

I get home, my toes and ankles bear a striking resemblance to the sausages hanging in the window of the Wurst Haus on Chapel Street.

Last week, when they were still doing their other show, I got a break from rehearsals in the evening. This week, we're running until almost midnight every night. It's probably a good thing Henderson and I put a pin in things for the time being. Even if I wanted to, I'm too tired for anything else.

We open in two days, which is a day earlier than the normal schedule. They had to do it, to accommodate the demand for tickets.

The demand for me.

It's unspoken but understood that this feverish pace is because of my presence here. I even feel a little guilty, forcing the cast to work at a breakneck pace to hit the stage a day earlier. I should do something nice.

"Maria, let's stop at the coffee shop. I want to see if she can bring up a treat for everyone either today … or tomorrow." Sometimes I forget that I'm not in LA anymore and things don't work as quickly here.

I leave Maria and Paisley in the car while I run into Dean's Beans. While it seems like half the population of Hicklam swings by the kitschy cafe for their caffeine fix, they usually aren't all in here at once. Today, it's wall to wall people, and the barista behind the counter looks as if she's going to collapse. There's a tall, skinny kid working frantically to foam a drink and failing terribly.

Maybe I should come back later. This doesn't seem like the most opportune time to put in a large catering order. As I'm about to slink out the door, Heidi—I think that's her name—spots me. Her eyes grow wide in panic. She shakes her head violently from side to side in an attempt to convey some sort of message to me.

I don't understand.

But then I see it and I know, and it's too late.

One person turns. And then another. Still another. Heads and eyes swivel toward me. It doesn't take a rocket scientist to see the recognition in their faces.

"Tabby!" someone screams. That's all it takes for the crowd to push forward, closing the gaps between them and me. The noise level rises, compounded by the hiss of the steam machine.

This is not good.

When I was a Sassy Cat, we always had a team of burly security guards to keep us from being flattened. I haven't had a security detail in years.

You don't really need one when no one recognizes you.

But I need it right now.

Above the din, I hear the door chime behind me and feel the rush of hot summer air as the door opens. The small hand slipping into mine tells me it's the last person who should be in here. She's likely to be crushed.

"Is that your daughter?"

"She's so big."

"She's so cute!"

"Who's her father?"

The last question has me gripping Paisley's hand for dear life. Nope, I'm not doing this now. I turn, scooping Paisley up into my arms and rushing outside into the bright sunlight where Maria is waiting.

"Holy cow! What happened?"

Clutching Paisley to my body with one arm, I grab Maria with my free hand, practically dragging her to the car. "Take her. Now."

Maria is surprisingly fast and nimble. She scoops Paisley from me, buckling her into her booster before sliding around into the driver's seat. I open the passenger door, but stop. I almost forgot what I should be doing. All these people—they're here for me.

For The Edison.

For everyone who's up the hill, busting their asses, dancing until their feet bleed.

"Hang on," I tell Maria.

I close the door and walk around the back of the car, where the crowd is spilling out onto the sidewalk. Smoothing my hands over my hair, I pull my sunglasses down. "Hi everyone!" I call. "Y'all surprised me before I'd had my coffee. How's everybody doing?"

The cellphones come out, and it's picture after picture. A few autographs for the more old school crowd. You know, the people my age.

God, I've missed this.

"You're really here! I wanted to be a Sassy Cat when I was little!" someone gushes. I smile until my cheeks hurt.

I'd forgotten what this was like. My chest is full and tight, in a good way. I feel alive.

"Mommy, are you coming?" Paisley yells through the rolled down window. "Rehearsal's not gonna wait. No one likes a late diva!"

My own words echoing back in my ears make me smile. I catch the amused look on Maria's face as she sits in the driver's seat, patiently waiting for me.

"Well, she's right. I can't keep the whole cast waiting. Thanks for coming out, and I hope to see you all at The Edison!" Might as well give the theater a shout out.

I hurry to the other side of the car, waving and smiling as I slide into the seat. I keep the pleasant expression on my face as we drive away, knowing that one last shot from a roving camera can end up splashed all over the internet.

"Mommy, are you famous like Daddy is? When did you get famous?"

My heart breaks a little that she doesn't know me in any other context than being her mother. On the other hand, maybe that means I'm not messing it up too terribly?

"I used to be famous. I was a singer in a group. With Mandy. You know, Tenley's mom."

Paisley already thinks Tenley is the bomb from their one playdate. She's making lists of the things they're going to play together the next time Tenley comes to visit, which should be in a few days. Mandy's coming to see me in a show.

"Can I have a sleepover at Tenley's? She has bunk beds."

I have no clue how my four-year-old knows about bunk beds,.but whatever. If that's exciting to her, so be it. "I'm not sure about a sleepover, but we'll see. I think we're going to visit when I'm done with my shows." I turn around to look at my daughter, sweet and innocent. "You know I'm an actress too. That's why we're here. I'm working."

"Yeah, but that's just your work." She says it so nonchalantly, like my work somehow doesn't mean anything.

Ah, the reasoning power of a four-year-old.

"Being a singer and an actress is work, honey. People pay me for my talent."

"Is the show going to be on Nick Jr.?"

"No sweetie, it's a live show. I perform every night."

She shrugs and looks out the window. "That's too bad. Maybe someday you can be on Nick Jr."

Actually, the Sassy Cats were once featured in an episode of *Maximus the Magnificent*, but ever since the tween star, Cody VanTwizzle, went off the rails with a porn career and human trafficking charges, the network made the show disappear. The only other show to get yanked so quickly was *Zoey 101* when Jamie Spears got pregnant at sixteen. Somehow, I don't think the two sins equate, but they got the same punishment. Either way, the Sassy Cats episode of *Maximus the Magnificent* is harder to find than a virgin at the Playboy Mansion.

My daughter doesn't know this about me. In my quest to fly incognito, I eschewed everything from my past.

That ends now.

"Actually, I was on Nick Jr. once. When we get back home to California, I'll show you the episode." I glance back to see a slack-jawed Paisley, wonderment on her face.

"Do you know Peppa Pig?"

I can't contain the laughter, and neither can Maria. "Nico was much the same when he was little. It never occurred to him that his parents were as famous, or even more so, than his favorite TV shows. They were just Mom and Dad, but Steve from Blue's Clues—now *he* was a star."

"Kids."

As we're pulling into The Edison, Maria's words continue to rattle in my brain. "Wait, so how does Paisley know he's famous if Nico never did?"

My daughter's voice pipes up from the back, four going on twenty-four. "Daddy told me that he has to pretend I'm not his daughter in public because he's so famous someone might try to take me. That's why that car was chasing us. Because Daddy's so important."

In an instant, my blood boils. If he weren't in the shape he was in, I'd fly back to California right now to kick his ass.

"I think it was just an accident. No one was chasing us." Maria soothes.

"And no matter what, I'll always be your mom first and foremost. I'm your mom, and then I'm in show business." These aren't just words; I know them to be true down to the depths of my being.

Even so, I'm still raging as we get to The Edison. "Maria, you can bring Paisley in. I think she's going to get bored quickly, but she can see how it goes. I want to share this part of my life with her."

And I don't ever want her to think I'm denying her or I'm ashamed of her.

"Hey, what's up? You okay?" Henderson stops me as I walk into the lobby of the theater.

I'm practically shaking with rage. "No, it's been a hell of a day, and we haven't even started."

"Slow down. What happened?"

The concern in his eyes appears genuine, but what the hell do I know? I thought Jonathan Spencer Maxwell actually loved Paisley. I bet he only takes her because Anastasia makes him. Hell, he could even be faking this memory loss to get out of seeing Paisley again.

Okay, so that's a little 1980s soap opera, even for me, but I wouldn't put it past the louse.

"I never knew my dad. I'm not even sure my mom knows who he is. I used to say it didn't bother me because what other choice did I have? Admit that I was a careless afterthought and a bother for the people who created me? That I didn't matter to the people who were supposed to love me most? You know, I wasn't even going to tell him he was Paisley's father. Better for her to have one parent who loves her totally than this crap. But I don't even know what I'm doing here. Do you know that Paisley doesn't even know I'm famous? I've denied it all for her."

"Which is very admirable. My mum never put me first. I don't know that she even could. Or wanted to."

And now my heart is breaking for Henderson. No wonder he's so gun-shy about relationships. He's never been loved either.

I slide my hand into his.

It's time to change that.

Chapter 36: Henderson

I wish I could hug her and take all her pain away. I don't know what she's going through with her daughter, but her hurt is obvious. Well, I do know what it's like not to be loved by the people who are supposed to love you unconditionally.

Her hand is in mine, so I squeeze it gently. I take her other hand, completing the circle between us. "What happened? Did I see Paisley go in with her nanny?"

"We stopped at Dean's Beans, which was mobbed. Apparently, they were there to see me. I started to get scared for Paisley, but then I thought about how that might reflect on The Edison. It was fine. Fun, even. I've missed being with fans. I didn't know how much until I got mobbed."

"I haven't been to town much this week, but I've heard a few people say things are busier. They're coming out of the woodwork to adore you." I squeeze Tabitha's hands again.

"I need it. I need their adoration. I think it's why I've been so lost since Paisley was born. I need someone to love me. Lots of someones. It's why I need to perform. When I'm not with Paisley, I miss her. But at the end of the day,

I miss singing more. And that's what makes me a terrible mother."

She looks so defeated.

"You're not a terrible mother. On the other hand, I may be the wrong person to ask about that. My mum was only seventeen when I was born. She wasn't ready to be a mum, so she didn't do a bang up job with it. Mostly stuck me with my granny or whomever would watch me. My dad caught wind—'coz he wasn't there either—and moved back to 'Straya to try to keep her in line. They fought like cats and dogs about who had to take care of me and why the other wasn't doing a good job. Finally, my dad got fed up, and we moved back to America. My mum didn't try to come after me. Didn't try to see me. I haven't seen her in over ten years."

"Ten years? Why so long?"

I shrug. "I stopped going back to 'Straya. My grandparents are gone. I'm not even sure where she is, and I got tired of chasing her. There's nothing left for me there."

I don't know if I've ever been so brutally honest with another person. Hell, I don't know if I've ever even been that honest with myself.

Tears fill Tabitha's eyes. "That's where Paisley is with her father, but I'm happy to be rid of him, I hope. He's not going to see her anymore. His shadow has been cast on me for too long. But on the other hand, I don't want to see her hurt."

"And I don't want to see you hurt," I say, my voice hoarse. From somewhere deep within, I feel a primal urge to protect her. I wish I had a magic wand I could wave to make all of this go away so she could find peace and direction.

She gazes into my eyes and I swear, right into my soul. "Don't you wish there was an easy button or something for life? To make us who we want to be instead of who we are?"

"But I lo—like who you are." I catch myself, stumbling over the word that *almost* came out. A word I've never said to another human. A word I never intend to say.

Yet there it is, buzzing around my brain.

"And I like you too, Henderson. I wish—"

"H, are you coming in? Oh Tabitha, good. You're here. We're on the party scene."

Damn Grayson and his meddling attention to time.

I'm still staring at her. She's staring back at me. Neither of us say anything.

Grayson clears his throat before muttering something and turning away.

"I don't know that I've ever admitted that to someone before," she says finally.

I know what she means. "Same here. I ... I feel myself opening up when I'm around you."

"I've been closed off for so long. It feels good. Better than sex."

I lift my eyebrow. Maybe I've been doing it wrong.

Tabitha bursts out laughing. "Okay, not better than sex, but ..." she tilts her head. "Yes, maybe. There are very few people in this world who know me. Hell, I don't even know if I know me. But when I'm with you, I feel like I'm the closest to me that I get. It feels ... right."

I know exactly what she means.

"I don't want this feeling to end between us." Her voice is almost pleading.

We've got three weeks while the show runs. Three weeks, and then it won't be like we're working together anymore. She won't be off limits.

Screw the limits.

"We've got to get in there, but I can't let this go. I want every single minute you have while you're here, and then when the show's done as well. This ..." I motion between us, "is too special to let go."

Tabitha leans in, kissing me sweetly on the lips. "Better than sex," she whispers, her lips still moving over mine.

"H, man, come on!" Grayson bellows from somewhere in the theatre.

I take her hand, not wanting to break contact. Afraid that if I do, this will all disappear the moment I can no longer touch it. Yet as I step to the heavy doors of the theatre, I can't help but realize it's impossible to hold onto her while holding onto The Edison.

Chapter 37: Tabitha

I should be running on empty, yet somehow, energy courses through my veins.

It's not like I'm getting any sleep. There aren't enough hours in the day as it is, so sleep seems like a frivolous waste of my precious time. I'll sleep when this is all over.

Except I never want it to end.

I pretty much love every single minute here. I love being up on stage, singing my heart out. I can't wait for the audience tonight, to feed off their energy. I'm ravenous for it, like a hiker starving in the woods.

I love that I can rehearse and perform, yet go home to Paisley every night. There's no craziness of jumping on buses and planes, never sure what city—or time zone—I'm in. I go home to my rental house, which is starting to feel a bit like home, despite the decor. I slide into Paisley's room and watch her sleep. In the morning, she slips into bed with me, snuggling in. After breakfast, Maria drives me to The Edison. Sometimes Paisley stays with me for a while. Sometimes she and Maria go off on an adventure.

But Henderson is always there. If I'm not onstage, I'm sitting with him. When we're not running a rehearsal, we're in his office, working on one thing or another.

Okay, we're kissing.

Nothing more though. That pin is still in place.

We eat all our meals together. At night, I slide down under my covers and call him like a lovesick teenager.

That's what I feel like too.

I call him before I go to sleep and text him the moment I wake up.

The one thing we're not doing is sleeping together.

I know, I'm shocked too. I do have a reputation to uphold and all.

At first, I thought it was because there was no time. I mean, there's not. During the day, there are always people around. Not to mention there's just so much work to be done. And at night, I want to have those moments with Paisley, even if she's asleep.

Plus, frankly, we're too old to have Henderson sneaking out in the morning before Paisley gets up. As soon as *The Greatest Showman* is done, there'll be plenty of time to figure this all out. Prior to Henderson, my sex life had been dry for over four years. Another few weeks isn't going to kill me.

I know it'll be worth the wait.

And in reality, I'm putting off sex because I never do. It's my go-to, instead of an actual relationship.

I want the real thing now. I won't mess this up by using sex instead of feelings.

As we pull up to The Edison, I can feel the change of energy in the air. It's like it's fully charged with a million little lightning bolts. Tonight is opening night.

The last time I went on stage, for the *weLoveMusic* Festival, it was the five of us. Despite the massive bombshells and blow ups minutes before, we stood backstage, in our circle, holding hands as one unit. This time, it's different. The cast is much larger. Yet in some ways, I could see us all linking hands and becoming one before the curtain rises.

I need to feel part of one unit again.

But even without holding onto someone's hands, I do. Here at The Edison, I feel like I belong. Or maybe it's not The Edison, but Henderson who makes me feel this way.

With him, I'm my true self. The Tabitha the world didn't know existed. The one nobody bothers to look for. The one I'd forgotten about myself.

When I'm with him, it's not about how many Instagram followers I have, or how many times my picture makes a tabloid site. It's not about who I might be sleeping with— obviously. It's only about us.

Everything in my life is falling into place. I feel whole.

The last time I felt this accepted was when the Sassy Cats were together. And even then, it wasn't on this level. I mean, I was so young and immature that I was only like half a person.

Thinking that causes me to pull out my phone and text Mandy. She's coming to the show tonight.

Immediately my phone rings. "I'm driving, so I can't text. Break a leg!"

I smile at my friend's voice. I can't wait to see her tonight. "Are you bringing Ben?"

"No, he's back in Nashville. It's my week with the kids. I had to get Reagan to take the boys. Tenley's coming with me, naturally. I think she's hoping to land a gig down there soon."

"I didn't know she was interested. Can she sing?"

Mandy laughs. "Not at all. Like, it's bad. Even Daniel couldn't help her. I kind of feel bad for her. She's as tone deaf as her father."

"Oh, Mandy, I can't wait to see you again. I love that I'm so close to you. Angie's coming to the show next weekend. Maybe we could all grab a late bite to eat or something."

"Tab, this isn't Manhattan. The restaurants there probably close by nine. You're in cow country. But we do need to get together. Maybe you and I can go down to see Angie before you head back to California? Okay, well, I'm pulling up and the holy terrors are about to hop in. See you tonight. Break a leg and love you!"

Back to California.

Her words ricochet around my brain, rumbling and grumbling, though I can't put my finger on why.

Of course I'll go back to California. It's where I live. It's where Paisley's father is. I have nothing out here. My life is back there.

So why does walking through the doors of The Edison feel like I'm sliding into my favorite, perfectly worn fleece pajamas? You know, the kind I never want to take off.

Maybe it's not The Edison. Maybe it's the feeling of performing. Yes, that's what it has to be. That feeling that in just a few hours, we'll be in hair and makeup and costumes and the audience will be filling the seats.

This is what I've been missing.

I immediately head for Henderson's office. It's been a whole six hours since I've talked to him.

It feels like a lifetime.

Before I can get there, I run into Leslie outside the bathroom; she's already in tears. This does not bode well for … anything. I wonder if Henderson was right about her being too dramatic to cast. On the other hand, he thought dating me was a bad idea, so what does he know?

"Leslie, are you okay? What's wrong?"

She wipes her face with the back of her hand. I notice angry red callouses lining her palm. I take her hand, looking more closely at it.

"Seriously, Leslie, are you okay? This looks bad. Should we get someone to look at it? You've really torn up your skin here."

"Yeah, I just poured some alcohol on it to clean it. It brought tears to my eyes." She waves her hands in the air, trying to fan the moisture away from her face. "I'll be fine in a second. I just don't want this to get infected."

I look again. It's bad. Several small tears and one big circular shaped wound in the middle of her left hand. Shaking my head I say, "What are we going to do? Do Henderson and Grayson know? Have you told Levi? Can you change the choreography?"

Again. All her numbers have already been restaged once, thanks to Jasmine's injury at my house.

While Grayson took my suggestion and hired Leslie because of her ballet form, Leslie has blown us all away, learning some tricks to perform while singing. While it's not what Jasmine would have done, it's a lot more than most people could have done in this short time span.

And her hand is paying the price.

Leslie shakes her head. "I'll be good. I need to air it out for now. I didn't use enough chalk last night and this morning. I'll tape it for tonight. I think I might have the seamstress bedazzle a pair of trapeze gloves to match my costume. I ordered them on Prime, so they should be here by tomorrow."

I blink, my gaze shifting from her face to her wounds and back again. She's seriously impressive. "Damn, girl. You are a badass."

Leslie pulls her hand from mine and shrugs. "Yeah, well, the hand is the least of my issues. I've been a ballerina for years. My feet have seen worse and still performed. I'm not saying it feels awesome, but you know, the show must go on. Is it really a show if someone's not bleeding?"

I know the kind of injuries Angie worked through on *Hollywood Dance Off!* and even some of the less-than-optimal physical conditions we suffered through while on tour. Leslie's right, the show must go on.

Still, her stock just rose in my book.

"You're my hero. But when this is all healed, I'm taking you for the most luxurious manicure this town has ever seen. Complete with paraffin and hot towels and a bottle of champagne."

A broad smile spreads over Leslie's face. "I don't even really know you, but I'm totally going to take you up on that. Can you find a whole body paraffin tank? By the end of these three weeks, I'm going to need to soak for about three years. This has all been so crazy."

I know what she means. "Well, you're a rock star to me. I've gotta run for a final fitting."

I don't know why I say that instead of admitting that I need to see Henderson. I mean, it's not like we're a *secret* or anything. People certainly see us together, but we aren't making out or holding hands or anything where people can see. It probably looks like I'm just a VIP cast member who he's looking to keep happy.

I mean, that's fine. He's already breaking his personal rule by dating an actress at work. I can let him work through his comfort zone and keep things on the DL for now.

As long as it's just for now.

I've kept one man's secret. I'm not keeping another's.

I head toward wardrobe, but then cut through the hallway to the back entrance to Henderson's office. I slide in quietly, tiptoeing up behind Henderson, who's hunched over the keyboard, typing furiously. Leaning over him, I whisper in his ear, "Have I ever told you how sexy you are when you work?"

Henderson snaps upright, pretty much knocking me over. I stumble back, slamming into a bookcase, knocking piles of papers over everywhere. "Jesus Christ, Tabitha! You scared the ever livin' piss out of me!"

I scramble to the floor, trying to pick up the mess I've created.

"Why didn't you come in the main door like a normal human being?" He slides out of his chair to all fours, trying to sort the chaos.

I sit back on my heels and shrug. "I ran into Leslie, who's a beast, by the way. She's tough as nails, and you were wrong about her. No drama, just a total professional. Just like you were wrong about dating me."

Henderson stills, his hand in mid-air. Finally, after a moment that feels like a year, he sits back and looks at me. His lips are pursed, an expression that gives me a bad feeling in the pit of my stomach.

What did I say?

"Tabitha, we're not dating. We don't date. Hell, we don't even sleep together. I'm not your boyfriend. Remember we put a pin in it?"

Whoa. Overreact much?

Where did this even come from? I start to answer, but he keeps talking. "You know how I feel about dating someone at work. Also, we don't have time to date. I enjoy spending what time we have together, but that's all it is. Spending time together. Talking some."

"Flirting." Our late night phone conversations have definitely included "what are you wearing" more than once.

"Well, sure."

"And sometimes we kiss." As long as we're locked away in his office.

His gaze darts to the door, which I'm sure is *not* currently locked. "I guess."

"Well, it wasn't someone else's tongue in my mouth."

He stares at me blankly.

"Do you flirt with anyone else?" I don't know why I'm pushing his buttons but I can't seem to stop.

He shakes his head.

"Do you kiss anyone else?" Now he's glaring back at me. Good.

"Then admit that we're something special."

Henderson's mouth opens and closes a few times before settling into a tight line. "This is hard for me."

"You think it's not for me? I don't know how to do this either. I have no idea how I'm supposed to balance being a mom and working and having a personal life. Hell, I don't know if I'm coming or going most of the time. But the only thing I do know is that I've never had these feelings before, and I'm not willing to let that all go right now. So freak out if you want, but get your shit together, Henderson, because I won't wait around forever for you to figure it out. I don't have forever here in Hicklam."

With that, I stand up and storm out.

Like my man Kenny says, you've got to know when to hold 'em and know when to fold 'em. I don't want to fold, but I may have to.

For someone who doesn't like drama, Henderson certainly causes a lot of it himself.

Chapter 38: Henderson

My whole life, I've watched how my mum did things, and then decided to do the opposite. She did such a bang up job with her life that any choices she made *had* to have been the wrong ones.

It's been a conscious choice on my part to play it safe. To not take risks—either with my career or my personal life. And certainly never to mix the two.

But now here's this damn woman who's turning my whole world upside down. And I don't know why.

She's just a person, not some sort of magical enchantress.

She just has long legs and a bright smile and sparkling eyes and a generous heart and a sense of humor, and for some reason, she accepts my bullshit.

Or at least she did.

I've always been focused on how my mum clung to each man, hoping he'd be the one, that it never occurred to me my dad was totally afraid of real commitment and real feelings.

I don't have time for this right now. We open in about nine hours. I'm not sure we're even remotely ready. My to-do list has to-do lists.

This is why I don't want to be involved with anyone at work. It's splitting my focus that can't afford to be split. Resentment swells in my chest.

Tabitha should've known better. I told her, and I told her why. She should know the show is the important thing.

She should have respected my wishes.

If she wasn't so funny and amazing with her daughter and giving, I wouldn't be drawn to her the way I am.

This is all her fault.

For being irresistible to me.

Dammit.

"Henderson, we're starting the last run-through soon. Final costume check in five. We need you out here!" Morgan's voice bellows. Whoever gave her a megaphone didn't think that one all the way through.

It may have been me.

I finish stacking the piles of paper and put them back on the desk. I unplug my laptop and grab my water bottle, as well as my notebook to write down last minute things that we'll need to fix before tonight's opening performance.

Grayson is booked solid, doing interviews and social media. He's going to want Tabitha to do some of it with him. Carson Reuben will undoubtedly make a visit.

I don't know if I should hug him or hit him.

Tabitha walks out in her costume, a sparkling, white satin ball gown that almost glows on stage. I'm not sure if the effervescence is coming from the fabric or from her. With everyone else in rich jewel tones and saturated hues, she stands out. It's unlike anything I've ever seen her in, and my brain short circuits at the sight.

Hug Carson, definitely.

I've seen bits and pieces of the costumes here and there, but never everyone all together with full hair and makeup. Erica and her team nailed the design element.

"Hang on, I've got to get some pictures for social media!" I yell, pulling out my phone. It's an effort to make sure I get the whole cast, and not just pictures of Tabitha. She's radiant and keeps swishing her voluminous skirts back and forth.

Morgan has the large digital camera out, also snapping pictures for publicity. We have a whopping two hours to get these out into the world. The tickets have long since been sold out, but these are great images for The Edison.

I have to remind myself again that this is about the theatre and not about Tabitha. She's just here to help.

But I also know she's here for me.

That tightness in my chest is back.

We wave people stage left and stage right, upstage and downstage, getting group shots and solo poses. Grayson looks ready to command not only the stage, but also the lions and elephants, not that we really have those in the show.

"They look so good," a quiet voice next to me whispers. I glance down to see Gloria, Grayson's girlfriend, with her hands clasped tightly under her chin.

"They do." I agree.

"Erica did a great job with her vision. She's so talented."

"They all are. So many of them belong on Broadway. Grayson especially."

"You know he'll never leave here again." Gloria says softly.

I look at Gloria. "What about you?"

She smiles. "Wherever Grayson is, that's my home."

A simple answer for a person in love.

Maybe this is why nothing has ever seemed simple to me.

Morgan grabs my phone to shoot some video. "Tabitha, can you sing a few bars?"

As she begins the chorus, my heart clenches. Not only is her voice so perfect, but now, with the lighting, she's practically glowing. The final assault, though, is the words she's singing.

No matter what I tell myself, this short time with her will never be enough.

But it has to be. It's all we have.

I'm so enraptured by her that it takes me a minute to process what I'm hearing. Little feet, running.

A little voice. "Mommy! Mommy!"

Maria calls out, "Paisley no! Don't touch!"

The tyke rushes by me. Without thinking, I scoop her up into my arms. Chocolate is smeared across her mouth ... and arms ... and shirt.

And now my shirt, which she uses as a napkin.

"Mommy! I wanna touch your beautiful dress!" Paisley calls out.

There's a resounding "NO!" from pretty much everyone inside the theatre.

Maria catches up, breathless. "I'm so sorry."

This little girl, who looks so much like Tabitha, is absolutely adorable, chocolate and all.

"Mummy's in a special dress that we can't touch."

She looks wistfully at the stage. "I want to look like a princess too."

I glance over at Gloria, who's laughing at the spectacle. Gloria runs the children's program, as well as helping Erica out in wardrobe. "Do we have anything that might fit the princess bill for our young princess here?"

"I'll go look."

"I can take her and get her cleaned up. I don't know how she made such a mess in such a short time. It was a fun size Hershey bar. There wasn't even that much chocolate in the package." Maria holds out her arms for Paisley. I hand her over and look down at my shirt.

This is a goner.

I need to change but don't have time to run all the way back to my room. "Gloria, maybe after you help Paisley out, you could find something for me to wear? Or can you run to my room and grab something?"

She laughs. "No problem. You probably shouldn't go near that white dress either, looking the way you do."

Was Paisley playing in a chocolate fountain or something? "I find it hard to believe that a simple choco bar can cause this much damage."

"You should see what she can do with a popsicle." Tabitha calls from the stage. I swear, Erica is standing in front of her, acting as guard. "Sorry."

Grayson, still in his full ringmaster regalia, squats at the edge of the stage. "I think we should run it."

A glance at my watch tells me we're running out of time. "Costumes for the first scene. We start in five."

"Looks like I got here just in time. Goodness, Henderson, what happened to you?"

Oh great. Carson Reuben is here.

As predicted.

"He was attacked by a Hershey bar and lost." Grayson trots over to us, still in his red coat and tails, carrying his top hat.

"More like a four-year-old wielding a Hershey bar," I add dryly.

"Well, look at you," Carson gushes. "Eat your heart out, Hugh Jackman."

Grayson spins, clearly enjoying the attention.

I hear the swishing of skirts as the movement of the voluminous white fabric catches my eye. "Carson. Grayson. Henderson," Tabitha greets us, nodding as she says our names. "You should do an updated version of *My Three Sons*." She laughs at her own joke.

I'm nervous, still being covered in the remnants of Paisley, to have this costume so close to me. I hold up my hand to warn her back. We have a way of gravitating toward each other without even realizing that we're doing it until we're somehow touching.

That would not be good in this moment, for a litany of reasons.

"Oh my God, Tabby Cat. Look at you." Carson reaches for Tabitha's hand and spins her, her dress swirling through the air.

Damn, Erica should win an award for this one.

"You look smashing, darling. Absolutely smashing." Carson continues, "Such a change from your usual ears and tails."

"I think I should only perform if I can wear a hand-crafted Erica Zheng original from now on." Tabitha laughs. Then she looks at Grayson. "You know I'm buying this from The Edison and taking it with me, right? I may never take it off."

"Certainly someone could entice it off of you, right?" I don't know why I say this. It's not like Carson is a threat or competition. Not in the least. Yet I feel the need to stake my claim.

Tabitha looks at me, her expression masked with stage makeup. I see her eyebrow lift slightly as if to challenge me. "Are you offering?"

Carson doesn't miss a thing. It's why he's so good at his job. "So, is this like a thing now? Are you Facebook official?" He motions between us.

Tabitha inhales. "You know, I like to keep my private life just that these days, but ye—"

"What Tabitha—Ms. Stetson—is trying to say is that she's here in a professional capacity and has maintained that throughout rehearsals. None of that backstage drama here," I answer curtly.

"So you two are not"—Carson looks from me to Tabitha and back again—"a thing?"

"No, we're not. We are only professional colleagues, though I've tried to make sure that Ms. Stetson's acclimated well here." I nod my chin to emphasize the point. I even fold my arms over my chest, forgetting that I'm covered in chocolate.

Tabitha's mouth falls open. Without saying a thing, she lifts the front of her skirts and is gone in a swish.

That probably could have gone better.

Chapter 39: Tabitha

I cannot cry. I cannot cry.

My makeup will run and ruin my dress. As it is, I have to put a shield on and have three people help me in and out of it so I don't stain it before the performances even start.

Hell, I can't even sit down backstage in this thing.

I've spent the last four years hiding and hiding my daughter because of a man. I won't do it again.

I'm also not wasting any more time on a man who cannot—or will not—accept me for me. And let's face it, Henderson's not there. I don't know that he ever will be. He's tried to tell me over and over, but I thought he would realize that we are something special.

I'm always going to be his Lucille. Attractive enough in a bar, but something's holding him back from going all the way.

Kenny Rogers really does have a song for every situation.

I could slap myself. *It's him, not me.*

It doesn't matter that he's the broken one, because it all still hurts just the same. But now I've got to stuff all those feelings way down deep so I can perform. Great.

Leslie, who's with me in the prep room, sees that I'm on the verge of falling apart.

I told you I'm not much of an actress.

"Tabitha, are you okay? Do you need something?"

I need someone who values me the way I value him.

"No thanks, I'm fine."

I hear a voice behind me. "Fine is what you say when you're anything but fine. Trust me, I should know." Gloria seems to do a lot behind the scenes, though, from what I hear, she's quite the performer herself.

"I'm not fine, but I'm trying not to cry right now."

Leslie reaches out, gently placing her wrapped hand on my arm. "Men are stupid. Trust me on that."

"I second and third that," Gloria adds, touching my other arm.

"But Grayson is great."

"Yes, but he's stupid sometimes too. And it took me a long time and a lot of bad choices to find him."

"Tell me about bad choices." Those brief few minutes in the back of the limo dance through my mind. Without them, I wouldn't have Paisley, but I wonder what my life would be like. "It's just that I thought what we had was different. I thought we were opening up to each other. I ... I don't share like that with a lot of people."

It's true. Aside from the other members of the Sassy Cats, and maybe Maria a little, I find it very hard to open up and let people in. Maybe this is why.

When you open up, you become vulnerable. They can hurt you with the ammunition you supply.

"Listen, Henderson can say anything he'd like, but it's as plain as the nose on my face that he's head over heels for you. I've only known him for a year, but I've never seen him like this before. Grayson said the same thing. He used to worry that Henderson wouldn't ever even entertain the idea of getting involved. It's like he can't help himself with you."

I appreciate Gloria's words, but they also make me feel terrible. Henderson doesn't *want* to want me. I'm like a craving that he's doing everything he can to resist.

Because he doesn't see me as a good thing in his life.

Why am I so bad, though?

I could be good for him. I guess the question is, will he be good for me?

I already have my answer. He's done this more times than I can count. He's had his turn at bat and struck out.

Jesus, he's got me so turned upside down, I'm using sports analogies.

I'm done with this bullshit. I'm done opening myself up. I'm done with Henderson Quade.

There. Decision made. Time to move on.

And any second, I'll start to feel better. Right?

Maybe Henderson's right. Maybe this drama isn't worth it. I should focus on Paisley and my career, whatever *that's* going to be.

Yup, that's what I need to do. Figure out my next plan.

I look at Gloria. "How did you end up here?"

"In Hicklam? I came to work with a therapist who specializes in PTSD."

Oh. I was not expecting that.

"Actually, I meant backstage at The Edison. Henderson's mentioned a few times about how you saved the theater with your performance last year. Why are you backstage instead of on stage?"

Gloria shrugs. "I went on stage to prove something to myself. Something I thought I'd lost. Something I *had* lost. But with Grayson's help, I found it again. I don't need to be on stage, like I once thought I did."

I consider her words. "I think I do need to be on stage."

She nods. "It's clear, it's where you belong."

I know she's right. But what I don't know is how to balance that with my daughter.

"I can't imagine going on tour with a preschooler, and I can't imagine leaving her behind."

Even the thought of that makes my heart clench. A different feeling than thinking of a post-Henderson life, but that's as it should be.

"Um, Gloria, can you show me that thing in the costume room?" Leslie asks.

Gloria looks at Leslie, confused. Then her eyes grow wide. "Sure. That thing I was telling you about is right over here."

I have no idea what they're talking about until I hear the low clearing of his throat. I inhale deeply, slowly letting it out before I turn to face Henderson.

I wait for him to start.

He looks nervously at his feet. "I could have handled that better."

I still don't say anything. He deserves to squirm. Payback's always a bit fun.

"Tabitha, you know I'm not comfortable with this. I knew it would create a mess. That *I* would create a mess of everything. I don't know how to put the two together without making a ... mess." He shrugs, obviously unable to find a better word.

But now I'm angry with him. Once again, he's pushed me away only to immediately pull me back. I'm sick of the yo-yo.

"I don't know what you want from me, Henderson. You go through life thinking that it won't be messy. Guess what? Life is messy. That mess is good."

He shrugs. "Mess hurts. It's chaotic and painful. I grew up in a mess."

"So did I, and yes, sometimes it hurts, but sometimes it's the most beautiful thing ever created. But you don't get to it by keeping everything neat and orderly. You can't create purple unless you mix your blue and red. You can't paint a sunset without all those colors swirling together on the brush." I'm not sure where all these deep metaphors are coming from.

Henderson looks at me, his hands in his pockets. He's wearing a new shirt, but I can still see a trace of chocolate on his muscular forearm. "But I know red and I know blue. I don't like all purples. Some purples don't work for me."

And suddenly, it's clear to me that I can't fix this. He has to want it. To want me. He has to *want* to grow. "No, but you won't know until you try. You're still the scared little boy you've always been. You're just older, but you're still the same. You just want someone to love you."

His eyes grow wide, hurt filling them. "But no one ever has. No one ever will. So why bother trying? It just makes a mess."

"Love is messy. People are messy. You have to accept their mess if you want to let them in. And no one will ever love you if you don't let them in. I'm trying to love you, but you have to let me in, mess and all."

"I want to, but I ... I can't handle the mess."

He's not saying this to hurt me. He's being honest. He's not ready. I should have realized I couldn't push him. But I have to be honest. "Then you can't handle me. Because I'm a whole lot of mess. But I'm a whole lot of just what you need too."

I turn to walk out. "Did you ever stop to think about how much you've missed out on in your life because you were afraid? Did it ever occur to you that maybe there were people along the way ready to love you, but you weren't ready to be loved? You've been alone all this time not because you weren't worthy of love, but because you rejected it?"

I swish out, ready to head to the stage. The show must go on.

Chapter 40: Henderson

The audience loves her. What's not to love? It takes us about ninety minutes to disperse the crowd following the show.

And this is show one.

It was … not our best performance, but the cast'll pull it together tomorrow. The potential producers won't be coming until next week, but I'm sure they'll have their ear to the ground for early feedback.

But none of it matters.

The Edison doesn't even matter.

All that matters is that Tabitha won't even speak to me. She won't look at me. It wouldn't surprise me if she blocks my calls and texts.

I would too.

I'm not worth it.

I wish I was. I could be.

I could be for her.

No, not *for* her, but because of her.

Regardless, this is not the time, nor the place. And when we have the time, the place will make it impossible.

I stand in the doorway, arms folded across my chest, watching the last of Tabitha's adoring fans fade off into the dark night. It's after midnight. The glow on her face is brighter than any full moon hanging in the sky.

Tabitha is in her element.

She turns and glances toward me. Instantly the light is gone from her face, replaced with a clouded scowl. Fair enough; I deserve that. Without saying a word, she walks away.

I let her go.

It's probably the best thing I can do for her.

She's barely out the door and I miss her already.

"It's only going to go up from here, isn't it?" Josh appears to my left. I glance over and then back at the door Tabitha just exited through.

"I think so, mate. She's a star."

"I still can't believe I get to musically direct her. And she's so fantastic. You think she'd be pretentious and snotty, like Julianna Rickey was. I mean, Julianna's big on Broadway, but did you know that Tabitha once performed with Prince? I can play six degrees of separation for *Prince*."

"Yes, actually I did know that. It's why her daughter's named Paisley."

Shit. I probably shouldn't have said anything. I don't know if that was a secret, like Paisley's paternity.

"That's the coolest thing ever," Josh gushes. "This whole experience. Daniel Vasquez complimented some of our musical numbers. I mean, Mandy Calhoun and Ben Reynolds actually listened to my idea for a show. They said they wanted to hear a song. Do you think they really mean it?"

I shrug. "I dunno, mate. I don't know them, but ask Tabitha if you should pursue it. She'll be straight with you." She's nothing if not straight.

Sometimes too straight.

Not to mention, she has a real knack for the show biz thing. We went with some of her casting suggestions, and they've all panned out so far. "Maybe run the concept by her? She's got an ear for this kind of stuff."

"Do you think she'd listen?"

I nod. "She's very generous. I think people take advantage of that a lot, but she's got a big heart."

And I broke it.

"I know The Edison is small potatoes compared to what Tabitha's used to, but part of me wishes she wouldn't leave."

You and me both, mate.

Into the wee hours of the morning, I lie in my bed, tossing and turning, waiting for much-needed sleep to descend. It doesn't. Images of Tabitha assault me endlessly: on stage singing, in my arms, as I denied her to Carson Reuben. The last one hurts, because I know how much it hurt her.

How much *I* hurt her.

I'd do anything to take that pain away.

Sleep finally claims me, but doesn't stay for long enough to leave me feeling anything but groggy and grumpy.

One of those things is unusual for me. The other is par for the course.

Still, we've a long day ahead of us, working out some kinks from last night. Several marks were missed and some transitions need smoothing. For stepping into the role on short notice, Leslie is doing amazing as Anne, but she's not fully there yet.

Another thing Tabitha was right about.

I probably should have cast her as Lise in *An American in Paris*. If only I hadn't been so worried about her causing drama. I wonder how much trouble there would be if I recast her now? We don't start rehearsals on *Paris* for another four weeks.

I'm going to have to run it by Grayson, obviously. Considering he downgraded Tabitha at the eleventh hour, he may support it.

Seems whether I'm involved or not, drama still follows me, like Pigpen and his cloud of dust. Having Tabitha here, while it certainly has ratcheted up the activity, has not been anything terrible.

Quite the contrary.

She brings an energy with her that makes me feel alive. Mum's energy was always so chaotic that it drained and scared me. I don't feel that with Tabitha. Actually, despite the complications and the risk, I felt … whole.

And now I'm broken once again.

I'm used to being broken. What I can't live with is the fact that I broke her too in the process.

If I couldn't give her me, I'll have to find something else to do to make it up to her.

But what do you give the woman who has everything?

Chapter 41: Tabitha

I could do this forever.

I mean, I can't, because we only have one day left of shows. Tomorrow's matinee is the last performance. I'm trying to soak in every ounce of tonight's run.

I can't believe I only get to sing this song one more time. At least with the Sassy Cats, I grew tired of the songs before I had to move on from them. I'll never grow tired of this song.

It's the summation of my life.

Never enough.

I glance out, searching for Henderson. The moment I spy him, I tear my gaze away. I can't help but seek him out. I keep telling my brain not to look, but she won't listen.

The only consolation is that he's in as much agony as I am.

Good.

Stupid idiot.

While it's directed at him, it applies to me as well. It wasn't like he lied to me. No, in fact, he was quite up front about not getting involved. Of all the people I decided to open myself up to ...

Still, I'm not thinking about Henderson anymore. I'm thinking about me. More specifically, what I'll do when this is done.

What I'm going to do to keep this feeling.

At the end of the show, I find not only Mandy waiting for me, but Angie as well. "Aw, guys! I didn't know you were going to be here!" I pull them both into a tight hug.

"You know I wouldn't miss this," Angie says, her voice muffled into my shoulder. "Hell, you flew out to New York to see me in everything I was in. Why wouldn't I do the same for you?"

"Yeah but ..."

"No yeah buts. I wouldn't have missed it for the world. You were so good up there."

"I had to see it again. You were good last week, but even better this week," Mandy gushes.

I hold onto my friends tightly, needing their comfort and support. As good as I feel when I'm on stage, the moment I step off, it all ends.

I didn't feel this way when I thought Henderson and I were a thing—or at least on our way to being a thing. I actually thought my life was falling into place.

Big fat ha there.

On the other hand, I can't give Henderson that power over me, like my mom did with so many men. I have something more to offer than sex.

I have my singing.

"I really like doing this," I admit.

"It's addicting, isn't it?" Angie asks. "Now you know why I run myself ragged. I can't quit it."

"I don't want to run myself ragged. I mean a few weeks at a time is one thing. I couldn't keep your schedule."

Angie squeezes my arm. "That's the best part about being a star. You get to pick and choose what you want to do. Tab, it's not like you have to work to put food on the table. The only reason you have to work is to feed your brain and soul. So, roll up to the buffet you like best and chow down. But walk away when you're full. You've got a little girl who needs you too. I only have Sergei who, while he sometimes acts like a toddler, can at least be self-sufficient from time to time."

I put my arms around my two best friends, pulling them in close. "Hey guys, there's an aftershow coffee house cabaret where the cast sings whatever they like while people have coffee and dessert. It's about the latest-night thing going here in Hicklam. Want to join me?"

I haven't been to the cabaret yet. Frankly, I didn't want to take away from the others by being there. But now I want to go and relax with my girls, and enjoy the super talented people I've had the pleasure of sharing the stage with. One last hurrah before this all ends.

Moments before Josh heads to the piano, I slide into a back table with Angie and Mandy in tow. He sees us come in and makes a beeline.

I see him take a deep breath, trying to gain his composure before he starts talking. "Wow" is all he can finally manage.

"Josh, you remember Mandy. This is Angie. Angie, this is Josh, our super talented musical director. He's even writing his own show. He showed me some of it last week, and it has potential. You should take a look at it."

Color fills his face, right to the tips of his ears. He bites his lip, trying to suppress a grin and failing miserably. He's sort of adorable when he smiles like that.

"Thanks. I'm still working on it. It's got a ways to go."

"You're off to a solid start. Keep going and let's see where it ends up."

Someone calls his name. "Gotta go start. I ... wow." He shrugs and turns to leave.

"Josh, if there's room ..." I motion toward the three of us. I didn't ask Angie or Mandy, but I know they're game for it.

"Did you just offer for us to sing?" Mandy asks.

"Of course I did."

"What are we going to do?" Mandy asks. "'Fur-ever Yours?' or what about 'Here Kitty Kitty?'"

Angie waves her hands. "Actually, guys, I have an idea. What about 'At the Ballet' from *A Chorus Line*? You know it, right? It would be perfect for us."

Of course I know the song, but not enough to sing it. Luckily, there's a stash of musical scores in Henderson's office. "Hang on, I'll go get the music."

I stand up and scurry out to the hallway where Henderson's office is. Tentatively, I push the door open. I should be relieved that it's empty, but that super stupid part of me is disappointed he's not in here.

I miss him.

On the shelf are stacks of books and scores from seasons past. I grab two copies of *A Chorus Line*, quickly opening to "At the Ballet." It is the perfect trio for us.

Wham!

Not looking where I'm going, I run smack into someone. I don't even need to look to know it's Henderson.

"What are you doing in here?" He steadies me by holding onto my forearms. I wish he'd never let go.

His hands drop.

"Grabbing music." I wave the books. "Angie, Mandy, and I are going to sing. Josh said we could."

"*A Chorus Line*?" He glances at the cover. "Good choice for the three of you. You have a talent for knowing what fits. You fit well with theater."

"It was Angie's suggestion. She's familiar with it because she was in the show. But she played Diana."

"So what part'll you sing?"

"I'll do Sheila, Angie will do Bebe, and Mandy can sing the Maggie part. It's the best fit for our vocals and harmonies."

Henderson nods. "See? You called it. Trust your instincts."

My instincts are to throw my arms around him and kiss him senseless.

Nope, not gonna trust my instincts.

"Well, I'd better go back out there." I gesture toward the cabaret room.

Henderson looks at me for a beat before nodding. He doesn't move from in front of me, and I don't know how to step around him without being rude.

He clears his throat. "I'm sorry Tabitha. Sorry I bungled this all up."

I close my eyes, not wanting to have this discussion— or any discussion—with him. Having it will only hurt me more.

"Well, you did and you ruined it. You weren't willing to take a chance with me, and you lost out. I'll be okay. This cat always lands on her feet."

I step around him and back out to my friends.

I may talk a good game, but my heart breaks a little more as I walk away. Why do I have to want the one thing in life I can't have?

As soon as I make it back out to Angie and Mandy, though, I feel better. I've got friends and a song to perform.

What else do I need?

We study the music, hunched over our table and not really listening to the other performers. I should be paying more attention, but I'm afraid I'm going to get up there and make a fool of myself.

This isn't like that karaoke night when I was three sheets to the wind.

I could use a drink. Or several.

Josh looks over at us, raising an eyebrow. I wave the book and nod.

"Okay, folks, for our last song of the night, we have a very special act. Our very own Tabby Stetson will be singing, along with her fellow Sassy Cats, Mandy Calhoun and Angie Aliberti. Please give them a warm welcome."

We weave through the crowded tables, waving and shaking hands with people. Once at the microphone I say, "Okay, so we've never practiced this song, together or apart. But chances like this come around once in a lifetime, so we're going to take it. I'm just so thrilled that these lovely ladies are here with me tonight."

I know, even before the crowd is on its feet applauding six minutes later, that I need to be doing this. I need to find a way to balance Paisley and myself. Because this is me.

And I need to honor that.

I spy Henderson in the back, his hands down by his side, watching me closely. He's not one to wear his emotions—other than annoyance—on his sleeve. Since he's not rolling his eyes, I'd say he is not annoyed.

I am, though.

I'm annoyed he let me go. I'm annoyed that he wasn't willing to try—to fight—for what was between us.

Still, at the end of this, I know that I did something for myself. I opened myself up in a way I didn't think possible. Now, I just need to find someone who appreciates me.

Someone who's willing to go out on a limb for me.

I look around this room, so full of love and energy. Damn, I wish that someone was right here at The Edison.

Chapter 42: Henderson

She belongs here.

Actually, she belongs on a stage singing to millions, but she's at home in this theatre. She is so Tabitha here.

For once, she's hanging out with the cast in the dorms. Mandy and Angie are with her. You wouldn't know that the three of them were once megastars. Right now, they're just like every single person here at The Edison.

Riding the high of a performance.

I hover in the background, in and out of my room. I want to be with everyone else, just so I can be around her. Walking away has been the biggest mistake I've ever made.

Even bigger than getting involved in the first place.

"I don't ever want to leave here!" I hear Tabitha say.

"You wouldn't be saying that if you were up here during the winter." Mandy laughs.

Angie chimes in, "You should see what she wore in February in New York. I'm surprised she has toes left."

Those ridiculous shoes spring to mind. God, if I'd only known what that evening had in store for me. Hell, I'd've handled so many things differently. I certainly buggered it all up.

And for the record, the drama didn't come from her; it came from me. Me being a dipstick.

Josh adds, "Okay, well then, we'll put southern climate on our list of needs in order for you to work with me on my show."

There's a gasp as the room collectively turns to look at both Tabitha and Josh. *His show?* Tabitha's going to do his show?

Tabitha laughs. "Nice try, Josh. I mean, I'm absolutely going to look at it some more, but don't quote me on anything yet." She takes a sip of her wine. "Wait, Carson Reuben's not here, is he? I mean, otherwise, he'll put out a press release in *Backstage Magazine* tomorrow, and it'll be set in stone."

"Worked out for you last time," Mandy adds.

Tabitha throws her head back, laughing. "I'd say it did, but it's not how I want to run my career. I'm impulsive, but that's going too far, even for me."

I drift out, thinking about what she said. Tabitha is a risk taker. However, her underlying instincts make them good risks with excellent payoffs.

An idea rattles through my brain like a boomerang. It's a risk though.

I hear Tabitha's laughter float out into the hall.

I flip through the pages of Josh's notes and music. Not that I had any doubt, but he's onto something here.

And then I see it. The song called "Purple Dawn."

You can't create purple unless you mix your blue and red.

I'm ready to make a mess.

I rush back to the office where I send out a frenzied email to Grayson. Despite the fact that I'm bloody knackered, I don't feel it as I outline my plan.

Once I hit the send button, my brain finally catches up with my heart, and the fear begins to seep in.

What if this is a stupid thought? What if it doesn't work? What if I lose everything?

It doesn't matter, as long as Tabitha is happy.

And maybe, just maybe, I can win her back along the way.

Chapter 43: Tabitha

I t's over.

I need to start packing to head back to California.

I don't want to go.

I have to go. It's time for me to get on with my life, whatever that is. No more rehearsals. The show is done. I'm finishing cleaning out the last bits from my dressing room. Erica will be shipping my costume to my house after it's been dry cleaned. I paid her and The Edison a nice chunk of change for it.

I can't just leave it here.

I'm leaving my heart here, and that's enough to leave behind.

I sit down, taking in this space for a few more minutes, trying to commit it to my memory and heart, where it'll stay forever.

"Oh, come on, can we at least consider it?" Henderson's voice, irritated, floats in from the hall. "It's a brilliant idea."

"It's an idea that has some merit. But it's too big of a risk. Plus, the cost." Grayson sounds tired.

"We made bank this summer because of Tabitha. We're comfortable to invest a little."

Henderson's words make my blood boil. I try to remember Maria's advice; they weren't using me, but we were in this partnership for mutual benefits. Except my benefits have run their course, and Henderson is looking to cash in on his for a long time coming.

"I'll raise the additional capital," Henderson pleads.

"You hate fundraising," Grayson scoffs.

My curiosity can no longer be contained, so I tiptoe to the doorway and peek out. Henderson's waving a stack of papers around. Grayson runs his hands through his hair, clearly already tired of this conversation.

"I reckon I do, but this is worth it. Trust me. It's going to be phenomenal. C'mon, have you even read it? Josh's been bugging everyone and their brother to take a look all summer."

Oh. Henderson's talking about Josh's show. He must want to do it here. I'd looked it over briefly, and it does look like it has potential. There's one song about the dawn that made me cry just reading the lyrics.

Well, my impulsivity's worked for me thus far. I charge out of my dressing room. "Grayson, you've got to read Josh's show. It's really good. If Henderson thinks you should do it, then you should."

Grayson looks from me to Henderson and then back again. "What do you know about this?"

I shrug. "I was in my dressing room, and you two were loud enough that I don't have to consider it eavesdropping. But I did look through Josh's stuff. He's very talented."

Grayson looks at me. "I thought you two weren't together anymore."

"Josh? I'm not with Josh. He's like ten years younger than I am. He's adorable and all, but way too young for me. I don't have time to train a puppy."

Henderson rolls his eyes. "He means you and me. And no, we're not together. She doesn't know anything about this. I went right to you, Gray, with my idea. I haven't talked to Tabitha about it—or anything."

Okay, so my heart breaks a little when he says that, but I'm used to that happening when Henderson is around. But wait, what is he talking about?

"I'm lost. Which isn't, like, out of character for me, but I honestly have no idea what you guys are talking about, other than Josh's show. If Henderson thinks The Edison should put it on, then I'd trust him with that. It could be huge."

Grayson looks at me and lets out a slow breath. "Henderson does think The Edison should put it on. This winter. With you as the executive director and producer. And a role, if you want the part."

Hold the phone. I can only process one part of that proclamation at a time and the winner is, "I thought you weren't open in the winter."

"We're not. Henderson thinks we should expand to a more year-round theater."

"That sounds exciting. I mean, you're pretty much sold out this summer, aren't you? There might be more people who wanted to come but couldn't."

"But there's a lot of extra expenses, including heat and electricity. It's not just the cost of the show. We've a little wiggle room, but probably not enough to do a brand new show."

"I told you, I'd work on funding," Henderson sighs. "I'll do everything I can to make this successful. Josh's show deserves a chance."

"How much do you need?" The words are out of my mouth without even thinking. "I want you to do Josh's show."

Henderson turns to look at me. "I want *you* to do Josh's show."

Is he crazy? "I can't do that. I'm not in any way, shape, or form qualified to do anything other than to write a check."

I mean, I can act and sing too, but what else could he want from me?

"Actually, Henderson's not wrong about this. You have a talent for this, Tabitha. Henderson wants you to produce and direct it. Of course, having your name attached to it would probably help sales."

I look at Henderson. "But I'd be working here."

"You'd be happy here. You are happy here."

I can't tear my eyes away from his. How does he know me so well?

"Tabitha, Henderson isn't looking for money from you. That was never mentioned in his proposal," Grayson says.

Why is he still here? I need Henderson alone to hash all this out.

"Money's not an issue, if that was what was holding you back. Josh has talent."

"So do you, and I want you to shine," Henderson says softly. "I reckon you'd be smashing at this." He glances over at Grayson. "Do you mind if we have a word in private?"

Grayson sighs again. "Tabitha, let me know what you think. I can see you need some time to process this as well. We'll talk, I guess."

I walk back into my dressing room and Henderson follows. I look at him, trying to process what all this means.

If there's one thing I'm certain of, it's that he wasn't looking for my money. But I'd be here, at The Edison. Again. Still.

"I wouldn't have to leave. I mean, I have to go home, but I could come back."

"There'll always be a place here for you, Tabitha." He shrugs. "If you want it, that is."

"I kind of think The Edison is the perfect place for me, actually. And I think I could be good for The Edison."

"I think you could too. And, if things go how we think they might, we'll need you here."

"How so?" I tilt my head, looking at Henderson. He's in his trademark soft T-shirt and jeans.

"The powers-that-be were impressed with *Showman*. They're trying to get a workshop date. If that hits, it'll probably land on Broadway. Don't be surprised if they offer you a part."

"I don't think I have it in me to do Broadway. Not with Paisley."

Henderson shrugs. "If you were located here, in Hicklam, the city isn't too far. It'd at least be more of an option. More feasible. This sort of thing takes years to come to fruition, but it'd be an option for you, if you wanted it."

"Why?" I still don't understand why he's doing this for me.

Henderson steps forward and takes my hands. "Because you belong here. Working here. It's the perfect fit, don't you see? The schools here are great for Paisley. She already loves the town and the theatre, and I bet you could even buy that house, if you really like it. You don't have to be here year 'round, but you can if you want. And you'll get to see Mandy and Angie as much as you want. You could even move up by Mandy and drive down." He pauses. "Or get someone to drive you because, well, you and directions."

He's thought of everything. Paisley does really like it here. She hasn't asked to go back to California once. And with us being here, I don't have to make excuses for why she can't see her father. The pressure there is off, and maybe someday, he'll remember that he has a daughter.

It really is the perfect plan, except for one thing; even though he sees the real me and knows what I need, Henderson doesn't want me.

Still, the idea of returning here fills my heart with hope. And just like I wouldn't make a decision for a man, I won't make this one because I can't have the man.

Tabitha Stetson: singer, actor, director, producer.

I like the sound of that.

"Okay, I'm in."

Henderson stares at me, still holding onto my hands. "Just like that?"

I shrug. "Just like that. I make decisions quickly. Some call it impulsive. I prefer to think of it as decisive. Plus, I really love being here. I love the people and the feel of this place. I don't want to leave."

You. I don't want to leave you.

But I'll have to get over that pipe dream and be content with whatever life brings me.

Henderson clears his throat. This is getting a little awkward with him still holding onto my hands. "I've got to tell you one more thing."

Oh no. What bomb is he going to drop now?

Chapter 44: Henderson

I drop her hands, and pace around her small dressing room. Grayson gave me a harder time than I'd expected, but he still came around. It didn't surprise me that Tabitha jumped right in. This is right up her alley. Not only that, she'll be smashing at it. There's only one thing I don't know.

If she'll take me back.

I need to tell her. It's now or never. "You were right."

"What?" She looks startled.

"You were right." I pace around the room, trying to figure out what I'm going to say next.

"Say it again. I don't think I heard you correctly."

I perch on the edge of her makeup table, facing Tabitha. "You were right. I wasn't accepting of love because I was too afraid. Afraid of wanting it—needing it—and being rejected. It was easier to reject it right off the bat than to put myself out there and be shot down."

Watching her for the past two weeks made me realize this. My whole life, I've been rejected. My mum, my dad, my career. I couldn't bear to be rejected by Tabitha too.

"But if you risk nothing, you win nothing," she says so matter-of-factly.

"And you lose nothing."

"You lose everything."

She's right, of course. Without her, nothing else mattered because I felt as if I'd already lost. "It used to be enough, what I had. Until I met you. I never saw myself falling in love. Being in love. Let's face it, I never had a clear vision of what love should be. To me, love was destructive and hurtful. Love didn't build you up. It tore you down. But now I see things differently. And everything I envision contains you. I can't see myself being anywhere but with you. In love with you. Forever."

Her mouth opens as a gasp escapes her perfect lips. "You ... lo ... love me?"

I lift my shoulders and then let them drop. "I think I do."

She folds her arms across her chest. "I'm going to need you to prove it to me."

"More than offering you the perfect job?"

She nods. "You messed up. Me taking the job here and working with you on Josh's show helps you out probably even more than it helps me. I need proof that you're willing to risk it, just as much as I am."

I bob my head up and down in agreement. "Anything."

Tabitha takes one, two, three steps toward me, closing the distance until our bodies are centimeters apart. I sit up tall, the scent of her filling my nostrils. I shove my hands deeper in my pockets, lest I embrace her before she wants me to.

God, I hope she wants me to.

Tabitha takes a finger and runs it lightly up and down my chest. "You see, Henderson, ever since the first night we met, I've been opening myself up to you. I don't know why. It certainly wasn't your bright and chipper personality. But still, I've put myself out there, and I don't feel that you've always taken the same risks."

She's not wrong.

I raise my eyebrow, daring her to continue. Her finger travels up, lightly brushing under my chin and stopping on my lips. She leans in and whispers, "Next Friday, you're singing to me at the coffee house cabaret. And I get to pick the song."

And then, before I can say anything, she starts laughing.

God, I've missed that delightful sound.

I take her face in my hands. "For you, I will. But no, I get to pick it. I have the perfect song."

This time, when I pull her lips to mine, I know it's going to be different. Better. Because this time, I can see where we're going, the two of us together. Actually, all three of us. I have a vision of our future stretched out long and happy in front of us. She's the one that I needed, and I'm so happy she found me.

We've got tonight, and now I want all the tomorrows. This time, it's going to last. I'll find a way.

Epilogue: Tabitha

O kay, you need to tell me your magic power." Josh sits down at my table, straddling the chair backwards like they do in TV shows. Somehow, it works for him.

"I don't have any magic powers." Well, Henderson says I'm magic in bed, but I'm not sharing that with Josh. Although, I do agree that what's between us is out of this world.

"No, seriously. He gave me music. He's going to sing tonight. How did you ... what did you ... we've been trying to get him up there as long as I've been here. How?"

I tip my head back with laughter. "I told him he has to do this to make it up to me."

"Do you know what he's singing?" Josh raises his eyebrow.

"He won't tell me."

Josh laughs. "I have no idea why he picked this song, but man, he's got it bad for you."

"Should I be scared?"

"Maybe a little." Josh shakes his head, standing. "I never pictured Henderson getting so whipped. Like, ever."

"I don't consider it whipped. He knows he messed up, and he's all about the grand gestures to make it up to me. Listen, I'm not complaining, and neither should you. I have a job, and your show is going to come to life. There's a lot to be said for the grand gesture. Remember that."

"I'll take that under advisement." I see Josh's gaze dart across the room to where Leslie is standing. Interesting.

I'm going to have to get that story later.

"Well, I'd better get to the piano," Josh says. "We don't want Henderson to be late for his big debut."

I shoot a quick text to Maria, telling her I'll be home around midnight. It's been nice putting Paisley to bed every night this week. But I like this balance of having some me time as well.

Who knew that this small town of Hicklam would help me find the balance my life had been lacking? Not to mention love.

Henderson takes the stage as Josh introduces him. He's tentative as Josh starts with the opening chords. But the minute he says "Lady," my heart absolutely melts.

Oh God, I love this man. He's singing Kenny Rogers for me. To me.

I can't believe he'd do this for me. Sing in public. The one thing he hates in life more than romantic entanglements at work.

I can't keep the tears from streaming down my face as he continues to profess his love, in the immortal words of Kenny Rogers. I stand up, unable to stay in my seat. I walk to him and take his hand. It's shaking.

His eyes are full of tears too.

I use my free hand to wipe first my cheeks, then his.

As he finishes the song, he pulls me in tightly. "I love you," he whispers in my ear.

"I love you too, and I'd love you even more if you'd sing 'Islands in the Stream' with me."

"Someday, we're going to have to talk about your unnatural dedication to Kenny Rogers."

Josh, overhearing, starts playing the song on the piano.

"Hang on, I need the words!" Henderson yells. The crowd laughs. Someone hands Henderson their phone with the lyrics cued up.

As I stand here, holding Henderson's hand, singing to him, and with him, all I can think of is how this all started. Ten seconds in, and it was the weirdest first date ever. Six months later, and I've found my home with him.

This, indeed, is the year for the real thing.

That night in February, we weren't even looking for each other. But what we've found is so much more.

It's everything.

The End

Acknowledgments

To the Love in the City Ladies: I was privileged and honored to be included in the group. Thank you for including me. Mission accomplished.

To Angie Colonna: Thank you for taking the time to answer my questions. I can't wait to see you back on stage.

About the Author

Armed with quick wit, relatable character, themes of resilience, and always a happy ending, award-winning and *USA Today* Bestselling author Kathryn R. Biel writes comfort reads. Balancing drama and angst with laughter and love, Kathryn weaves stories that will whisk you away for a few hours and have you rooting for the underdog, whether it's through sports romance, romantic comedy, or lighter women's fiction. By day, Kathryn is a pediatric physical therapist and Chief Domestic Officer of the Biel household. By night, when not writing, Kathryn can be found at the dance studio, knitting, watching sports with her husband and son, cuddling with her four cats, embarrassing herself on TikTok, and doing absolutely anything to avoid cleaning her house.

Kathryn is the author of 21 books, including the award-winning *Live for This*, *Made for Me*, and *The UnBRCAble Women Series (Ready for Whatever, Seize the Day,* and *Underneath It All)*.

Stand Alone Books:
Good Intentions
Hold Her Down
I'm Still Here
Jump, Jive, and Wail
Killing Me Softly
Live for This
Once in a Lifetime
Paradise by the Dashboard Light

Boston Buzzards:
XOXO
You Belong with Me
Zero to Hero

A New Beginnings Series:
Completions and Connections: A New Beginnings Novella
Made for Me
New Attitude
Queen of Hearts

The UnBRCAble Women Series:
Ready for Whatever
Seize the Day
Underneath It All

Center Stage Love Stories:
Act One: *Take a Chance on Me*
Act Two: *Vision of Love*
Act Three: *Whatever It Takes*

If you've enjoyed this book, please help the author out by leaving a review on **your** favorite retailer and **Goodreads.** A few minutes of your time makes a huge difference!

www.ingramcontent.com/pod-product-compliance
Lightning Source LLC
Chambersburg PA
CBHW031339020726
47499CB00005B/1332